Praise for
THE FIXER UPPER

One of *New York Post*'s Best New Book Releases

One of *USA Today*'s Best Rom-Coms of August

"By turns witty and tender, observant and heart-wrenchingly romantic in a thoroughly modern way. I will be thinking about it for a long time to come."

—Jenny Bayliss, author of *The Twelve Dates of Christmas*

"A wry, modern take on a rom-com, as funny and fierce as it is clever and warm."

—Abigail Mann, author of *The Wedding Crasher*

"A fun, fast read. A sweet childhood-friends-to-enemies-to-lovers romantic comedy that I could totally see being a movie!"

—Abby Jimenez, author of *The Friend Zone*

"Sweet and deftly plotted, *The Fixer Upper* will have you rooting for Aly to not just get the guy, but to get it all." —*USA Today*

"If you've got a problem, including a boyfriend in need of some serious motivation to change his life, Lauren Forsythe's *The Fixer Upper* is sure to give you some inspiration." —*PopSugar*

"There's a lot to love about Lauren Forsythe's latest foray into romantic, humorous women's fiction . . . *The Fixer Upper* has rom-com screenplay written all over it." —*Reader's Digest*

"Female readers, many of whom may feel that they carry the emotional burden in their relationships with men, will find that

Lauren Forsythe's debut novel, *The Fixer Upper*, hits pretty close to home. Billed as a 'sassy feminist rom-com,' the book is a lot of fun, full of cheeky one-liners and a cast of characters both sharp and heartwarming . . . giving the reader time to ponder their own relationships while giggling at the absurdity of others'."

—*Christian Science Monitor*

"This is for all the women who realize halfway through a long-term relationship that they've been carrying the entire weight of the emotional baggage. I can already tell you that people are going to relate to Aly's storyline and can already see fans calling for a Netflix adaptation!" —Bookstr

"Walking the line between rom-com and tale of self-discovery, Forsythe's debut delights with sure-footed plotting and an endearing cast . . . Charming characters and quick wit make for a fun, breezy romp . . . [The] primary focus here is on Aly learning to love herself enough to stop putting everyone else's needs before her own. It's entertaining [and] readers looking for a smart, empowering blend of romance and women's fiction are sure to be pleased." —*Publishers Weekly*

"Forsythe understands the contemporary romance genre and writes with confidence. With likable characters and good pacing, this debut novel offers a great second-chance romance."

—*Library Journal*

"Aly's desire to stop being a people-pleaser and start working on herself is relatable, and her journey to personal fulfillment follows a satisfying arc . . . A pleasant [look] at the importance of taking responsibility for your own happiness." —*Kirkus Reviews*

ALSO BY LAUREN FORSYTHE

....

The Fixer Upper

DEALBREAKERS

A NOVEL

LAUREN FORSYTHE

G. P. PUTNAM'S SONS · NEW YORK

PUTNAM
— EST. 1838 —

G. P. PUTNAM'S SONS
Publishers Since 1838
An imprint of Penguin Random House LLC
penguinrandomhouse.com

Library of Congress Cataloging-in-Publication Data
Trade paperback ISBN: 9780593422533

Printed in the United States of America
1st Printing

Book design by Elke Sigal

For every woman who had a list in her head,
and a life that turned out nothing like it.

And for Shaun. Just because.

DEALBREAKERS

CHAPTER ONE

"My favorite book?" The man across the table from me rested his chin on his hand and considered the question. He hemmed and hawed, thoroughly enjoying thinking about his answer. As he had with all five questions I'd asked him since we sat down fifteen minutes ago. He was not giving me much to work with. But maybe he was shy. A shy, bookish type, with a sharp jawline and a love of double-chocolate-chip cookies. Promising. "I'd have to say . . . *mine*. The one I'm writing. I haven't finished it yet, of course, but it's going to be important, you know?"

Oh. All that promise, just fizzling away.

Now, I knew from the Dealbreakers app that Michael, thirty-six, university lecturer and avid cyclist, *loved* talking about his novel. Three other women who'd been on dates with him had mentioned it in their notes. But none of them had mentioned how he chewed with his mouth open and kept making these patronizing "humph" noises when you said something he didn't expect.

I knew I should have listened to them; usually I did. But the crop of available men was becoming smaller and smaller. And an interest in creative writing hadn't seemed so bad, hardly a real dealbreaker. I just had to give him a chance.

"Oh wow," I said dutifully, sipping at my wine and wondering why, even with the world's smartest tech at my fingertips, I couldn't meet someone who fit my criteria. I tapped my feet on the sticky floor of the Dragon and Treasure, weirdly comforted by its consistency. Was my favorite pub a little rough around the edges? Sure. But it had two things I loved: an easily accessible exit, and my best friend, smirking at me from behind the bar as she watched me bolster myself in the face of disappointment. Oh, also, the burgers were good.

As Michael started to explain, in minute detail, the intricacies of his novel, I let the comforting background noise of the pub wash over me. I noticed a young couple standing at the bar, his hand in the back pocket of her jeans. I smiled faintly at Old Reggie, who always sat in the corner by the fake fireplace, drinking his pint of bitter. Was it polite to ignore Michael and his apparent creative genius? No. Had the man asked me a single question since we'd met? Also no.

Some people dated because they liked dating, but it was hard to imagine that those people were not a) young, b) bored, and c) in want of a free meal. I was not dating for fun. I was thirty years old, and I was behind schedule. I had set criteria, a timeline, and places to be. Preferably in bed with a hot-but-sweet guy who thought I looked cute in my badger pajamas, always let me eat the peanuts from the kung pao chicken, and knew I liked to be asleep by eleven on weekdays.

I didn't think my dealbreakers were unrealistic:

No smokers
No tattoos
No swearing
Stable job
Lives locally
Close with family
Wants kids

My best friend, Meera, had looked over my shoulder when I'd written that list, sitting at this very table ten months earlier, when I'd decided I was finally ready to start dating again. She'd snorted and shaken her head.

"So you want someone boring and willing to procreate? That's it?"

"Boring and willing to procreate *with me*, Meer."

I wanted, and still want, someone reliable. Someone who would stay.

But the sound of Michael's chewing was making me want to stab him in the hand with my fork.

"Editing's just for people who aren't as dedicated to their craft as I am. That's why I never change anything I write. I wrote it with *intention*, you know?"

I clenched my teeth into an approximation of a smile and nodded.

"The creative process is so fascinating . . ." I said blandly, hoping that trailing off would send a signal.

Come on, please ask me something about myself.

"So . . . what about you?" Michael said suddenly, looking expectant, and I gripped my glass in relief. Okay. Maybe this was just a bad start. He was employed and hadn't sworn and didn't seem like the type to be covered in biker tattoos. I could take him home, and Mum would be impressed. So maybe this could be salvaged?

"Um, well, I'm head developer at a start-up in the city—"

"Ooh," he exhaled, shaking his head, "start-ups are risky. Lots of them fail. That's why I picked something solid, like working at the university."

Ah, academia, that traditionally well-paid profession.

"I guess we're pretty opposite, the classics teacher and the developer!" I chortled, hating myself, tapping my star-and-moon necklace against my collarbone. It was a reflex, a comforting move to soothe myself.

"That's pretty," Michael said suddenly, gesturing to my necklace, a small smile on his face. For a moment, hope bloomed. In that warm smile I tried to imagine another date, a laugh, a kiss, a future. A story where I'd say, *You know, I wasn't entirely sure about your dad when I first met him. He's still working on that bloody novel, too!*

My hand stilled on the silver charm on my chain, and I tried to press down on that weird sense of grief. I shouldn't be wearing this necklace anymore. "Thanks, it was a present."

"Professor, by the way," Michael said, and I frowned in confusion at the switch in conversation. He paused and repeated himself: "I'm a professor, not a teacher. And I'm assuming you'll give your job up when you have a family, yes?"

I blinked. "Sorry?"

He looked up, that dark hair so flawlessly coiffed, that eyebrow raised perfectly. "These future children you plan to have. You said in your bio you want kids. So you'd give up your job to raise them, yes? That's very important to me, and I don't intend to compromise *my* career."

"Of course," I said faintly, lifting my wineglass to my lips, desperate for the last dregs. "Why would you?"

"So you would? How refreshing." He went back to

focusing on the "snacks for the table" he'd ordered and then promptly pulled over to his side when they arrived.

Nope. I was tapping out. Twenty minutes was more than enough time to give someone the benefit of the doubt. I looked over at the bar in desperation, catching Meera's eye. I tapped my fingers on the side of the table three times, and she rolled her eyes. She finished pulling a pint and dropped it off to Old Reggie on the way, offering him one of her rare, sweet smiles. Then she tilted her head at me, as if to say, *Are you sure you need saving, Rina? It looks like such a fun time you're having.*

I widened my eyes, pouted a little. *Yes, help me, you cheeky cow! Save me!*

Meera nodded, barely holding back a smirk, and in five strides she was standing over our table.

"There's an emergency," she said woodenly, not even trying to sound convincing as she pulled her dark hair back into a ponytail. "It's terribly important. Timmy's fallen down a well."

"What?" Michael frowned. "Excuse me, you're interrupting a first date."

"Gosh, I never would have guessed, what with all this simmering sexual tension." Meera was not subtle, but she got the job done.

"I'm sorry, I have to go, emergency and all that." I stood up and put a tenner down for my wine. "Nice to meet you—good luck with the book!" I took Meera's hand as she wove us through the crowded pub to the back room and out to the small patch of fake grass the staff called a garden. It was just a fenced-off square of land around the side from the actual garden so that the staff could have a breather in peace. I leaned against the wall and closed my eyes. Why couldn't I seem to get this right? Every single date, even with my thorough research on Dealbreakers—none of them had worked. No one even had potential. No second dates, in the six months since I'd created the app. I'd completely given up on attraction, sexual tension, desire, focusing only on the important things . . . at the very least, if my dating life was going to be a disaster, I wanted it to be a hilarious disaster.

"You owe me." Meera sucked on her vape. "Again."

No longer the good Indian girl I'd met on the first day of secondary school, Meera had gradually morphed into a tattooed badass with an undercut and a nose ring. Guess that was what happened when no one was around to make you stay the same. No relationship to hold you in place, no parents to mourn the transformation of their sweet girl into the angry bartender. You could become who you were meant to be. The sarcastic, dry comebacks and desire to ignore the touchy-feely bits of friendship, however, were exactly the same as when we met, nearly twenty years ago.

"Put it on my tab," I said brightly, blowing her a kiss.

Then I grabbed my phone and opened the Dealbreakers app. "There were *definitely* some details missing on Michael's bio, that's for sure."

"Oh, you mean the opinions of random women on the internet didn't lead you to your perfect match? Shocker." Meera rolled her eyes but grinned at me.

Dealbreakers was an app overlay. Basically, you opened it on your phone and it pulled through data from all the different dating apps. Whoever you matched with, on whatever app, you could see a bunch of notes from previous women who'd been on dates with them.

What I'd found out, in my months of feverish dating, was that people lied about who they were online. And sometimes even *they* believed those lies.

So, I decided the only thing you could trust were reviews. Which was why I created the app and shared it discreetly on a female coders forum. Since then, it had been gradually building momentum: more users, more dealbreakers, red flags, and the occasional "good egg" badge to indicate the guy was super lovely but just not for you.

I was proud of it. It was working. Hundreds of women had left comments and hopefully had saved themselves time by not dating someone who wasn't right for them. That was the thing that I didn't have, and exactly what dating required: time. Time to message with someone for two weeks before meeting them and realizing you hate their Mickey Mouse voice or the way they pick their nails. Endless dates with men who said they loved kids or were close to their parents or any other thing you wanted to hear. And the hiking? Why did everyone on dating sites love hiking? I'd never met anyone in real life who liked it.

This was my way of leveling the playing field. And okay, it didn't always work, but this way, a dud date was never truly a waste of time, because you could give notes to help other women. And maybe one of those would want to be Michael's adoring, book-reading, barefoot baby mama. But that wasn't going to be me.

"They were right, I just needed to see for myself. He looked so good on paper." I quickly typed out a note about the chewing, the book, and the expected halt of his future wife's career the minute she pushed a baby out. "Besides, now I've saved some other woman time. It's all for the greater good. No date is wasted."

Meera raised an eyebrow at me. "If there's no laughing or shagging, it's a date wasted." She blew out a smoke circle.

The door opened behind us and Bec poked out her head, rose pink hair catching the light, and nodded when she saw it was us. Another one who had started school as one thing and had butterflied into another. Bec was our puzzle piece, our balancing act. I was about control, Meera was about chaos, and Bec was about having the most fun possible. Some days I felt that if I didn't have my friends, I wouldn't be anyone at all. When we were together, I felt most like myself. Which was probably why Bec always arrived at the pub when she knew I had a date planned.

"Ah, late as usual," Meera said, grinning at Bec. "Where were you when Miss Marina needed rescuing from her latest bad idea?"

"I live by my own clock, you know that." She held up a plate at me. "Marco gave me a bacon sandwich for you. Is this a thing? Why do I never get bacon sandwiches when I come here?" She handed it to me and pulled out her pack of cigarettes.

I wrinkled my nose. "It's pity pig. Every time I bring a date here, Marco makes me a bacon sandwich to soak up the alcohol and disappointment."

"It's his way of thanking you for the business." Meera laughed. She'd been working at the Treasure since she dropped out of law school, and Bec and I had been coming here ever since. So yes, we came for birthdays and Thursday nights and Bec's last-minute hen do, but mainly we came because I could depend on my favorite bartender rescuing me with a raised eyebrow and my other best friend walking me home after. Safe and practical: my favorite things.

"Another dud?" Bec asked. "What was wrong with this one?"

I opened my mouth to reply, but Meera didn't give me a chance.

"Self-important, arrogant, too much aftershave, and he wasn't smart enough to immediately fall to the ground and worship at Marina's tiny, ugly feet."

"Hey." I threw a bit of the crust at her. "Excuse me. My feet are normal size and no uglier than everyone else's."

"What did Dealbreakers say?" Bec asked, twirling the vintage ruby-encrusted wedding band on her finger absentmindedly.

"That he was a self-important, arrogant . . ." Meera started, then grinned. "She gave him the benefit of the doubt. Lowering her standards already."

"He mentioned wanting kids in his bio! He had a puppy in his profile picture! Sadly didn't make up for the absolute 1950s nonsense that came out of his mouth. I should have trusted the women who came before me." I held up my hand. "I've learned my lesson. The sisterhood knows best."

And they did. It had been months of work, but there were good-sized files on almost all the men on most dating apps. The problem was it started to make me wonder if there was anyone out there for me at all. The goal was to only focus on your personal dealbreakers. Rude to the waitstaff? No way. Terminally clumsy? Not a big deal for me. I was particular; I wasn't insane.

"Well, I think you should be proud that your dating skills are improving, even if your choices aren't," Bec said supportively, reaching over my shoulder to pull a piece of bacon off my plate.

"What dating skills?" I laughed. "My ability to see that someone isn't a good match within thirty seconds of sitting down?"

"Her ability to completely ignore whether she wants to have sex with someone?" Meera offered thoughtfully, tearing some crust off my sandwich.

"No, the small talk and getting-to-know-you bullshit. Mere months ago, our Marina was still using cue cards to think of things to say! And look at her now—she's got a date down to under twenty minutes."

I looked at her. "I . . . appreciate your positivity. I think."

She laughed, and then held up her hands like she'd suddenly remembered something. "Oh! Moving this conversation to a more Bechdel-approved zone for a moment, I got you a present!" Bec said, pulling off her horn-rimmed glasses and cleaning them on her harlequin-printed top.

"Oh God, what? You know I don't have the space." I'd been staying in Bec's spare room, which was starting to feel smaller and smaller every day I stayed there. It had been 241 days. The walls were starting to cave in.

"Don't worry, no one gives stuff anymore. It's the gift of us! I signed me and Meera up for your pottery class."

"You what?" I yelped.

"You WHAT?" Meera repeated, with feeling.

"You said you were struggling with it, and I wanted to support you having a hobby that isn't trying to meet the perfect man or find the perfect flat or pitch the perfect bug fix." Bec looked at me, her beautiful round face suddenly pinched and serious. That face said, *Be ungrateful, I dare you.*

"It'll be fun!" she cajoled. "Just like being back in Mrs. Jacob's art class."

"You were the only one who was good at art class," Meera said faintly. "Marina and I spent time scratching our names into the tables and throwing paint at each other."

"Well, sure, but *you* need to do something fun, and Marina needs to continue doing something she's shit at."

"Hey!" I sighed. "The teacher said I was getting better."

"I think your teacher is developing astigmatism," Bec said, grinning. Then that determined look returned. "Say thank you, be gracious, move on."

"Thank you," Meera and I mumbled in unison.

It had always been this way. Meera the cynic, me the perfectionist, Bec the chaotic free spirit. Of all of us, Bec was currently winning the adulthood race, which no one would have guessed. Including her.

The girl who had no idea what she wanted to do with

her life and started sweeping up hair at a London salon while she figured it out now owned that salon. Four months ago, I'd introduced her to Matt, a guy I'd gone on a date with because he was also a developer. We had too much in common, so I introduced him to Bec (plus, he didn't like travel and really loved reptiles).

They dated for three weeks and got married on a Wednesday. And as a very thoughtful wedding present, when my landlord increased the rent on the flat I used to share with Adam and I couldn't afford it anymore, they let me move into their spare room. I'd gone from planning my own wedding (secretly, on a hidden Pinterest board) to living with newlyweds. My five-year plan was not quite on the money, apparently.

All my stuff was in storage. I visited every few weeks, just to remember I had stuff. I had the things that made up a life. Baking utensils and throw cushions and a welcome mat. I missed my vintage glasses from the charity shop and having dinner parties where I served things on odd plates. Sure, it was just stuff, but I missed it. As soon as I found the perfect flat, I'd move out and reclaim it.

"Come on, I'll walk you home," Bec said, holding out a hand to me, which I immediately took and squeezed. This was our routine. I'd book a terrible date at the Treasure, and Bec would walk me home. At the beginning, it was a safety thing, but I was starting to think she wanted to be there to console me. Either way, my best friend wanted to hold my hand, even when I was taking up her office space and stopping her from having newlywed sex on the kitchen floor. I was lucky.

"Thank you, really. I don't know what I'd have done without you giving me a place to live," I said as we walked down the quiet streets toward the beautiful Victorian terrace that housed Bec's flat.

"You need to stop thanking me." Bec squeezed my hand and shook it a little in admonishment. "It's nice to have you around. And when you find your Insta-worthy ground-floor flat with a garden and a book nook and enough natural light to grow a tomato plant, I'm sure I'll miss you."

"You think I'm being too fussy?" I winced.

"I think you're being exactly who you are." Bec smiled, shrugging. "And who am I to tell Marina Spicer not to be her wonderful self?"

"I should lower my expectations," I said as we padded along in the growing darkness. "I know I should. I just . . . I *loved* my flat. It was perfect."

It was. My flat with Adam was a labor of love, which was what happened when you'd been with someone since you were fifteen and moved in together instead of living in halls at uni. You had enough time and space and disposable income from never making any new friends to . . . nest. To build up a collection of beautiful art in frames instead of posters Blu-Tacked up in dorm rooms. To fill a vintage bar cart and repaint old furniture on the weekend until your friends came around to visit and their jaws dropped at how you had your shit together. How you were a grown-up.

"I know," she said sagely. Poor Bec, she must have been tired of this conversation. And how many times I'd lamented losing my gorgeous living space in the past few months. It was easier to moan about that than it was to talk about Adam leaving. Easier to pretend hardwood floors and a truly shocking amount of natural light for East London mattered more than the man I'd been with my whole life walking out. Until I'd lost the flat, his departure almost hadn't seemed real.

I was getting sick of talking about it myself.

"So, how's work?" I asked, changing the topic and learning from my experience with Michael. Ask questions, listen to the answers.

"Actually, I convinced Marjorie to give bright violet streaks a go." Bec grinned, grabbing her phone to show me. "She looks amazing."

"Marjorie who's eighty-five?"

"Eighty-five and started one of the most prominent fashion brands in the city. She's a local legend." She held up a hand to her chest, as if overcome. "And I had an impact on her daily life. What a thrill!"

"I love how you love stuff."

"How about you? Create some sort of terrifying AI that's gonna take over the world and enslave us all?"

"Nah, that's next week." I snorted, then sighed. "Still in a war of words with marketing."

"That guy with the snarky emails?"

"Yep, it's all passive-aggressive pleasantries. He's taken to responding to my emails with a simple 'k' of acknowledgment, so I know I've really pissed him off." I grinned. "It's better than coffee. Really energizing, you know?"

"So unlike you to be confrontational." Bec snorted, and I nodded.

"Some people are worth the work." I laughed and felt my phone vibrate in my pocket.

"Is your presentation tomorrow?"

I took a deep breath and slowly exhaled, making a face. "I'm going to try to get a promotion. I never should have accepted the first offer. And I miss running a big team. I can't keep going backward." *In all areas of my life.*

Bec made a face and took a deep drag on her cigarette. "How you feeling about the public speaking?"

"Like I'd rather knock myself over the head with a Lego spaceship, which, incidentally, my bosses have on display in their man-child office."

Bec's laugh turned into a cough, and I felt my phone buzz again. I checked the screen.

I passed that shop in Dulwich where we bought the flamingo glasses today. They have a huge flamingo in the window! Made me think of you.

I stopped walking to look at it and thought, not for the first time, that deciding to be friends with the person who walked all over your heart with their muddy size-nine Adidas was probably not the best idea.

After a moment of silence, Bec ventured, "Adam?"

I nodded, and she peered over my shoulder.

"Bastard."

I turned to look at her, laughing. "What deserves that response?"

"The fact that he thinks he even has the right to message after what he did." She pretended to growl, baring her teeth. They'd been friends once, too. We all had. I'd won them in the separation.

"People are allowed to grow, Bec. They're allowed to want different things," I defended, knowing it was true. "I just wish he'd told me before I started taking prenatal vitamins and took a stupid job at a dopey start-up for the great maternity package."

Before I knew it, we were standing in front of Bec's flat, out on a leafy suburban street, quintessentially London. We perched on the front wall as she lit up her final cigarette of the night.

"Well, tomorrow, when you make your big, exciting pitch to become a boss-arse bitch, that dopey bro start-up is gonna start raking in the cash and making an impact. And you're gonna be at the heart of it."

I said nothing but crossed my fingers. One step closer to being a head of development. To running a team. To training female coders and making an impact on the industry. One step closer to that five-year plan, that version of myself with the swishy hair and the capsule wardrobe and the flat with a garden and a picture-perfect husband.

I thought back to that text message from Adam. I remembered that shop. Remembered buying those flamingo glasses, laughing and clapping my hands as I discovered them, his arms around my waist. He used to say my ability to be happy with the simplest things was one of my best traits.

Wasn't it the simplest thing in the world to meet someone, fall in love, make a life?

As I followed Bec in through the front door and watched how her husband's eyes lit up with delight at her return, I promised myself it was all coming to me. I was doing everything I could. I would make it happen.

I'd developed an app to save women time when dating. How hard could it be to fix a failing start-up?

It all started tomorrow, and this time I wasn't letting it slip through my fingers.

CHAPTER TWO

He was needlessly combative when I said I didn't like the Beatles. Like, let people have their opinions.

Marina Bambina! *Come stai?*"

I tried not to cringe as I looked up from my desk. Harriet, who sat opposite me, raised her eyebrows and then turned on her megawatt smile for the bosses.

The two CEOs of LetsGO, Joe and Joey, were exactly the kind of guys you'd expect to run a start-up—loud, engaging, and endlessly confident even when they didn't have any reason to be. I liked Joe better, by a fraction, but only because his dark hair fell forward over one eye like the emo boy band front men of my youth. He was also *slightly* quieter.

Joey was shorter, with light hair, and he'd made a habit of wearing a pocket square in a jacket over his raggedy T-shirt, with ripped jeans, like he'd bought it as a start-up CEO starter pack.

He also constantly spoke to me in a broken Italian-Spanish-Portuguese hybrid, even though I'd said three times that I was from Forest Hill. I'd made the mistake of mentioning my mum was half Italian. But she didn't even have a decent lasagna recipe. The most "exotic" thing about me was that I was known by name at my local kebab place.

"Hey, boss." I saluted, and Joey grinned, wiggling his wireframe glasses from behind his ears. He seemed to both love and hate being reminded he was the boss. I don't know if he wanted to feel cool or if it reminded him that he was responsible for this heavily invested-in (and yet very much not "up") start-up.

"Now, *Marina*, we're all rowers on this great ship, right? There are no bosses, only guides on the journey." Sometimes I wanted to punch him square in that handsome jaw.

"Right." I sipped my coffee and smiled. My face was starting to hurt.

Joe arrived, never far behind his business partner, like the two were mid-thirties Ant and Dec, always looking for a chance to perform their double act. The two Joes.

Joe liked to wear turtlenecks, even in spring. Like he was the Steve Jobs to Joey's Zuckerberg. I felt a strange affection for them, like they were little boys playing dress-up in need of some guidance and a hug.

"Ready to blow our minds this morning?" Joe asked, and smiled warmly, pushing his dark hair out of his eyes before getting distracted by his phone.

"Oh, absolutely. Data organization may *sound* boring, but I promise I have gifs." I grinned. My work persona was so cheesy. I spent most of my day internally rolling my eyes at myself.

It was *hard* to talk to people. All that water-cooler chat everyone went on about? It physically pained me. Fifteen minutes trying to scrounge up conversation about the weather, and I felt like I was dying. I didn't know if it made me awkward or rude, but I'd really rather just turn up, do my job, and go home to the people I already knew and liked. People who didn't ask me if I got up to anything nice at the weekend. Because I didn't really have anything cool to say anymore. Apart from pretending that pottery was a legitimate hobby rather than something I forced myself to do every week like an endurance test in how crap a person could be with clay.

And LetsGO did this whole spiel about how we were a family, but all it meant was longer hours and more people trying to pretend the pressure wasn't getting to them. Next time I saw "work hard, play hard" in a job ad, I was passing. *Hard.*

The idea was cool, though, and our fancy glass offices near Canary Wharf definitely looked all #girlboss. Even if the coffee was awful and the Friday free pick 'n' mix didn't really make up for the commute costs. LetsGO was a website that helped you book activities in the city. Whether you wanted something low-key or adventurous, we could help you find something unique to do. The idea was that there was so much cool stuff going on, there was no need to be bored. It was a great concept.

But spending hours a day rearranging said activities on the site in a war with the marketing department was killing me. *Couldn't you just do this? It should be easy . . .* Grr.

I turned to Joe and Joey, suddenly desperate to make my point before they disappeared with their coffees into the conference room.

"Hey, guys, I was thinking . . . if you like what I present on today, the idea . . ." I cleared my throat, which was suddenly dry. "Maybe you should let me implement it? By making me head of development and growing the development team?"

Harriet was sitting at her desk with her oat-milk latte, tapping her fluffy purple pen on the headphones that clearly had no music playing. At my question, she wiggled her eyebrows and gave me two thumbs up, mouthing, "Yaaas, bitch!"

I snorted and fought a smile, focusing on the CEOs.

The silence seemed to last a lifetime, their faces blank as if they'd never considered the idea before.

Suddenly Joey punched his fists into the air, and I jumped back.

"GOD, Marina, I LOVE your energy! Yes, that is the kind of entrepreneurial spirit we need, right? Go-getter mentality."

He looked at Joe, who nodded thoughtfully and tilted his head. "I didn't know you were interested in management, Marina."

Five-year plan, baby.

I shrugged. "I'm always looking for opportunities to grow."

"Well . . ." Joe looked back at his partner, who was so enthusiastic he looked like he was going to take off into space. "Let's hear your presentation, and then we can talk."

I nodded and took a breath.

"See you in there," Joe said kindly, and they headed toward the conference room.

I checked my watch. Yep, everyone was starting to get up from their desks. I tried to tamp down on the panic. I took a deep breath that sounded like a gasp.

Harriet suddenly appeared in front of me, holding a

glass of water. I downed it in three gulps, desperately thirsty, trying to think about anything but the potential embarrassment of the presentation not going well. Of Joe and Joey tilting their heads to the side, pity in their eyes.

Harriet widened her eyes and tugged on one of her red pigtails, a modern-day Pippi Longstocking. If Pippi had grown up into a coder who liked death metal.

"Yes to asking for the things you want! But . . . you realize no one *made* you do this?" she said, her dark eyebrows raised in judgment, looking at the empty glass of water. "You volunteered to do this presentation."

"I saw a chance for improvement; it's my responsibility." Even if it made me want to vomit.

Why do you want to be the boss, Marina? I'm not sure it's suited to your temperament, darling. Running a team would stress you out. Some people are lions, and some people are . . . beavers. My mother had been her typically anxious self this morning when she called to wish me luck.

Nope. I could do hard things. That was what being a grown-up was all about. And my future swishy-haired, "all together" self needed me to step up.

I exhaled, standing up and pulling my favorite blue blazer over my T-shirt and jeans. I popped in my lucky earrings, the ones with little blue pom-poms on them. Harriet nodded and led the way.

The conference room was full of people milling around, sitting on tables or leaning against the frosted-glass walls. A few at the front lounged on lime green beanbags, and I walked slowly to the front to set up my laptop. I tapped my star-and-moon pendant on my collarbone with my thumb, the nervous habit somehow comforting. I should really stop wearing the damn thing.

Harriet settled right at the front, nestled into a beanbag, picking at her ripped jeans. Ravi chucked himself down beside her and waved at me. Our little team. The team I was fighting to grow and lead.

I took a deep breath and imagined my lovely future flat, with my ideal green velour sofa, and my Insta-perfect bar cart with the neon sign above it. My happy place. I could do this.

"Guys! Hey there!" Joey decided to stand on a table to get everyone's attention, which was entirely unnecessary. "We've got a treat this morning! An amazing presentation from our own development manager, Marina! Marina . . . blow us away!"

No pressure.

I looked out at the sea of faces I sort of vaguely recognized. The bright white walls and large windows looking out over the city made me wince a little. I wanted to wear sunglasses in the conference room. Most people sat on top of the desks in the room, rather than in the chairs behind them, swinging their legs like children. A few leaned against the walls, expecting this to be a quick five minutes.

Huge motivational posters with cheesy sayings like *Follow your dreams* or *Work hard, play hard* lined the walls. Things that were vague and unhelpful but generally positive. The Joes loved that kind of stuff.

Behind me, a screen came to life, and I fiddled with the tablet to make sure the right slide was showing, peering over my shoulder. I looked back out at the people I worked with and wondered if it was bad that I knew so few of their names.

I knew Martha from marketing, that permanently concerned frown making lines in her forehead. I recognized Tara from reception, and the two guys in HR, and the constantly hooting twentysomethings from the sales team who seemed to always be high-fiving each other and throwing packets of crisps across the office. They all seemed to look at me blankly. Most of them probably couldn't pick me out of a crowd if they'd tried.

"Hi, all, I'll try to keep this quick, promise!" *Great, not exactly a power move, Marina.* "Joe and Joey have very kindly let me share some thoughts with you for how we organize the events on the site. The problem we have is categorization." I clicked through my presentation on the screen and a mock-up of our current site appeared, with all the different activities we offered. "Now, you might find someone who is a bungee jump enthusiast who also wants to spend an afternoon feeding llamas on a farm, but I'm imagining the crossover level isn't that high."

Polite tittering from my audience. *Okay, keep going.*

"What . . ." I coughed, and recovered. "What I think we're missing here is the group element—people aren't booking these excursions alone. They want to do them with friends. Lots of them would work for hen or stag dos—raft building and vintage makeup tutoring sessions? You can see it, right?"

Joey was nodding his head like a mad person. I clicked along, and my next mock-up appeared. I watched their faces, engaged and surprised, like they weren't expecting the nerd in development to have something to say. Possibly because I hadn't, really, since I'd started. I felt a weird sense of excitement—this was actually going well!

"So we need to think about groups," I said confidently, pointing to my mock-up. "We make it easy to share the booking info, we let you book for a group and split the up-front costs. Maybe we even create a space to share photos of the day or to send messages. These could easily be turned into reviews and promotional material for the marketing team." I gave Martha a smile, and she blinked in surprise. "People are going to want to use LetsGO with their friends, and we need to own that space, making it as easy as possible for them to get excited."

I looked around the room and found people nodding, smiling, generally shrugging positively. I wasn't the only person who had ideas, I knew that, but I was the first person who'd made a presentation like this. Our start-up was very good at fancy benefits and boozy freebies, but we had no direction. We were run by two guys who thought everyone decided on a Friday morning to flit away for a ski holiday in the Alps and could afford the last-minute fees. Any direction was a step in the right direction.

Joey clapped, so slowly I would have thought he was being sarcastic if he had the capacity. But no, he was just trying to start a round of applause. Luckily no one joined in, because we were all too incredibly English for such an unnecessary show of enthusiasm.

"That's brilliant, Marina! That's the kind of initiative we need, seeing a target market and just BOOM—going right on in there."

I beamed, relieved. I could hear Meera's voice in my head: *You were a very brave girl and now you deserve a nice wad of cash and a pat on the head.*

"Ahem." A man lounging against the far-right wall lazily lifted his hand as he coughed, just enough effort to get our attention. He looked like the wall was the only thing keeping him upright, his brown curly hair ruffled beneath a beanie, his green T-shirt creased, and his jeans ripped. He was a thirtysomething dressing like a nineteen-year-old, and I immediately disliked that smirk.

"Yes?" I clipped, irritated. "Did you have something to contribute?"

He grinned at me. "Yeah, actually I do." The man's Northern Irish accent was distinct but soft, and I watched as a few people looked at him quizzically, trying to figure out who he was. Clearly they had no more idea than I did. He pushed off the wall, smoothing down his top just to make us all wait a little longer for his thoughts. Anticipation.

Of course, a bloody storyteller.

I raised an eyebrow and extended a hand. "Well . . . ?"

He met my eyes in a challenge. "Well . . . it's a very good idea, love. Except for the fact that it's utter bollocks."

The gasp was so distinct that after a moment everyone laughed with discomfort.

"No, hear me out," the stranger said, smiling at the response and then having the *gall* to wander up, standing right in front of me. "What's missing here from . . . sorry, what was your name again?"

I was going to kill this man. Future me was melting

away like the Wicked Witch from *The Wizard of Oz.* This smooth bastard was ruining everything.

"Marina," I offered through gritted teeth, and he actually *winked* at me. Winked!

"Ah, Marina! *That* makes sense," he said, with a recognition I didn't like. "Well, what *Marina* here is missing is the clearest option of all—dates."

I frowned. "We've designed a really intuitive calendar, so I don't—"

He laughed, short, sharp, and lyrical, like he was moving up a scale. I noticed the looks from the women in accounting, taking in those bright eyes and pouting mouth, as if those features could make up for the fact that he was a cocky arsehole ruining my life.

"See, that's exactly my point! Not dates . . . *dating.*" He raised his eyebrows at me as if it was the most obvious thing in the world. "We're offering some of the most exciting activities in the city. When do you want to be doing something exciting and impressive? On a date!"

This guy is cracked. I looked at Harriet, who rolled her eyes.

"You often take your dates skydiving, do you?" I threw back, and he grinned, sticking his hands into his pockets.

"Let me guess, you're more of an only-one-glass-of-wine-it's-a-weeknight gal?"

Well, that certainly felt like a personal attack. And like someone had been reading my diary.

I took a breath and assumed a wide smile. "Well, dating as a woman is dangerous enough. You never know what kind of maniac you could end up spending an evening with. Chaos and spontaneity are cute in movies. Not so much on a Wednesday-night date with an accountant from Balham when you don't know if he'll murder you."

"Or bore you to death," Harriet added, trying to be helpful.

The man's lips quirked automatically, but he assumed a concerned expression.

"That does sound . . . not fun." He turned to his audience— *my* audience—and addressed them. "And isn't that what we're trying to fix here, really? Helping people have *fun*?"

I had my hands on my hips and heard a soft growl escape my throat before I even noticed. He did, though, my unknown saboteur. He grinned at the sound, those green eyes holding my gaze for a little too long, daring me to look away. I clenched my fists and refused to back down. I didn't know how long we just stood like that, staring at each other, but thankfully Joe stepped in to break the stalemate.

I knew it had to be bad, because Joe's solemn face was suddenly owllike. "Well, this is *quite* the debate. Are we the premier destination for groups of friends looking for a good time, or are we here to help you impress your beau?"

He pulled at the neck of his black jumper like he was being strangled.

"Our activities aren't suited to dating; that's not what we've been going for! We never have," I said, appealing to the sales team, who shrugged and nodded.

"Just because *your* dates are uninspired doesn't mean everyone else's are," the guy threw back, and then before I could respond, he added, "And even if they are, we should be the ones to change that! Just because we've been doing something a certain way, it doesn't mean it's the right way."

For the briefest moment, I tried to imagine any of the dates I'd been on in the past six months being somewhere other than a carefully chosen bar with clear lighting and an easy escape route. Why on earth would I waste time doing something cool with someone who might very well be yet another dud? It was upsetting enough spending eight quid on a glass of wine that I didn't even finish most of the time.

I snapped back to the room, where I stopped even pretending to be polite, throwing up my hands as if I'd lost control of them. "Sorry, who *are* you?"

The man threw his head back and laughed, and Joey jumped in, clearly overexcited and bouncing on his toes like a toddler.

"Ah, excellent question! This, team, is Lucas Kennedy.

He's one of our very talented freelance copywriters who has been working remotely from Belfast! Our marketing team will be familiar with Lucas's skillful copy and great ideas, but he may be a new face to everyone else!"

Lucas Kennedy. Of course.

I felt my jaw clench so tightly I worried I'd give myself a headache. I purposefully softened my features as I listened to him, so clearly loving the spotlight.

"Just here testing out the waters, whether it's about time to become a Londoner and all that," he announced cheerfully, then dared to look at me. I could feel myself about to explode.

"*You're* Lucas Kennedy," I breathed, almost shaking my head but managing to stop myself.

He grinned. "Lovely to finally meet you in the flesh, Marina Spicer," he said, hands in his pockets. "You are *exactly* how I imagined."

Lucas had been a thorn in my side since he'd started working for LetsGO. An endless array of requests and ideas and demands. *Why can't we just do this? How hard would it be to do that, really? Are you saying it's impossible, Marina? Is it too hard for you?* The guy never stopped, and when I ignored him, he went over my head. Which was how I'd spent last Christmas Eve as the only one in the office, making system changes dear Lucas had convinced the Joes were *essential.*

He was selfish, he was bossy, and he thought he was smarter than everyone in the room. As if knowing which version of "they're," "there," or "their" to use was a real life skill.

My email sign-off for Lucas Kennedy simply said "regards," and that was only because I couldn't sign it "burn in hell."

I ignored him completely and turned back to our bosses.

"Did you want to try my idea, or are you convinced people are willing to spend a good chunk of their income on impressing perfect strangers they may have nothing in common with?"

Lucas snorted. "Spoken like a woman who has never been on a decent date."

I felt my jaw drop, and prepared to say something I would probably regret, when Joey jumped in.

"Well, hasn't this debate been INVIGORATING?" he boomed, like he was an MC at a disappointing open-mic night. "This passion, this energy, this . . . STRENGTH OF CONVICTION . . . this is what we want from you guys! And Marina and Lucas have really shown how much they care, how much vision they have for LetsGO! I think we owe them a round of applause!"

Everyone dutifully complied, looking a little bewildered.

"So, what's the answer, boss?" Lucas said. "Because I've got to be frank with you: doing it her way is not going to showcase the copy in the way it deserves. We need to think about the user here."

I frowned at him and his attempt at being reasonable. "And doing it *his* way is going to screw up my perfectly coded algorithm. Which is all *about* the user."

Harriet *woo*ed from her beanbag. "Woo-hoo! Sexy algorithms, user experience, yes!"

Everyone laughed, and I felt myself take a breath. The man had gotten under my skin when he was four hundred miles away and I couldn't see his expressions. Now I was positively ripping my hair out to throttle him with it. I was better than this.

Lucas just grinned, good-natured and irritating as hell, leaning against the nearest wall like he didn't have a care in the world. I watched as the women in the room considered him. Would they side with the quiet woman with the good idea, or the man with the pretty green eyes who promised a world where men took the time to plan dates? Where single guys logged onto a website and compared evenings out, paid deposits, and surprised them with quality time and romance? Most of us were thrilled with a McDonald's drive-through on a Thursday night or a man who didn't ask about our sexual preferences in the first five minutes.

I watched them watch him. The hope was the killer.

Joe and Joey moved aside for a moment—"Talk among yourselves"—as they stepped into the hallway to confer.

"You must be *so* proud of yourself, turning up and making quite the stir," I hissed at Lucas under my breath.

He looked, as apparently was his default, amused. "You're just so easy to annoy, Spicer. If anything, it makes it *less* fun."

I clenched my fists and my jaw, speaking quietly. "Why today? Why couldn't you leave me with one idea, one moment when you don't bounce over like a Labrador desperate to tell me that *actually* the ball should be a different color, or a different shape, or forget the whole thing because dogs prefer chew toys?"

He turned his whole body then, suddenly straight-backed so I could see that, yes, he was capable of standing up, and yes, he was tall. I felt my neck twinge a little as I looked up, refusing to feel dainty, refusing to look away. I took a moment to note the tattoos covering his forearms, beneath his rolled-up sleeves, silly little drawings dotted in every free space. He clicked his wrist, a few leather bracelets jangling slightly. There was a disarming line in Lucas's eyebrow as he raised it, considering me.

"Is this about the Christmas campaign?"

I pressed my lips together, staring past him, crossing my arms. "You mean the one where you went over my head to the Joes to demand I make radical changes to the release I'd been working on for *months* and I had to sit here alone trying to fix it to your liking on Christmas Eve?"

He winced, opening his mouth, but I held up a hand.

"Nope, not finished. *Maybe* it could be about the site update, when you decided you knew better and crashed the upload feature. Or when I pitched a different series of article buttons to *help you* and you didn't even say thank you." I lowered my voice again, eyes flicking to the door. God, this was all over, really. I couldn't compete with Lucas's energy or charm, or the way people in the room seemed to be looking at him like he was their best friend when they hadn't even heard of him until now.

I sighed, trying to come to terms with my defeat. "Or it could be that I just wanted *one time* where I shared an idea and you weren't there to crap all over it."

"Wow, you really don't like me." Lucas blinked, honestly surprised. A small part of me thought he might apologize now that he knew what he'd done. Instead, he looked at me, overly thoughtful. "I'm not sure I've had anyone hate me before. A nemesis . . . how fun."

I held back a growl, but barely. He smiled lazily, like he knew it drove me crazy.

"It's like the company says, Spicer: collaboration is the sweet fruit on the tree of success."

"That doesn't even—"

I stopped talking as Joey bounded back in, bouncing on his heels as Joe followed more calmly behind him. He held his arms out wide, reminding me of a circus ringmaster. Except the elephants had gone rogue, the tent poles were slipping, and the tiger was eyeing the crowd.

Joey waited for silence, another fan of anticipation. Why did everything have to be such a *show* all the time? Why did the ice-cream cart in the office on Thursdays need to have sparklers on it, and why was I still finding glitter in my bra after that fun run for charity? Why couldn't work just be *work*, so I could focus on the more important parts of my life?

"What we need"—Joey grinned, raising an eyebrow—"is a good old-fashioned vote."

I felt my eyes go wide in panic.

"Team!" Joey stood up on the table again. "You are experts in your fields, and you are experts in what it means to be LetsGO! What do you think? Do we vote for Mr. Kennedy and his romantic notions of effort and energy in date planning?" He was clearly enjoying himself. "Or do we follow Miss Spicer's suggestions, on the importance of friendship, togetherness, and shared experiences?"

"There is a third option!" I heard a voice I recognized and didn't like that mischievous look on Harriet's face as she raised her hand.

"We do not compromise here! Halfway between an

omelet and a cake is a terrible mess!" Joey announced like he was some sort of spiritual leader.

Ravi frowned and whispered, too loudly, "Surely halfway between an omelet and a cake is a pancake, which is known for being delicious?"

I offered a one-shouldered shrug. Ravi still got annoyed that the Joes couldn't do metaphors.

"It's not a compromise, it's a suggestion for more research!" Harriet responded, holding out a hand for me to help her up. I pulled a little too forcefully. "Why don't we send them on a bunch of activities and see if the activities are better suited to dates or groups? Marina and Lucas can each take notes and give feedback. Do the activities, try the drinks? *Then* we can vote properly! In vino veritas, after all."

Cheeky cow, she knew they loved Latin.

Joey lit up, and I jumped in before Lucas could. "I'm happy to go and do research and give feedback, of course."

Lucas shrugged. "Sure, it's good to get a real sense of things. And my evenings are pretty empty while I'm visiting." I watched with interest as the female contingent of the room took a mental note of that fact. "There are only so many times you can watch *Moana* with your niece without going mad."

They all tittered and swooned, and I gritted my teeth. Trying to make himself all sweet and relatable, the bastard.

"Great! So you'll be our test duo!" Joey nodded, and my clenched teeth were the only reason my jaw didn't fall open. It was nice to see Lucas Kennedy, *the man who knows everything*, suddenly speechless. "We'll send you to five different LetsGO activities and you can give feedback! Lucas, you could even write about them! A little column to keep you busy while you're here!"

"I . . . uh . . . You've got it, boss." He looked at me like he was hoping I'd argue. *See, if you'd just kept your mouth shut, none of this would have happened. Now we both have to play along.*

"Sounds like a great challenge," I said, smiling politely, trying to drum up that enthusiasm they loved. I watched as Lucas's face fell. "I'll take notes and mock up some opportunities on the site. Lucas can write his little blog . . ." I paused to smile sharply at him, watching as the passive-aggressive jibe landed. "And then everyone can vote!"

"Okay! Brilliant. All in favor?" Joe said loudly, and everyone held up their hands. "Cool, the crowd has spoken."

As everyone filed out, Harriet gave me a double thumbs-up, and I glared at her.

"What was that about?" I yelped, grabbing her arm.

"Um, saving your ideas from being rejected outright?" she offered, shaking her arm free. "Getting you a bunch of activities and meals for *free*? Giving you some semblance of a life?"

"I have a life. What I didn't have, until today, was a need to spend an unholy amount of time with my nemesis," I hissed, making the mistake of looking up at Lucas just as he looked at me.

He sauntered over, hands in pockets, shoulders permanently in a half shrug. "Come on, now, 'nemesis' is a bit strong, isn't it?"

"It was your word!" I exploded.

"And I'm willing to be edited," he said smoothly, reaching past me and offering a hand to Harriet. "Lucas Kennedy, copywriter."

She took his hand, tilted her head, and held on for just a tad too long. "Harriet Graft, junior developer. Team Marina."

He smiled like he didn't even hear the warning. "Well, isn't she lucky?"

Harriet wasn't sure what to do with that, so she looked at the ground and blushed.

I turned to face him, not sure whether I was going to yell or plead. "What do you get out of this? I'm trying to get a promotion; this is my chance to get a fully funded team, to really have an impact rather than just fixing bugs and running behind all the time."

Lucas considered me, and for a moment, I thought he might show some remorse. He had his hands in his pockets again, like none of this really mattered to him. But it was a facade. Because beneath the ruffled brown hair, and the *Space Invaders* top, and the three-day stubble, I saw that throb in his clenched jaw. And those green eyes promised war.

"Wow, that sounds like it's really important to you," he said, nodding and waiting until I nodded back, a flicker of hope at a reasonable response. Then he grinned. "Maybe you should have given a stronger presentation."

I opened my mouth in shock. "So you get nothing out of this except to mess with me?"

He shrugged one shoulder, looking across the room at the bosses, in a discussion by the door. "Maybe living in London on a copywriter's wage isn't so easy. Maybe our fearless leaders are paying for a very nice hotel for me while they decide if we need an in-house writer rather than a remote freelancer. Maybe I've got other reasons to be in this expensive city."

I blinked, focusing on the important bit. "They're paying for your hotel room?"

Lucas just smiled. "But then again, maybe there's nothing in it for me apart from correcting your work, yet again, Marina Spicer. You make collaboration irresistible."

I was going to kill this man.

"So 'nemesis' *was* the right word."

He just grinned, wiggling his eyebrows.

"*Fine.*" I held out my hand, exhaling like it was all too boring for words. "I guess. Let the best person win."

Lucas Kennedy took my hand and squeezed it briefly, holding eye contact as he grinned. His hand was warm, his fingers firm as they dared to stroke the inside of my wrist, just once, so unexpected I wondered if I'd imagined it. But that smile didn't waver.

"Oh, don't worry, love. I absolutely will."

CHAPTER THREE

What a suave fucker!" Bec hooted as she reached across the table for the nachos. "Did you punch him?"

Bricking It was a new pop-up restaurant on the same road as Bec's salon, and she'd been invited to their opening week. So far it was a riot of colorful red and orange walls, uncomfortable leather seats, and dangerously reasonable beer prices. Which I was getting through a little too easily after my encounter with Mr. Kennedy.

"No, no, I did not." I took a gulp of my pint and sat back. "But God, I wanted to. I imagined it, like truly meditated on it. It would have been wonderful."

Meera snorted, picking up a jalapeño popper and considering it like it was a magic trick she couldn't figure out. "I just once wish you would lose your shit. Like, properly.

Lose your shit before you lose your mind, you know?" She stuffed the morsel in her mouth and briefly closed her eyes in delight.

"You should put that on a T-shirt." I rolled my eyes and pushed back from the table, collapsing farther into my chair. "But seriously, what am I meant to do?"

"You're meant to *win*, of course." Bec shrugged. "This guy has nothing on you. You're the queen of research, a problem solver. Practical and level-headed."

"You're his worst fucking nightmare," Meera supplied, mouth full.

I paused and looked at them both, their brightness shining even in this loud, vibrant location. I looked down at my jeans and T-shirt, then tapped my star-and-moon necklace.

"Wow, you guys make me sound so exciting and fun," I deadpanned, only half joking.

Meera rolled her eyes. "Am I gonna have to make you listen to that podcast about external validation again?"

I shook my head, grouchy. "There's no dirt on him, I've looked! You can't believe I'd be in an online war with a man and not do a social media search on him." I sighed. "Some days you just need one bad picture of a guy in a mullet or Crocs. But nothing. He doesn't exist."

Across the restaurant, a waiter dropped a tray of glasses and everyone cheered. I made a sympathetic face at the poor kid, who was scrabbling to sweep up glass and trying to ignore the furious blush on his cheeks.

Bec raised an eyebrow and tilted her head at me, holding her glass like she was waiting for me.

"What?"

"Focus, Rina. I think you're forgetting the most important thing of all here: you have a secret weapon."

I frowned. "I know Harriet said she'd kill a man for me, but I think she was being hyperbolic."

Bec pulled her fingers through her pale pink hair and shook her head. "You don't think creating an app that shows the weaknesses and flaws of a whole bunch of men across the country is an advantage at this point?"

Meera pointed at Bec. "That's a fucking epic idea! You said he seemed like a charmer, right? No wedding ring?"

I made a face and thought of how Lucas bit his lip after he smirked at me, finding my discomfort just so hilarious. How happy he was for me to know when he was watching, looking back with a challenge. That dimple in one cheek that had the women in sales fanning themselves jokingly that afternoon.

"That man is most definitely not the marrying kind. But that's not what Dealbreakers is for!" I said. "It's to help people find someone they're truly compatible with and to save them time. Not to just list bad traits. I created the good-egg badge and everything!"

Meera blinked slowly for effect. "What in the flying fuck is a good-egg badge?"

"Sounds like the patriarchy insisting Girl Guides know how to poach, fry, or scramble appropriately." Bec laughed, sipping at her lemonade.

"It's basically the Matt badge, for the lovely ones who just aren't right for you."

"Well, I do appreciate you bringing some random guy to our house party and declaring he was my soulmate." Bec smiled, raising her glass in a toast. "Definitely the best way to find a husband. Ten out of ten, would recommend."

"We're getting sidetracked," Meera said, gesturing at my phone. "Go find some dirt on the dickhead so you can be the winner."

"Knowing that his cock tilts to the left is hardly going to help her in a professional competition," Bec offered, and I choked on my beer.

"Depends on how she uses that information." Meera raised an eyebrow and smirked.

I typed Lucas's name into Dealbreakers and waited for that satisfying "ping" sound. The scanning screen came up, a bunch of punky little black and red love hearts loading as they pulled together all the data from every different dating app. And there it was—ding, ding, ding, we had a winner. Hinge, Tinder, *and* Bumble. His main profile photo was sweet, clearly taken abroad, where his brown curls had tinted in the sun, his skin was tanned, and his wide smile boasted that dangerous dimple. His eyes crinkled with humor, and I briefly wanted to know what he was laughing about.

And then I remembered he was the smug demon standing between me and my future and clicked on the comments tab.

"Holy shit," I breathed, eyes glued to the screen.

"Penis bends to the left." Bec nodded sagely, sucking up the last of her drink noisily through a straw. "Told ya."

"No, it's . . . he . . ." I blinked, refocusing on the screen. "He has nearly a *hundred* dealbreakers listed."

Meera shrugged. "Break it down for those of us who don't need technology to get laid. Is that a lot? What's the average?"

I paused, thinking. "The highest I'd seen before this was about twenty-five."

Bec smiled, looking for the bright side. "So, it's a numbers game, right? He's been on a hundred dates and each woman found one awful thing about him?"

"I made it so there's a maximum of six dealbreakers per date," I explained, scrolling frantically, "and Dealbreakers has only existed for six months, so . . . either it's a lot of dates with dealbreakers or a few dates who had a *lot* to say about him."

I watched as Meera did the math in her head. "Let's

hope it's the latter. Much more interesting. Much rather he was the worst man on the face of the earth, and all women agree." Meera snorted, stretching out her shoulders like they ached. "Come on, give us an example. How close to the earth's core is this guy living?"

I scrolled, trying to take them all in.

"He was on his phone the whole time we had dinner. And then he left early. I'm sure he had a date with another girl."

Meera shrugged. "I'm sorry, didn't you double up only a few nights ago?"

"Yeah, but I gave them my full attention before I bolted," I replied, looking for another. "*He hates dogs.* Who hates dogs? *He kept calling me the wrong name. He dropped a drink on me and didn't even really apologize.* Here's a good one: *He didn't offer to pay, and we had to split the bill down to the penny.*"

Bec pursed her lips. "Well, some of these are personal taste . . ."

"He *hates dogs,*" I yelped, vindicated.

"Sounds like a dickhead, as expected." Meera shrugged, rubbing her eyes. "Keep researching—I'm sure there must be something in those criticisms that's the key to his defeat."

I looked at her, the sag of her neck and the way her eyes drooped.

"Hey, are you okay?"

That smile was switched straight back on. "Me? Babe, I'm always okay. It's you two who need looking after."

Bec looked up, vaguely amused. "I need looking after?"

"You married a man three weeks after you met him; you need a keeper."

Bec rolled her eyes. "I have my own business in central London, I can do a liquid-liner cat's eye on the bus, and I seasonally change my duvets to ensure appropriate weight for the weather." She raised an eyebrow. "I fell in love quickly, I knew what I wanted, and I made it happen. That's not silly; that's efficient."

Meera looked at me, as if expecting me to back her up, but I raised my hands, refusing to get involved. Meera had never been in a relationship (at least not on purpose, and she was always very surprised when she was alerted to the fact), and she found the whole thing a bit nonsensical.

"Different people, different styles. No judgment from me," I said.

"Oh yes, because you're so accepting of different approaches." Meera laughed a little too harshly. "The woman with the checklist and the race against her biological clock."

"Hey," I said, a little hurt, "I don't question how you guys do things. I'm not a bad person for not wanting to date someone who swears or has tattoos or doesn't want kids."

"I mean, we have tattoos and swear, and you love us." Meera held up her hands.

"I don't have to bring you home to my mother." I signaled to the waitress that we needed another round of drinks. She smiled and gave me a thumbs-up.

"Penny loves us, perhaps too much," Bec countered.

"Too fucking much," Meera added, offering a smile.

I shook my head. "You don't get it, I don't have the time. They were used to Adam, they liked Adam. And now I have to find someone and get back on track. I want everything to be smooth."

Bec looked at me, a little concerned. "Honey, life is messy. No one's saying you have to get married in the next few years. If you want a baby, you can do that on your own. You tell the story. Your parents will deal with it."

We paused as the waitress set down mine and Meera's pints and Bec's lemonade, thanked her, and waited for her to leave before resuming. I didn't know how to make my friends understand.

I pressed my lips together. "That's not the point. That's not the story I've written for myself. That is not the plan. I want the flat and the marriage and someone who wants what I want. Adam doesn't get to take that from me just because he wants different things."

Meera sighed, like she'd had this argument with me a

hundred times before. "I'm just saying . . . there's nothing wrong with having a little fun."

I didn't want to say anything about how Meera didn't really seem like she was having fun anymore. The one-night stands and creeping out, the blank face as someone approached her as if they knew her. The ex-sort-of girlfriends who resurfaced whenever she was too tired for something new.

"So, how are you going to beat Lucas?" Bec asked, realizing that the conversation needed to change. I tapped my thumb against my collarbone, feeling the silver chain, and tugged on it slightly as I threw her a grateful smile.

"I guess I'm going to read all these comments and find out what kind of guy he really is. And if there's anything in there that will help me win, I'm going to use it."

"You could message some of the women who left comments, see if they can give you some ammunition?" Meera offered, downing the last of her previous pint. It was an olive branch.

I shook my head. "That seems too far, doesn't it? Him being"—I swallowed—"an *enthusiastic* dater may not give me any insight."

"Or he's not a Lothario, he's just incredibly crap at dating," Meera offered, pouring the dregs into the new pint and laughing as I wrinkled my nose.

"You already know he's scared of dogs. Do you wanna borrow Muffin?" Bec offered, apparently serious.

Meera fought a smile, and I laughed. "Thank you, love, but I don't think your mum's tiny Pomeranian is going to put the fear of God into the man."

"That thing is the devil in a fluffy bodysuit." Bec frowned. "But you're doing this, right? You're going to war? Because you deserve the things you dreamed of, and you took this job because of Adam and you should have everything you want."

I felt a little tearful. Bec had every reason to be tired of me and my nonsense by now. It had almost been a year. And instead she had taken me in and was my unfailing cheerleader no matter what.

"Thank you."

"Is that a yes?" Meera leaned in, then half sang, half yelled, "War, what is it good for? Getting Rina's promotion. SAY IT AGAIN!"

I tried not to laugh, but failed, shaking my head and pushing her arm. "Shh! Yes, yes, okay, I'll go to war and destroy my nemesis and get my promotion and fix my future!"

Meera grinned and nodded. "And no mention of babies and boring husbands. Excellent."

As we finished our drinks, talk turned to other things,

and I thought of Adam, apologizing for my confusion as he explained he'd never wanted any of the things he let me believe, his brow furrowed in sorrow. He'd never wanted to hurt me, he'd said, but he couldn't pretend anymore. He wanted to live, he wanted to grow. Try new things with new people. I thought of those first few dates after he'd left, getting dressed up and nervous, brimming with hope and prepped conversation cue cards, always ending in disappointment and outrage.

And then I thought of Lucas Kennedy, that dimple that appeared in his cheek as he'd smiled wildly and told me he was going to win. Charm and a nice smile were the worst skills a man could possess.

And I was immune to charm, and smiles, and all that nonsense he loved. I wasn't getting sucked in by the innocent questions and the quick one-liner retorts. Because I had a future to think about. A future that depended on making this job work for me in a real way.

I didn't have time for mercy. I had a plan and a timeline. My thirty-first birthday was approaching, almost a year since Adam had left. And what had I made for myself? There was no new, exciting single life. Just a series of dates that went nowhere and a collection of disappointing pottery under my bed.

I was going to win. Because I needed this. No, I *deserved* this. I had done my time, paid my dues. I had good ideas, and when I won this competition, I was going to walk up to Lucas Kennedy and hold out my hand for him to shake. I was going to grip his hand and stroke my thumb across the back of it and see how *his* eyes widened in surprise. And I was going to tell him the best person won.

I wondered how he'd take defeat, all solemn and serious, or childish and silly. Whether he'd laugh and pretend it never mattered anyway, or throw a hissy fit and storm out.

I couldn't wait to find out.

I had a life to build, and no one was getting in the way anymore. Not Adam with his leaving, or the random men on dating apps with their lying. And certainly not Lucas Kennedy with his lyrical laugh and single dimple.

He was going down.

CHAPTER FOUR

Nice guy, but my God, he was clumsy. Spilled beer on my dress, got caught on the chair in the bar, broke a glass. I wouldn't mind, but he seemed to. A lot. Good in bed, though.

The first assignment had arrived on my desk in a jade green envelope.

"The Joes asked me to document this on social media," said a young girl with huge gray eyes and a single white-blond plait, leaning over my shoulder to take a photo of the envelope. "I'm Marie, by the way."

"Nice to meet you." I nodded, then winced. "So we need to send you photos?"

She nodded, gave me a Post-it note with her number and email address, and disappeared like I'd imagined her.

The envelope suggested something fancy, like a masquerade ball. I was relieved to find it was nothing like that at all. The note gave us a time and address, and I wondered how much notice I was going to get before each activity. Would it always be last minute, on the day? I mentally ran through my tasks for the day and checked in with Harriet to make sure she was on top of it all.

"I've got it." Harriet had a turquoise pom-pom headband on, her red hair in little pigtail buns. I couldn't stop looking at it all. "You focus on getting our development team, getting that promotion. Do it for women in tech everywhere, desperate to see a woman in charge."

"No pressure." I rolled my eyes, and she smirked, stretching her arms out in front of her and clicking her wrists. "I don't even know how I *win* at what is essentially a date," I said, pulling at my hair and daring to glance across the main space to where marketing sat on the other side. I could only see a tuft of hair under a green beanie, and that was enough to enrage me.

"Well, it's his job to prove it is a date and yours to prove it isn't, right?" Harriet shrugged. "So you stay friendly. Do not—and I repeat, Marina—do not let the man charm you into acting like it's a date. I've seen stronger women than you fall prey to a fake dating daydream."

She shook her head sadly, as if remembering fallen soldiers. I just blinked. I only understood about 70 percent of what Harriet said most of the time. But that 70 percent was usually spot-on.

"I think my abject hatred for the man kind of kills the mood."

"Says a woman who has clearly never had hate sex." Harriet shook her head. "For shame. Just . . . keep imagining you're there with friends, keep reframing it. Take notes and I'll help you make an amazing presentation when you're done."

"Thanks." I smiled, and Harriet saluted.

"Team Marina, till the end."

Bad Mother Chuckers was in an industrial estate in South London, the kind you felt like you'd accidentally wandered into and worried you might be about to uncover a crime scene. I walked briskly, making mental notes as I entered under a symbol of two crossed axes. There was no way ax throwing was romantic. I'd practically won this one already. If anything, it felt like a gift from the Joes, like they knew I'd have to blow off some steam the longer I had to listen to Lucas's nonsense.

To be honest, I was kind of looking forward to ax throwing. I'd never done it, and it seemed like a great way to release tension. The wrought iron entrance and flickering faux candles inside gave a sweet medieval vibe, and everyone hanging in the bar area in front of the reception looked relaxed. Even in the afternoon, people chatted in groups, as if they were meeting for a green juice after the gym. Was ax throwing the new cardio? I pulled out my little notebook from my back pocket and wrote that down.

I bet this was good for mental health. And broken-hearted people. They should do an anti-Valentine's party!

Okay, I was going too far. I reined myself in, dropped my shoulders, lifted my chin, and looked around for Lucas as I reached the reception desk. I heard him before I saw him, that laugh echoing as he leaned against the bar, chatting to the bartender, right next to reception. The bartender was nodding and smiling, as if he was thrilled to be in conversation. What was with this guy?

I took a moment to just look at him, so relaxed, that dark curly hair tucked into a green beanie, his arms tensed as he leaned on the bar, so engaged in what the bartender was saying that it was like he had tunnel vision. Of course people would love you if you made them feel like the most interesting person in the world.

When he turned to see me, I thought he was going to switch back to that clearly competitive and unpleasant man I'd met in the office, but no, he smiled and waved. He was wearing another childish T-shirt, this one with a retro pink Care Bear on the front, with the words "Take care!" underneath.

"That's what you'd wear if this was a date?" I couldn't help but exclaim as he came over. Had he worn that T-shirt to work this morning? I'd been purposefully avoiding his existence.

Apparently nothing I said could shock this man. He just laughed and shook his head, eyes bright with humor. "Hello to you, too, you charmer."

I blushed, irritated with myself. "Erm, hi."

"And no, I probably wouldn't wear this perfectly excellent T-shirt on a date, but luckily our task is to assess the suitability of the *activity*, not the *company*."

"Well, thank goodness for that."

He raised an eyebrow. "The feeling is mutual, believe me. I don't date kiss-arses."

"And I don't date hijackers."

He tilted his head in surprise, that smirk still playing around his lips like he was permanently amused.

I helped him. "My presentation?"

"Oh, that. Yeah, I prefer to think of it as collaborative idea improvement."

"You can choose to see my boot up your behind as a therapeutic colonoscopy," I growled. "Won't make it hurt any less."

He laughed again, which irritated me even more.

"Do you ever just swear like an adult?"

"When we've got a whole beautiful language to use? No, it's lazy."

He rolled his eyes. "Of course it is." Then he swept his hands in front of me to suggest I lead the way. "Shall we start what's sure to be a *delightful* chance to spend time together?"

I rolled my eyes back and walked past him, heading toward the welcome desk. Our guide, Devin, talked us through how ax throwing had become popular and showed us the technique. I asked endless questions, making tiny chicken-scratch notes in the black leather notebook I whipped out from my back pocket.

"Aren't you meant to be all techie?" Lucas tilted his head as I scribbled away, and I raised an eyebrow.

"You're angry I have a notebook?"

He held up his hands like he wasn't there to fight. Liar. "I'm intrigued. I thought you were all about 'the best ways to optimize performance.'"

I could hear the quote marks.

"This is about that app I recommended to improve your editing," I yelped, pointing my pen at him. "I *knew* you were angry about that!"

"Increase speed, not improve. You need a human to edit."

"Tell that to spellcheck, grandad." I rolled my eyes and then looked back to Devin, who regarded us with surprised amusement.

"I get a sense you guys are going to be quite competitive." He grinned at me, and I smiled back, gesturing to Lucas with my thumb.

"Well, if you can print out a picture of this guy's face so I can put it on the bull's-eye, I'm sure I'll be one hundred percent more accurate."

Lucas snorted and tried to disguise it as a cough. "Enough smack talk, let's do this."

"And here's me thinking I wouldn't get an insight into your dating life," I retorted, and picked up an ax.

I loved watching the spin of the ax and the sound it made as it thudded into place. We were lined up in rows, like bowling, and everyone around us looked like experts. A woman next to us was using throwing stars—*throwing stars!*—and I found myself transfixed. It was like a movie. A revenge movie.

I smirked as Lucas took his first throw and the ax clattered to the floor, nowhere near the target. There was no way this was a good date idea. The tiniest amount of male insecurity and the whole evening would go down the drain.

"You know, I somehow don't think watching someone fail miserably at something is an aphrodisiac," I said lightly, pretending to make notes as he took another throw. This one skimmed the side of the target but still missed.

"You don't think being crap at something but laughing about it would make a good date?"

I thought about my pottery class and all those mangled lumps of clay I had in my room. I still couldn't make a vase. And yes, I was still angry about it.

"Depends on whether you find failure attractive, I guess." I shrugged one shoulder and smiled.

"You're trying to get a rise out of me, Spicer, but you're barking up the wrong tree, love. I've got a lifetime of failure behind me. I have no problem being shit at things. I'm good at all the things that matter."

He threw the last ax haphazardly, and this time, at least, it hit the target. Just about.

"Woo-hoo!" He jumped up in surprise, and I pressed my lips together so I didn't smile. He looked like a child who'd been told he could have cake for dinner.

"Getting the hang of it," Devin said with approval, and gestured for me to come up as he went to collect the axes.

"Dare I ask what these things that matter are?" I said as I walked past Lucas, and he just took a sip from his water bottle and smirked at me.

"Oh, I really wish you would."

Better not, then.

I assumed the position for my turn and felt myself get nervous, weirdly aware of my heartbeat as I threw the first one. I could feel Lucas watching me, and I wondered if he was willing me to fail or hoping I'd succeed. It was hard to tell. I put my entire body into my throw, hurling the ax over my head and watching it spin before it landed in the center of the target.

"Yes!" I jumped around in a circle, celebrating.

"Someone's a natural!" Devin exclaimed.

"It's all the pent-up rage, needs to escape somehow," Lucas deadpanned, making his own notes on his phone and taking photos of the decor.

"Are you sure you'd want to bring a girl somewhere she could have access to deadly weapons?" I retorted as I threw another. I watched as it effortlessly arced through the air and hit the bull's-eye. I gave Lucas a smug smile, enjoying the moment of shock on his face. "This is clearly better suited to a breakup party."

"People have breakup parties?" He looked to Devin. "Do you have any of those?"

"We have . . . angry groups of people, particularly around Valentine's Day, sure." The guide shrugged. *I knew it.*

"How else are you meant to celebrate a lucky escape or heal a broken heart?" I dared to look at Lucas, weighing up the ax in my hand.

Lucas looked back at me, as if the answer was obvious. "Whisky and Johnny Cash, obviously."

"Cliché."

"The best things often are," he offered, watching as I lined up my throw, as if trying to work out exactly how I was doing it. Just as I released the ax, he said, "So, which bastard broke your heart?"

I wrenched my shoulder in shock.

We both watched as the ax hit the base and, seemingly in slow motion, ricocheted off and back toward us. Or, more precisely, toward Lucas.

"Down!" Devin roared, and we all jumped.

Lucas ducked, but I still heard a yelp at the sound of impact, and again as the ax clanged on the ground.

"Holy shit." I rushed over to where he was half crouched, half sprawled on the floor, holding his hands to his face. "Did it hit you?"

His voice was hoarse. "Am I hallucinating, or did the ever-so-prim-and-proper Miss Marina say a curse word?"

I growled. "Lucas. Are you okay?"

"As if you care, coldhearted wee wench that you are."

I rolled my eyes. "For goodness' sake, let me see."

"So you can finish the job?"

I put an authority into my voice that left no room for argument. "Lucas."

He lifted his hand, his light eyes on mine as I surveyed his face, wincing a little.

I gasped dramatically, and his eyes widened.

"God, what? Why are you making that face? What's wrong?" He looked to Devin, who was peering over my shoulder. He shook his head, relaxed.

"Just think you'll find it hard to smirk with half your face missing," I said in a horrified voice, and then laughed. I watched as his eyes narrowed when he realized I was joking. "You're *fine*. You're probably going to have a bruise on your cheekbone and there's a *tiny* cut."

"I did say not to distract whoever's throwing," Devin added gently. "It rarely happens, but bounce back is always a possibility. Are you okay?"

"I'm fine, cheers." Lucas turned the charm on again, somehow seeming even more friendly now that he was overlooking his ordeal. When Devin went to get us a couple of beers from the bar to prepare for our next round, Lucas turned to me, cupping his cheek.

"You *do realize* that if you kill me, you don't get the promotion by default?" Despite his whining, I offered a hand to help him up. He hovered, like he wasn't sure I wouldn't drop him, but accepted my offer. His hand clasped mine, and I tried not to think about whether my own were clammy. His fingertips were rough, and I wondered if that was from hours of typing and whether mine were the same. He used me as a springboard and jumped up like a spaniel, seemingly ready for his next adventure.

"Believe me, if I were trying to kill you, it would be done already," I deadpanned, "with absolutely no evidence or motive. I listen to a lot of true crime podcasts."

"You're only sounding cooler by the moment, Spicer."

I suddenly felt the need to justify myself. It wasn't my fault! But also . . . he could have been hurt. *Oh no, is that guilt? I don't need guilt.*

"Look, there's no way I could have purposefully done that. If you hadn't distracted me with some dumb question just when I was throwing . . ."

"It's not dumb to want to know how recently someone was dumped when you've got to spend time with their delightful personality for a work project." Those green eyes were wide and honest. I spent a moment wondering whether they were field green or lagoon green, and then remembered that I didn't care.

I fixed him with a stare. "I have *not* been dumped." *Not recently.*

"So you're just . . . angry? That's your personality?"

"When people mess with my carefully laid plans just to boost their ego? Sure. Besides, if you weren't so clumsy, it wouldn't have hit you."

"I'm not clumsy," he said quietly, like a seven-year-old who had been told they had to go to bed. He knew I spoke the truth. And Dealbreakers had already prepared me. Clearly, he was touchy about it. I didn't even need to press on the bruise.

He looked so sad for a moment that I actually took pity on him.

"Do you want to cut this short, and I'll take you to

A-and-E to get checked out?" I offered, halfhearted, watching as he checked his cut in the reflective surface of the bar.

"Ah, so *now* we're getting to your idea of a good date. Do you maim all the men you meet?" he replied, irritating as ever.

"Only the ones who deserve it. I guess that's a no?"

He shook his head. "I am a professional; I will soldier on. Especially upon promise of a free beer."

I sat back on the stool at the tall table in front of the throwing station, raising my hands in defeat.

"But thank you," he said, suddenly serious. "I appreciate the offer."

I nodded, silent, unwilling to weaken my resolve. Stronger women than me had broken over sincerity and pretty eyes. And most of them had gone on to complain about him on the app.

I'd spent last night reading those reviews of Lucas. The number one dealbreaker listed for Lucas Kennedy? He made women think they were the center of his world. And then he never called them again.

I could see it, that charming half smile on his full lips, the playful winks, the compliments thrown out casually. He'd overwhelm them with charm, a full offensive from an experienced general, and then after coffee, or dinner, or the next morning, he'd tell them they were beautiful and special and perfect, but he just wasn't ready for anything serious.

The worst dealbreaker of all—wasting women's time.

Devin returned to break the silence, placing two beers and a plate of curly fries down on the high table. "Don't let it spook you!" he said to Lucas. "Take a beer break, and when you do your next round, alternate turns. And don't wind each other up!" He laughed as he departed.

"Might as well tell the sun not to shine!" Lucas replied, digging into the food with the enthusiasm of a man who hadn't had a real meal in weeks.

"So, we gonna continue?" I said, dipping a fry in ketchup then mayo before he could eat them all. He wrinkled his nose at my condiment choices but wisely chose not to comment.

"And subject us both to more of this endlessly witty back-and-forth? I'm too tired to keep up in my damaged state, Spicer. You've broken me." Lucas shook his head dramatically.

"Well, that's heartening," I said, crunching away. I took a sip of my beer and closed my eyes. Okay, there were worse ways to spend an afternoon on the company dime. And yes, I might suck at pottery, but I was secretly an expert ax thrower. Who knew?

He laughed at my response, and when I opened my eyes, he was poking his cheek.

"Stop doing that, you'll make it worse." I flapped my hand at him.

"Aw, good to know you care." He grinned, and I took a deep breath, wondering whether I had the energy to carry on with this.

"You know, you make it really hard to like you."

"Well, I appreciate you trying."

I fought a laugh. "Shall I go first this time?"

As I lined up my ax, I took a deep breath and threw. It hit the target with a satisfying thud. When I turned around, Lucas was crouched on the floor, hands covering his face. "Is it over? I just can't take it anymore!"

I didn't manage to hold in the laugh that time, and he smiled like he'd won a point.

Charm me all you like, mister. I know exactly who you are. It won't work on me.

I held out my arm. "Go on, prove to me how attractive losing is."

Lucas shrugged, went to collect my ax, and squared his stance, taking a deep breath. I watched, just a little hopeful that he'd actually hit the target this time.

"If you make your feet a little wider . . ." I offered before I could stop myself.

"Shh, you've already maimed me, you don't get to distract me, too."

"I didn't maim—"

The ax hit the bull's-eye, and I found myself clapping as he celebrated. When he turned, I put my hands by my side, my face impassive.

"You know your problem, Spicer?" he asked as he strutted back to the table.

I walked past him to collect the ax and rolled my eyes. "Yes, it's *you*. You're my problem. You and your big mouth getting involved in *my* project."

He shook his head, leaning forward on his forearms on the table. I tried to ignore the rather pleasing tension this created in his biceps, his T-shirt sleeves straining a little. I focused back on his face. "Your problem is that, actually, you quite like me."

I paused, trying not to laugh. "Impossible."

"No, really." He smiled. "It's okay. Happens to the best of people despite their intentions. Like, it pisses you off, but you actually like me."

"Is this how you think you make friends? Just walking around insisting people like you until they give up?"

"Come on, be honest. Just the *teeniest*, *tiniest* bit." His eyes actually twinkled. *Twinkled.*

I paused, thinking about it. "You're charming," I admitted.

He clapped his hands. "Okay, so now we're—"

"But I don't trust charming people," I interrupted, waving a hand. "Charm is just a lie with a pretty face."

"Oh." He looked genuinely perplexed. "So . . . I guess I should just be relieved you think my face is pretty?"

"And who knows how long that'll last if I get my hands on another ax?" I said lightly, and took my throw without even really concentrating. Bull's-eye. Again.

"So now we know how you are with something you're good at, how are you with something you're bad at?" Lucas asked seriously, making notes on the back of a stained napkin.

"Pretty awful," I said honestly. "I don't like being bad at things. Who does?"

He raised a hand, then grabbed his beer. "If I suck at something, it means I've tried it. There's a big old world out there. And honestly, as cool as it is that you're some sort of idiot savant at ax throwing . . . still means you're an idiot, right?"

"What was that about being charming?" I huffed, and got out my notebook. "Look, putting our ever-entertaining repartee on hold for a moment: Real work—you'd bring a date here?"

He looked around and ticked off on his fingers: "It's fun, it's unique, it's affordable, the snacks are good, it's memorable."

"Memorable."

"Everyone wants a good start to their story, right?" He

shrugged. "When you're telling your engagement story, you want to say, 'We went on this amazing date and had this wonderful time,' not 'We had an awkward drink in a shitty pub and had sex because we were drunk and now we're together because we're scared of being alone.'"

I blinked. "Feel like I learned a lot more than I needed to about you just then."

"Me?" He leaned back. "I'm an old-fashioned romantic, through and through."

I snorted. "Sounds like it. You do realize people don't meet like that in real life? That's a rom-com movie fantasy. People meet at work or on apps, and years later, with hindsight, they make up this story about how they knew all along to make it sound more interesting."

He winced. "Ouch, cynic."

"You think anyone's ever met arguing over the last pair of gloves at Bloomingdale's, or because he made a bet to turn her into the prom queen?"

"So what I'm gathering here is that you hate romantic comedies?"

"No." I shook my head. "In fact, I love them. I love those big epic moments where everything comes together and the music swells and fireworks go off in the background. But those moments aren't real. And believing in that stuff can get you hurt."

He raised his eyebrows. "I dunno."

I threw up my hands. "Do you wait to see what I have to say or decide to disagree in advance?"

"I just mean . . . no, most of us don't get big, dramatic meet-cutes or crescendos before the credits roll . . . but fireworks exist. There should always be fireworks. Otherwise, what's the point?"

"Suddenly I understand why you'd spend forty quid on an ax-throwing experience for a date you don't even know that well." I shook my head, judging him.

"Because I'm a classic romantic?"

"Because you can't bear not to be the most popular guy in the room. You need to be liked." I smirked.

"So good of you to work on curing me of my debilitating problem." Lucas rolled his eyes, irritated. "Go on, then, your turn. Why does this work for groups? Your gaggle-of-angry-hags meetup or whatever."

"It's empowering, it's energetic without requiring skill, it's well priced, and you can get a good competition going between groups. Food and drink would be good for birthday parties. And if there was a group of people here with us, they'd see me wiping the floor with you."

"Fair." Lucas stood, looking around. "So this first one's a draw?"

"We won't know until the end, I guess."

He toed his boots on the floor and looked up at me.

"So, the Averages asked me to write up our days out for the blog," he said as we started walking toward the exit, falling into pace with each other.

"Averages?" I paused, then it hit. "Joes. Funny."

"Do you want to check what I've written before it publishes on the site? Make sure I'm not describing you as a gorgon or exaggerating my terrible maiming at the hands of Marina Spicer?"

He held the door open for me as I walked through, and I nodded my thanks.

"Thank you. But weirdly"—I paused, knowing I was going to regret saying this—"when it comes to that, I trust you completely."

That smile was megawatt, undeniable. It shone so brightly, I was a little off-kilter in the limelight. This was a dangerous smile. It was a smile that said you were the most important person in the room. The most beautiful, the most interesting. And for the briefest second, it was intoxicating.

It was actually hard to breathe in the face of so much . . . unabashed fondness. Like I'd impressed him, surprised him, delighted him.

And then I suddenly remembered every woman on Dealbreakers who had thought she'd found her soulmate in Lucas Kennedy, the man who made you the center of his universe for as long as he stuck around.

"I knew it," he said, pointing at me as he started to back

away down the street. "You like me! You trust my writing and respect me as a human being!"

"I do not!" I called back, irritated.

"You do, you really do!"

"Good-bye, Lucas."

"But . . . we're going the same way!" he said, laughing after me as I walked off. I bit back a smile and focused on how Lucas Kennedy was the one thing standing between me and my future plan. Between me and my beautiful flat and my brilliant job and, somehow, my future relationship and the family I was eager for. It all started with this job, this task. This was where everything fell into place for me.

And yet, when I was safe on the bus back to the office, with no flirting copywriter to distract me, and no need to be spiky and clever with my retorts, I thought about that smile, and how nice it had been for someone to look at me like I was the sun coming out. No one had smiled at me like that in a long time.

I'd missed it.

CHAPTER FIVE

As I waited for the bus to tonight's date, my phone rang. HOME flashed on the screen, and though I supposed I should update it, my parents' landline would always claim that title.

"Hello?" I decided to walk to the next stop; it was easier to keep moving if I had company.

"Hello, petal," Dad chimed, "I'm making that curry recipe. How many teaspoons of garam masala?"

I half rolled my eyes. Dad always had to call for a reason. Even if he had no reason at all.

"Two teaspoons." *And you know that because you've been making this recipe for longer than I've been alive.* "What's up?"

"Just wanted to talk to the youth of today. Feel relevant

and up to date. Very important to stay on top of these things." I heard the smile in his voice.

"What are you up to?"

"Eh, the same. Always the same. Driving, of course, and I fixed next door's stupid plumbing, nearly had the whole street underwater! And I've been chatting with your mum about your birthday . . ."

Ah, here we go. It was a warning call.

"Got a few weeks yet, Dad. Happy with a gift voucher," I said, certain that wasn't what he was calling about.

"Of course, well, actually your mum did have an idea for your birthday present. It is sort of a voucher. And I, well, I'm not sure it's a good idea, but maybe I'm old-fashioned and I'm missing something, so if she mentions it, just be kind, hey, pet? She's thinking of you. She wants you to be happy."

"You're making me worry . . ."

"No, it's just, you know, best intentions and—"

"IS THAT MARINA?" I heard a yell in the background.

I half laughed. "Hand over the phone, Dad."

I flagged down my bus, tapped my card on the reader, and gave the bus driver a smile that he didn't register. As I bounced down the aisle to take a seat, I heard my dad's voice whisper, "Remember what I said. Best intentions."

There was a fumbling sound as he passed me over to

Mum, and I held my own phone away from my ear in anticipation.

"Darling!" Mum's voice always boomed. Dad was a reserved cabbie who liked to find out about his riders' lives. I often said he should charge more and call it a therapy cab. Mum, on the other hand, was a school administrator who took no shit and was only slightly angry about never making it as an actress. She was the queen of her local drama club though. No one could project to the back row like Penelope Spicer.

"Hey, Mum, how's it going?"

"How did your presentation go?" Honestly, I was touched she'd remembered. She tended to react enthusiastically and then immediately forget stuff that didn't directly impact her. Mum's strength was in celebrating the wins. You got an A on a test, she threw you a party. You got a new job, she called the local paper to see if they could mention it. Your long-term boyfriend leaves you after more than a decade and . . . she tries to fix it. It was best to keep Mum in the dark about things that weren't going perfectly.

"It's . . . ongoing." I explained the situation briefly, lowering my levels of vitriol where Lucas was concerned.

"Well, not everyone needs to be a leader, my love. You had a perfectly good job doing the website at that university. We don't all have to shoot for the moon, Marina. We're proud of you no matter what."

Mum's brand of acceptance always made me feel like I was expecting more than I was capable of, more than I was worth. And that she'd read a very specific book in the nineties about important parental catchphrases and had never quite moved on.

"It's a good job, with good perks."

"Like pick 'n' mix Fridays?"

"Like great maternity pay and good health coverage."

"Hmm, so you're still planning on having a family, then?" Oh God, I'd walked right into that one. My Mother and the Case of the Biological Clock.

"Yes," I said, feeling like a sullen teenager. "Why?" *Just because my boyfriend dumped me doesn't mean I can't still have children one day.*

"Oh, it's just good to hear, darling. I get worried about you out on all these dates, playing the field. That's what you call it, right? Living that hashtag ho life?"

I cringed so hard it felt like my muscles would never relax.

"I'm just meeting people, Mum. That's how you get to the baby-making bit. Finding a willing participant."

"I didn't need to date around to know your dad was the one. I just looked at him and—"

"It was perfect, I know. It's not like that now, Mum. And even if it was, you met Dad at school. That didn't exactly work out for me."

"Speaking of, Patricia said Adam's doing very well. New job, really thriving," Mum said breezily, as if she had no idea how that would hurt.

"That's great," I said through gritted teeth. "I'm happy for him. And I'm thriving, too, you know."

"I know, that's what I told her. 'Patricia,' I said, 'you can be proud of that boy all you like but you know he'd not be anywhere near as successful if my Marina hadn't helped him along all those years.'" She sounded so satisfied.

I slapped a hand against my face in horror. "You didn't say that. Please, Mum."

"Well, it's true! Adam was a nice boy, and if you ever get back together I will be happy as a clam, but he wanted to be a rock 'n' roll star, and you made him get a real job."

"He still wants to be a rock 'n' roll star," I mumbled. "Look, please don't talk to his family about me. It's awkward."

"Marina," Mum said firmly, and I knew one of her this-is-really-a-pep-talk moments was coming, "you have nothing to be embarrassed about. He left *you*. He wasted *your* time. He's the reason you may never have the chance to have kids. Quite honestly, he should be ashamed."

"People are allowed to change, Mum," I tried weakly, looking out the window as the bus trundled on, wondering if everyone else out there had these sorts of conversations with their mothers, or if they were from sane, normal families.

"Nonsense. People don't change if they love you."

Ouch. Time to switch the subject. I closed my eyes and said faintly, "Dad mentioned something about my birthday?"

She gasped theatrically. I could imagine her putting her hand to her chest. "Naughty man! But yes, I had a rather genius idea for your birthday, darling. It was Doris at work's idea, actually, her daughter did it. She's a lesbian, you know."

I did know.

"So . . . what is it?" Keeping Mum on track was a full-time job.

"Oh, freezing your eggs, darling!" She clapped her hands down the phone. "We can give you the gift of time! Can you think of a better gift than *time itself*?"

I wanted to ask if she could go back to when I was fifteen and Adam Phillips asked if I fancied going out, and make me say no so I saved over a decade. And if not, then this wasn't the gift of time.

The bumping movement of the bus was making me feel sick, the way it trundled and crawled through traffic, seemingly getting no farther than when I'd stepped on. I pulled on one of the windows, but there was no air.

Just noise and fumes. I sat back down, unsure of how I'd got here.

"I . . . honestly don't know what to say." I blinked, trying not to be hurt. I made my voice gentle, pleading. "I'm thirty, Mum. I've got time."

"Less than you think, darling," she said softly. If we'd been having this conversation in person, she would have tucked my hair over my shoulder, skimmed my cheek with a pastel pink nail. But on the phone, when Mum had an idea and a chance to fix things, she was like a bulldozer: impossible to negotiate with. "I'm not trying to be unkind, I'm just trying to make sure you have choices. We'd never planned to have children, but we had other things in our lives."

Oh yes, please tell me again how you'd never planned to have children, and yet here I am.

"I have a full life." *Or I will, once this promotion starts everything in motion.*

She didn't even reply to that. "You're a practical girl, darling. I'm just being practical. There's nothing to be ashamed of. Sometimes life doesn't work out like you planned." We both knew she was lying now. If you were Penelope Spicer, life turned out exactly as you planned, or you hadn't planned well enough. "Plus, there's a discount on the egg retrieval and we can pay for the storage for a year as your present. Then next year you can take it over. They call it a freezer fee, isn't that cute?"

"Oh adorable," I said dryly. "I've got to go, Mum, I'm going to miss my stop."

"Okay. Love you!"

"Love you," I repeated with a lump in my throat.

With an ax in my hand I'd felt like I could conquer the world. Now I was just a woman running out of time.

Really, after that, the last thing I wanted to do was go on a date. But, as my mother had so eloquently pointed out, I didn't really have time to waste. And something about that made my chest constrict and my stomach churn, like there was a countdown timer above my head that everyone else could see except me. And I was almost out of time.

Desperate for something to do instead of drinking my glass of wine too quickly and jiggling my leg like a nervous rabbit considering making a break for it, I opened my work email. Today's activities with Lucas had thrown off my work schedule, and I needed to catch up. This afternoon I'd resolutely put my headphones on and kept my head down, trying to ignore his lounging figure spinning in his office chair across the way. He'd caught my eye once and winked. I hadn't looked up for the rest of the day.

And now, an email from him, with a link to the site.

His article, already. Damn, he worked quickly. But as I opened the link and scanned the page, I realized he'd kept his word. He could have made me sound like a murderous gorgon, and yet he'd made me sound . . . fun? Interesting, even. Our irritating back-and-forth read like top-level banter, and I was impressed by my own wit.

> *While my date might disagree, there's something vaguely romantic about nearly getting your head knocked off by a beautiful warrior woman. But maybe that's just the head injury talking.*

Oh, you smooth bastard.

I sipped at my wine and tried to remember he was playing a game. We both were. But he was talented, no doubt. The women in the office had softened toward me today. Like his proximity had humanized me in their eyes. They'd all asked how the date went when we got back to the office, tittered about my near miss with the ax. Talked about how *nice* Lucas seemed, how it must have been *so much fun*! I couldn't tell if they suddenly thought I was nice, or they just wanted to figure out if I was standing in the way of their shot with Mr. Perfect.

They were welcome to him.

I checked my watch. David, an accountant from Leeds, was ten minutes late. Not a great start, but not necessarily a dealbreaker for me. Things happened: traffic, work, life. If the wait reached fifteen minutes, though, I'd be reconsidering. People's time mattered.

David had good reviews on Dealbreakers; people said he was a little quiet at first but polite and driven. He had two dogs; he loved living in London. He was close to his family, but not too close. He had a five-year plan, and his photo, while a little blurry, didn't include the arm of a woman who'd been cut out of the picture, a random child he was using to show he was appealing, or him holding a giant fish, as if he needed to prove his survival skills. So already, good start.

"Hi, I'm so sorry I'm late. Are you Marina?" The man who was standing in front of me was . . . well, even using the word "*man*" was a bit of an overstatement. Oh my God. In the picture he'd had stubble. He'd looked older. His age range was set to thirty plus.

This is a child.

"David?" I blinked, and he nodded and sat down, grabbing the menu.

"I think there's been some mistake," I said suddenly, and watched as his eyes widened. "How . . . how old are you?"

"Oh," he said, suddenly sheepish. "That."

"Yes, that."

"Age is just a number. Isn't it worth getting to know each other first and finding out if we're compatible before we worry about things like that?" He looked so hopeful, but I couldn't stop myself from shaking my head in horror. I had done my research; I had read the reviews. All I wanted was *one* person who could meet my needs. I didn't need romance; I didn't need a big, beautiful story or fireworks exploding in the distance as we kissed. I just needed someone who was the person they said they were. It didn't seem like a huge ask.

And yet . . . here I was, disappointed, again. I wanted to cry.

"Do you want to start a family in the next two years?" I said blankly, daring him to try to talk his way out of it.

"I . . . uh . . ." He tried to hide his horror, and failed. "No, I'm still finishing university."

"Exactly. So age does start to matter, doesn't it?"

"I just . . . I seem to do better with older women—"

I felt my jaw drop, and stood up, almost knocking my wineglass across the table in my hurry to get out. I caught it just in time, steadying it on the table, trying to find the strength to even have this conversation. *Older women.* Of course, women in their thirties were "older women" if you were still basically a *teenager.*

David held up his hands in apology. "I meant women in their thirties! I don't know why, but they seem to get me more than girls my own age!"

I clenched my fists in frustration and heard my squeaky

angry voice escape: "Well, that seems surprising, as your brain hasn't even finished developing yet!" I took a breath and wiggled my fingers, trying to find a way back to being a responsible, reasonable human being. Not just a walking disappointment machine. "David, I am trying to find a life partner. I want to have children. I've got things to do, and I don't have time to waste on someone who is still figuring out how to separate their washing in the machine." I felt myself crumbling, on the edge of falling apart. I took a deep breath. "Just . . . put accounting student on your damn profile, would you?"

He nodded, as if scared.

"I'm gonna go. Good luck with your studies." I downed my wine, placed the glass on the table gently, and walked out without looking back. Was it incredibly rude of me? Maybe. Would I potentially laugh later when Bec snorted about taking out a boy toy and what time he had to be home for din-dins? Sure. But right now, all I felt was overwhelming disappointment.

Weirdly, I thought about what Lucas would think of it all. How he'd chuckle and feel sorry for "the poor lad" and wonder if I'd been unfair. No harm in just being polite, was there? he'd have said. Why not take the time, get to know someone, be surprised, learn something new?

Boundaries and expectations mattered, though, right? What use was wasting each other's time, just to be polite?

I'd had years of my life wasted; I was behind schedule. Even if I had liked David, even if there had been an immediate connection and he'd made me my funniest, wittiest self . . . I wasn't giving up my future. Not for anyone. Not again.

CHAPTER SIX

Another dud?" Harriet asked as I sat at my desk the next morning, headphones hovering on the way to my ears. She looked particularly colorful today, a bright pink and yellow kilt over ripped black tights and a dark, nearly purple lipstick.

I smiled, trying to remain cheerful. "I don't want to talk about it."

"I'm sure it couldn't live up to the joyful experience of trying to kill Lucas Kennedy with an ax," she said, raising an eyebrow and pulling on her bright red braid.

"So you read the article." I sighed, putting the headphones around my neck and leaning back in my office chair. "How am I meant to compete? He writes a funny blog that everyone in the office loves, and I come up with . . . a PowerPoint presentation?"

Harriet took a moment to consider. "You know, I don't think it's a bad thing. He's making you the star of this whole thing. Like he's trying to convince you that these are good date locations, but he's also trying to date you. In a way."

I said nothing, just blinked, unimpressed.

"Not the answer you wanted, I get it." She held up her hands like I was going to shoot. I softened my facial expression. "Just . . . he's raising your profile. Besides, I think you should do a glorious page mock-up for Bad Mother Chuckers and share it so you're even. If everyone in the office is invested, you need to start showing your work."

The minute she said it, I felt a spark of inspiration jolt through me and twitched my fingertips, considering it.

"Ooh, she's in creation mode." Harriet saluted, recognizing that look. "Get to it, let me know if you need any feedback."

I spent the morning doing what the woman said. If I wanted to win this, it wasn't enough to go along with it and do my part; I needed to show it. I needed to make these people see my side. And sure, I wasn't natural with the small talk or remembering people's names (I was too busy trying not to forget my own when it was my turn to talk), but I didn't need to be Lucas Kennedy. I didn't even need to be liked. I just needed them to believe in my vision for the direction of LetsGO.

And even as Lucas's hijacking of my project annoyed me, at least people were interested. We hadn't had much direction since I'd started here, and the fear that the money and pick 'n' mix were going to run out soon was on a few people's minds, I was sure.

I mocked up a page and emailed Marie, the Joes' PA, for any photos that Lucas had given her, unwilling to ask him myself. She was apparently in charge of this little competition of ours anyway.

Then I designed a group booking system, making it look like a group had uploaded their photos separately, commented on the event, asked questions, and left reviews. I'd made it look like Bad Mother Chuckers had responded and thanked them, offering a discount voucher. And then I messaged Bec for a little creative help. Within fifteen minutes, she emailed me a drawing I'd asked for, and I added it to the page. It was a cartoon of a grown man, crouching down as an ax bounced above his head. I used Photoshop to make it look like all these uploaded photos were Polaroids, and when you clicked on the page, it generated a photo collage. In the center were Lucas and me, smiling toothily in the photo Devin had insisted we take before we left. I could almost feel how my teeth had clenched as I stood just far away enough to make it clear this was not date territory. And, of course, Lucas looked relaxed and happy, even with that slight bruise forming on his cheek.

I'd built an imaginary world in which I was not only friends with Lucas Kennedy, but we had a whole group of people who would go ax throwing with us. Who would leave comments joking about competing, and who stole the last curly fry, and who was going to win next time. I may not have been a writer, but I was clearly good at imagining the unimaginable.

When I showed it to Harriet, she muffled a squeal. "This. This is exactly what I meant. Fucking epic." She raised her hands and then lowered them. "I bow down to the princess of . . . page layouts. Send it."

I paused, unused to sharing stuff on the internal system unless it was a development update that no one read or an announcement no one wanted. I wasn't used to showing off. But there, from yesterday, was Lucas's link, his friendly winky-face emoji mocking me as he'd told the whole office he'd written about our "date." I had to do the same.

Within five minutes, likes and comments poured in. People who had never spoken to me in the office now were "LOL"ing and congratulating me on a job well done. Hashtags #TeamMarina and #TeamLucas had started, and I wondered what was really happening here. I peered through the glass walls of our office pod into the main area and out to where marketing sat opposite us. So far, I'd only been able to see a tuft of hair beneath yet another beanie. The back of his neck as he leaned forward in his chair.

And then I heard it. His light, loud laughter was easy to recognize. I felt my pulse race a little and then shook my head. But before I could turn away, Lucas leaned back in his chair, head turned to face me, and grinned the brightest, most delighted smile. A smile like that could destroy a woman weaker than me. He tilted his head and held up both hands in a silent clap. I twirled my hand in an approximation of a royal thank-you and turned back to my desk.

Twenty minutes later, Marie arrived with another envelope, ruby red this time.

"The Joes are really going big on the production value for this." I snorted, and Marie nodded, a world-weary expression on her young face.

"I think they're just excited there's something to talk about, you know?" She shrugged. "Oh, loved the cartoon, by the way. Super cute. Glad you didn't behead him, though. Seemed like a close call for a while there."

With that, she disappeared and I was left wondering whether my behavior suggested that I would actually behead a man for getting in the way of my promotion and whether that was something to be worried about or proud of.

I was frowning when Lucas suddenly stuck his head around the doorframe, even though the glass walls made that pointless. He waved his red envelope. "There's something ominous about a red envelope. I thought we could open them together."

"Afraid?" I snorted, then held up a hand. "Don't make a maiming joke, it's getting old."

He nodded, then leaned against the doorframe. "Open on three? One, two . . ."

He tore it open before I could get to mine, and I yelped. "You said three!"

"I lulled you into a false sense of security!"

"Why?!"

"Because . . . it's fun?"

When we looked at the cards, his face fell. I, on the other hand, couldn't stop smiling.

"Smug doesn't suit you, Spicer." Lucas sighed, adjusting his jumper.

"Are you pouting because this is clearly suited to groups or because you're crap at escape rooms?"

"No, I'm just hoping being claustrophobic isn't going to put me at a disadvantage!"

I looked at him, wondering if he was really claustrophobic or was pretending vulnerability to lure me into going easy on him. I raised an eyebrow. "Hmm."

Lucas held up a hand. "Scout's honor. Anyway, looks

like we need to leave now if we're gonna make it. You ready to go?"

I grabbed my jacket and closed down my laptop. "Yep, one second. Also, no way in hell you were a Boy Scout. Way too wholesome."

"Oh come on, I'm always prepared." He laughed, stepping back as I sidled past him, waving at Harriet. "Ask me what's in my pockets right now."

"No." I led the way to the lifts, him following me like an overexcited golden retriever. I noticed the rest of the office looking our way and smiling. Some gave me a thumbs-up.

"Come on . . . you'll be impressed!"

"But will I be disgusted?" I put a hand on my hip.

"No!" Those wide eyes spoke of innocence. I didn't believe him for a second.

"Okay, but if you suddenly pull out a stack of condoms because you're prepared . . ."

Lucas looked a little affronted. "I'm a gentleman, Spicer. Jesus." He opened his hand and revealed a Swiss Army knife, three elastic bands knotted together, a small ball of rather fluffy Blu-Tack, and a fun-sized bag of jelly beans.

"Why?" I asked, stepping into the lift and waiting for him to follow.

"Team Marina!" someone yelled from the office as the doors closed, and we looked at each other. Suddenly, the elevator was a little too close for comfort, those green eyes and smirking mouth a little too easy to pay attention to. He seemed to take up so much space, the backs of his arms brushing mine as I rearranged my bag and coat. I jumped slightly at the electric jolt and reached for the button. He still hadn't said anything, just looked at me knowingly, like he was in on a joke I knew nothing about.

"Why do you have a bunch of rubbish in your pockets?" I repeated, annoyed at how low and soft my voice seemed. Why was there no air? And why was he *still* smiling at me?

"Because, you never know how things are going to turn out."

I did not like the confidence in that smile. Time to pull myself together. Even if some small part of me wanted to ask what aftershave he was wearing.

I assumed my unruffled professional persona, shook my head, and staunchly faced the doors. Ensured absolutely no part of him was touching me. "I know how things are going to turn out. That's what careful planning is for."

"Oh yeah, you foresaw going on a bunch of dates with me in order to win your promotion?" Lucas tilted his head, that little secret smile on his lips again. "Come on, Spicer, you don't have to control everything, you know?"

"Going on a bunch of *not*-dates with you and proving

you wrong is going to be the easiest promotion I've ever got," I bluffed. *No, my careful planning is down the drain in every area of my life, thanks for pointing it out.*

"I love when you get all fiery." He grinned and waited as the doors opened at the ground floor, gesturing for me to step out first.

I checked the directions on the card, and luckily our destination was only a five-minute walk away. We stepped along in silence for a while, the streets surprisingly quiet before the influx of workers were let loose for the evening. Lucas didn't say anything, just strolled along beside me, hands in pockets. I watched him watching everything with curiosity, his gaze tracing other people, their interactions, his lips quirking up briefly at the sight of a pigeon eating a slice of pizza on a bench.

"Ah, London. Everything I was promised and more besides." He grinned again, nudging me with his elbow. I stepped just out of reach and watched his smile falter a little.

"Would you say I'm hostile?" I suddenly asked, thinking of David last night and my abrupt escape from the pub. Now with the comments on the page I'd made, and the #TeamMarina hashtag, I was starting to wonder. Had heartbreak made me hard?

"Only to me, and I kind of enjoy it." Lucas shrugged one shoulder. "Why?"

This was not the person to be vulnerable with. He was my nemesis.

"No reason."

"Nothing wrong with taking names and kicking arses, darling," he said lightly, letting me walk in front slightly as we weaved through the streets. "And I find your dedication to being generally pissed off at all times sort of adorable."

I gave him a death glare, and he clapped a hand to his chest. "See, that. Be still my heart. You're trying to kill me again."

"I told you, charm doesn't work on me."

"Maybe that's why I just can't seem to help myself." He stopped in front of a red door in a dark alleyway. It looked almost as if we'd come the wrong way.

I checked the paper again.

"Are we sure this is it?"

"Only one way to find out," Lucas said, and leaned forward to turn the handle.

Inside, it was a different world. The ceiling was draped with vines, fake bunches of grapes hanging down, soft mood lighting making it look like a mysteriously luscious haunted castle. A wrought iron bar was almost built into the wall, where a gothy girl with dark red lipstick and heavy eyeliner waved us over.

"Welcome to Mistress Octavia's Mysterious Bacchanal

and the Case of the Missing Wine," she intoned, a strange smile on her face. I watched as her eyes rested on Lucas, trying to figure out the relationship between the two of us. Her clipped, perfect fifties English accent, found on old movie reels, suddenly fell away as she asked, "Is it just the two of you?"

I gave Lucas a satisfied grin, as if to say, *Told ya.*

"Is that unusual . . . sorry, what's your name?" He was straight into full-on charm mode. Typical.

"Nadine."

"Well, Nadine, lovely to meet you. Is it unusual to have a pair do the escape room?"

She nodded and shrugged. I raised an eyebrow at Lucas, smug in my certainty that this was going to be a win for me.

"Now, now, don't get ahead of yourself, darling," he said, shifting to the side slightly and drawing me with him, his hand on my waist as someone holding a tray of drinks walked past us into the gloom. I stepped away, trying to ignore the warmth. "Still loads of time to let me win."

I met his eyes, just for a moment, and saw the dare reflected there. We were both here to win. No matter what. Did he think casual physical contact was going to freak me out enough to back down?

"But it'll still be a wonderful time!" Nadine assured us, making me jump. I focused all my attention back on her. I wondered if she was an actress doing this gig in between West End shows and adverts for lip-plumping serums. She looked famous already. I needed to figure out how to work a bold lip. It was one of those grown-up things I was sure would change my life, if I could just make it work.

"Follow me." She beckoned after we'd put down our coats and bags. Lucas snorted at the trusty notebook in my back pocket again but said nothing, gesturing for me to go first, following close behind, that hand hovering at my back. I glared at him, but he didn't notice. He was too busy being that curious kid again, his eyes everywhere, on everything.

We stepped into a strange room, full of old furniture, weird lighting, and . . . I mean, I'd never *seen* a sex dungeon, but the vibes were distinctly sex dungeon–esque.

"Welcome, intrepid travelers, to the vineyard of Mistress Octavia. This very location is the site of a yearly bacchanal where a select group of unique guests come together and celebrate the weirdness and wonder of Octavia's seemingly magical wine."

"Oh really?" Lucas nodded. "What's so magical about this wine?"

"Well." Nadine smiled at him, a particular smile I was starting to recognize on the faces of women when Lucas did that smirk-and-raised-eyebrow thing. Give them a week, and they'd be writing dealbreakers on the app like the rest of them. "This particular vintage makes guests rather . . . uninhibited. For these very special yearly parties."

"So like . . . wine, then," I said, and Nadine deflated a little.

"Yes." Her reply was clipped, and the script became infinitely more recognizable now. "Follow the clues to find the missing wine before the party and you'll win a bottle for yourselves. You've got ninety minutes. Ring the bell if you need clues—you're allowed three."

She left us in the dark, looking at each other.

"Did you have to do that?" Lucas asked, suddenly close. I had to tilt my head back to reply.

"What, ask questions?"

"Shit in her porridge." He sighed, looking around. "She has a job to do."

"Yeah, sure, that's what you were irritated about. How do we start this thing?"

A spotlight appeared in the middle of the room, highlighting a bunch of letters hanging on strings from the ceiling, hovering over a glass table. They were Scrabble tiles, creating eerie shadows in the light. We couldn't see much beyond that, so it seemed like a good place to start.

Lucas pointed. "I guess there's that."

"'The vintage you know, the visions you'll see, to free yourselves from mediocrity,'" I read on the placard underneath. "Wow, on the nose."

"As if you've ever known mediocrity." Lucas squinted, then slipped his hand into his pocket and pulled out a pair of glasses. "Okay, let's see."

I wasn't sure why, but something about that small action made me soften a little. Like there was a part of him he hid. I liked him with glasses, suddenly frowning like a dad trying to read the menu in a fancy restaurant. Somehow less dangerous.

I realized I was smiling at him the same moment he did. I didn't give him time to say anything.

"I think we need to pull on the letters that spell out the right word," I said, reaching for one at the same time as him, our fingers brushing, and pulled my hand back like I'd been stung.

"Oh God, it's 'wine,' isn't it?" Lucas laughed, apparently not noticing my hand in midair, and tugged on the Scrabble letters in order to spell out the word.

When the light went out, another red spotlight lit up a far part of the room and we jumped, bumping against each other. He smelled like spice and warmth, soap and fresh laundry. I didn't move away that time, unsure of where to go without tripping.

"You still don't think escape rooms could be a good date? Being locked in a dark room with someone while you find clues about a sex party?" Lucas whispered, holding out a hand to help me across the uneven floorboards. I ignored his offer and stepped past him, focusing on the faint lines on the floor.

"Yeah, if anything, it's awkward."

"Nah." He shook his head, looking around. "I don't do awkward."

"I get that," I replied. "I imagine you just charm the awkward out of any situation."

Lucas paused his perusal of the room to look at me. "Was that a compliment?"

I pretended to think. "Did it *sound* like a compliment?"

The light was dim, but I still saw that grin, the way his eyes crinkled as he laughed. "From *you*, darling, yes. All those hateful barbs sound like compliments when you say them in that soft, throaty voice."

I rolled my eyes, sure he couldn't see me, but he laughed again.

We looked at the lit-up cabinet with a bunch of keys inside, all different shapes and sizes on different shelves. But there was no way to open it. I went up on my tiptoes, reaching to fiddle with all the items on the top of the cabinet, trinkets in a bowl, looking for a hidden switch.

"Wait, do that again!" Lucas yelped, clapping his hands, and watched as I picked up a coin from the dusty ceramic bowl. "It's a magnet!"

Sure enough, the key started moving in line. He sat on

the floor, his eyeline focusing on the movement of the key as I stood, tracing the magnet along the top of the cabinet.

"Okay, brilliant, to the left, a little more," Lucas breathed, and adrenaline rushed through me as I became hyper-focused. It was so odd how such a silly little activity could make you feel alive. Like part of a team. A thrill.

"You're so close, so close!" he said in a low voice, excitement building. "Just to the right, then you can let it drop."

"How do I do that?" I whispered back.

"Just yank the magnet away, I guess?"

It was worth a shot.

"Okay, now!" I pulled the coin back, my fingertips clutching too tightly, and the key clanged into a pocket at the bottom of the cabinet.

"Yes!" Lucas held it aloft, jumping up from the ground. He moved in as if to hug me, then paused, inches away. We stood like that for a moment, statues in the near-dark, unsure who was meant to push and who was meant to pull. Whether to advance or retreat. I licked my lower lip and held my breath, not sure why the dark made everything so much more intense. I could hear him breathing.

The key slipped from his fingers and clattered to the ground, jolting us back to reality. Lucas laughed, reaching down for the key and then stepping back from me, so I could no longer feel his warmth or smell that soap and spice.

He coughed and held up a hand. "Can a nemesis get a celebratory high five?"

I laughed and hit his hand with mine. "Okay, on to the next."

Don't talk about it, just move on.

We scanned the room for lights and eventually found a crack of blue light underneath a door. At least, it had to be a door. We dropped down to the floor, rested on our hands and knees, our heads together, peering at the wall that seemingly had no entrance. I leaned forward, and my nose brushed his shoulder. Lucas flinched, knocking me back in surprise.

"Sorry," we both whispered, then laughed. He reached out a hand to pull me back to sitting, fingertips extended down my wrist. I shivered.

He let go and started feeling around the edge of the space for a hidden lock or latch.

"Is any of this really making sense?" I asked. "Like should something about the story reveal the entrance?"

"Do you wanna check the bookcase? Maybe a book will open the door like one of those secret rooms," he offered. "I always wanted to find one of those as a kid."

"Me too! My kingdom for a secret book nook."

I pulled myself up and carefully shuffled over to the bookshelf, fingertips trailing across the spines as I struggled to see the titles in the low light.

"Just try all of them!" Lucas urged, but I didn't want to. I wanted it to make sense. Besides, picking the right one would save time, rather than pointlessly looking for answers in the wrong place.

When I got to a book titled *Love Potions and Elixirs for a New Era* by Octavia Eleanor Barlett, I knew I'd found it. I pulled the book out from its place on the shelf, and I heard the hidden door in the wall click, a sliver of light visible around the edge. But when I went to push it open, the door was still locked.

"The key from the cabinet!" I shouted, scrabbling over to Lucas, following the sound of his voice.

"What?" he said, and I moved toward the sound, unable to find him. I should have looked down.

In my excitement I tripped over him, fully falling on top of him, until we were both tangled on the floor. There was half a second of silence where I was only grateful it was too dark to make eye contact. Was that his stubble against my cheek?

"Um, sorry," I said, frozen.

"Sorry enough to move?" Lucas asked, his voice tight as he shifted, sitting up and taking me with him. I felt strong hands on my waist, guiding me back ever so slowly until I was no longer on top of him. I felt breathless as I scrambled back on the floorboards to get farther away.

"Sorry!" I said again, my voice high and on the edge of hysteria. Why did he smell good? That wasn't fair. Almost a year of failing to find a future husband, and stick me in a room with a man who smelled good and had good hands . . .

I was stronger than this. The darkness had a lot to answer for.

When Lucas spoke again, there was none of that tension of the moment before, as if he wasn't affected at all. He just laughed as I dusted myself off. "Come on, total movie moment. See, there's a method to locking two people in a dark room on a date, right?"

"Wishful thinking," I managed to croak out. "Chuck me the key?"

He slid it along the floor, our fingertips touching.

"Thanks," I rasped, unsure why my throat was dry. The book revealed a code, which needed to be punched into a hidden safe in the back of a creepy armoire. We then had to rearrange the contents of the safe into Lady Octavia's initials—*OEB*—and, eventually, an almost holy light shone down on a trick floorboard that popped up to reveal a dusty wine bottle.

I grabbed the bottle and brandished it above my head,

shouting "Champions!" just as Lucas yelled "Yes!" and grabbed me around the waist to swing me around.

The minute my T-shirt slipped and his thumb touched my skin, he seemed to realize what he was doing and set me down, before stepping back. "Sorry. Not very appropriate nemesis behavior."

I tried to look suitably peeved, even as I felt heat creep up my neck. "Yes, very inappropriate. But also, we won!"

"Nice to be on the same side for once," he replied, and Nadine suddenly appeared from behind a door that had been there all along.

"Did you have fun?" she asked, focusing on Lucas.

"We really did!" He nodded before looking to me for confirmation. I nodded, but she wasn't looking at me.

"You finished it pretty quickly." She looked anxious. "Normally people get a lot more time out of the experience."

"Well, this one"—Lucas pointed at me—"is all about the efficiency."

Nadine led us toward the exit, stopping at the reception table to offer us a branded tote bag containing a bunch of promotional stuff and a couple of reusable glasses. "For your wine."

Lucas took the bag, held it open for me to slide in the wine, and then looped it over my wrist and up onto my shoulder. I blinked.

"Well, if there's anything else you need, anything at all, please do get in touch," Nadine said to Lucas, those huge eyes hopeful as she bit her lip.

"We absolutely will do, love, and I'll definitely leave a review on how brilliant this was. You have a good day!" Lucas clearly had no idea how her face fell as he gestured for me to walk ahead, then opened the door.

See, now I was intrigued. We stood in the funny little side street that suddenly looked less murderous, and I couldn't help myself from commenting.

"You know you could go back and ask her out. Don't mind me."

"What are you talking about?"

I widened my eyes, gesturing to the door with my head. "Your charm offensive hit a willing target."

He frowned at me, then I watched as the realization landed. "Sweet Jesus, woman, she was a child! She was probably born in the noughties!"

"Oh, so there are limits," I said lightly, smile on my face. "I took you for an equal-opportunities shagger."

"You seem to have a lot of opinions about me for someone you've mainly interacted with by email for the past year." Lucas frowned.

Well, that was fair. He didn't know I had access to feedback from every date he'd been on in the past six months. I suddenly wondered what reviews of me would say. In the early days back on the dating scene, they'd probably say that I was an unstable mess, bottling up emotions and firing questions until every man felt like he was being interrogated in an international incident. Now it would probably say I was rude, I didn't take the time to get to know them, just decided it wouldn't work, and moved on before we could even order a starter.

Something about that made my stomach hurt, and it must have been that that made me say: "Do you want to go sit in the park and share this? We did win it together."

His mouth actually fell open, and I followed up before he could say anything.

"Plus, we need to compare notes. Even though it's quite clear I've got this one locked down."

"Don't worry, I wasn't about to take it as a sign you liked spending time with me. Only that you're a consummate professional. You lead the way."

I nodded and strode off, suddenly feeling vulnerable. As we walked, I heard him answer his phone. "Hey there, darlin', what's shaking?"

I rolled my eyes. Of course. *Let's not forget who he really is, Marina.* Probably lining up a date for tonight, and I'd read the unlucky lady's feedback myself tomorrow morning in the cold light of day.

The temptation to look at Dealbreakers again as we walked along was overwhelming. To remind myself of what a mess he was. Sure, we had a good time, but the man hated dogs and I very much had a future mapped out with a black-and-white collie called Doughnut. Doughnut was nonnegotiable. And what that had to do with Lucas Kennedy, I had no idea, but I felt myself getting angry at him, like I wanted to go and tell him off for hating dogs, and having tattoos, and the pack of tobacco he always had in his back pocket, and convincing every woman in a ten-mile radius that he wanted to be her knight in shining armor when really he wanted to be her one-night shag in stripy boxers.

I could hear him speaking soft and low on the phone for the short walk to the park, and I wondered whether the girl on the line was going off on him for something. Maybe he had someone back home.

Maybe it was none of my business.

I flopped down on a patch of grass, pulling out the bottle and glasses.

He nodded, held up one hand, and mouthed, "*Sorry.*" "Darling, I've really got to go, I've got a work thing. But I'll see you tomorrow night, okay?"

The voice on the other end squeaked and then was gone.

"Sorry about that, it's—"

"None of my business," I said quickly, and handed him a glass. "Here."

I unscrewed the cap on the wine and poured, his then mine. Lucas leaned in to sniff it, his eyes watering a little. "Whoa, pungent."

"Well, it's magic wine." I shrugged, clinking my glass against his. "Bottoms up."

We both sipped and made identical faces. It was awful.

After a moment's silence, Lucas tried again. "You do . . . you do realize a lot of the time, I'm just trying to be friendly, right?" He sounded hesitant, like it mattered what I thought.

"Oh sure, you're Mr. Friendly. You're the whole welcome parade." I snorted.

"It's my nature! I don't see what's so wrong with wasting a bit of time on some chat. You don't know how someone's day is going. An honest smile and asking how they are can go a long way."

I raised an eyebrow. "Okay, Mother Teresa. Tone it down a bit."

"Cruel woman." He shook his head. "Fine, down to business—what did you think?"

I nodded, sipping the wine thoughtfully. "Super fun, great for groups, quirky storyline. Winning something out of it is a nice touch, too. Thumbs-up from me. Be great for a birthday party."

"I think it works as a date, too, though," he argued, and I made a face. "You disagree with me—shocker."

"I'm not trying to be difficult, I just mean for most people being stuck in a dark room together with no way out unless you outsmart a randy ghost is not the most romantic thing."

To be fair to him, he considered that, half nodding.

"So those charged moments when you get a clue right, when you make eye contact as you realize something, when you can put into words what the other is trying to say . . . those aren't special?" he asked, his hand skittering near mine on the grass, then moving away again. I didn't dare look up. Not now. I focused on watching that hand.

"You think it . . . creates a false sense of intimacy?"

"I think you've just stuck two people who do want to shag in a dark room together and made them feel very clever about themselves. Surely that's an aphrodisiac?"

I tried to ignore the weird jig my stomach was doing. It felt like my intestines were being wrung out like a flannel.

I gave a considered, one-shouldered shrug. "It would have to be a very specific stage of dating, though, right?"

He conceded, nodding, looking me right in the eyes as he spoke, ever so slowly, as if he didn't want me to miss anything. "Sure, it would definitely need to be before they've slept together. The tension doesn't exist otherwise."

I tried to think of something to say, to seem unaffected by those green eyes.

"You're also forgetting the possibility that they don't work well together, or they fail the mission." I made a face. "Two huge risks—finding the person you're dating is stupid, or finding they're a sore loser."

"I'm assuming from your expression that the second one is worse?" he said, incredulous.

"Absolutely."

"You'd rather be with someone who was dim as long as they weren't competitive?"

"I'd rather be with someone who wasn't good at escape rooms if they didn't complain about it for a week after, sure. Being subject to someone else's moods is not fun."

Lucas looked at me like he was considering asking more, but he didn't, simply sipped the wine and winced a little. "There really is a reason they give this away. It's awful."

"It's magic."

"It's fucking disgusting," he retaliated.

I gave him a grin. "It got us working together well. That makes it a miracle beverage in my book."

Lucas laughed his quick, rich laugh and held up a glass in a silent toast. Then he sipped and tried not to cough up a lung.

"To be fair, working together has never really been our problem."

"News to me," I said, and he bared his teeth at me.

"No, really, when we have to do the professional stuff, chatting about work, debating ideas . . . that's the easy stuff."

I frowned, sipping at the wine, and then frowned some more. "I'm going to regret asking this but . . . what's the difficult stuff?"

"When we get caught up in this whole antagonists storyline. I'm not your bad guy, and you're not mine."

"I have a year's worth of emails and a bunch of random activities to write up that say otherwise."

Lucas sighed, looking up at the sky like I was impossible. And I probably was.

"Maybe I could have been a little less . . . effusive in my criticism."

"Which time?"

"All of them," he said carefully, watching me like I was a bomb that was about to go off. He reached over and topped up my glass. "So, have you found a new flat yet?"

"What?" I blinked, pausing to sip and wince.

"You were looking for a place. Hence the presentation, promotion, and our delightful nemesis ways?" He laughed, and I laughed with him.

"I'm too fussy."

He opened his mouth and shook his head, pretending to be shocked. "You? The queen of laid-back? Solid believer in just letting the universe handle it? No!"

“Ha, ha.” I settled on my stomach on the grass, resting my chin on my hands. “I’ve got standards.”

“Famous last words.” He winked, and I reached into my back pocket to throw my notebook at him. He caught it in one hand and then grinned at me, surprised.

“Go on, tell me about this beautiful flat you want that doesn’t exist.”

“It exists. I just need to find it,” I said with certainty.

“I’m sensing a theme.” Lucas grinned. “But go on, I’m all comfy, tell me a fairy tale about a world far away from moldy basements and mice named Gus Gus.”

I took a deep breath. “I’m not asking for much. Just natural light and a breakfast bar where I can sit and eat one of those croissants you put in the oven, like a frozen one? Because it feels fancy but takes no time. And I’d drink my coffee and then go and sit in my little window seat and read my book, and my plants will all be happy because they’ll have sun and sunshine makes you happy . . .”

When I snuck a look at Lucas, he had this soft little smile on his face, like I’d surprised him. Like I was cute.

“What else?” He leaned in, and I found myself accosted by green eyes paying me way too much attention. *He makes you feel like the most important person in the world, and then he’s gone.* Dealbreakers had warned me. So why did his gaze still send a warmth from my stomach to my fingertips? Stupid, awful magic wine.

"What?"

"What other things make you happy?"

"Why?" I almost barked, and Lucas laughed.

"I'm not trying to extract secret codes, Spicer. I'm just trying to get to know you. You know, like a person."

"Uh . . ." I searched around wildly, then felt the grass beneath my fingertips. "Picnics and strawberry picking. The good dumpling place near work. Dogs wearing socks. Looking up at the night sky and feeling insignificant, in a good way. Really bad dad jokes, usually told by my dad. Sunflowers and garish sparkly trainers, the sound of little kids laughing, and too many marshmallows in hot chocolate."

He beamed at me. A full-watt, devastating grin.

"What?" I went on the defensive. "What's wrong with any of that?"

"It's just . . . it's really nice to finally meet you, Marina Spicer."

He looked back up at that perfect early-evening pink sky and said nothing else.

And that was how we spent the next twenty minutes, drinking shitty wine, sitting on the grass as the sky darkened, and saying nothing at all.

I tried to ignore the realization that it was better than most of the dates I'd been on in the past six months.

The bastard.

CHAPTER SEVEN

He told me I was really special. He remembered all these details of things I'd said, he was the perfect gentleman. And then he was just gone. I felt like an idiot. I thought it had been the start of something.

The next morning, when I came into the office, there was a solitary sunflower sitting on my keyboard.

I tried to fight a smile, and Harriet raised an eyebrow. Then I remembered. This was not the plan. I did not have time to be charmed by Lucas Kennedy. He was a shag-about-town with multiple women on the go, a never-ending need to woo everyone around him into loving him, and I did not need to be wooed.

Case in point, when I looked across the office, where he

was surrounded by a gaggle of coworkers, all hanging on his every word and laughing loudly, he looked up and met my gaze, smiling. His eyebrows raised as if in expectation. I crossed my arms and raised an eyebrow. "Why?" I mouthed.

"Why not?" he mouthed back, childish and exaggerated.

Impossible man.

The days had taken on a nice pattern, though, I had to admit. I spent the morning going through my normal work with Harriet and Ravi, working on our plans to improve the site. I ran a workshop with Harriet to help her pitch ideas, reveling in the power of leading and teaching someone. Okay, I hated pitching, but I knew Harriet would be excellent at it. And most days I preferred helping her grow more than I did almost anything else. She was so hungry for everything. It reminded me of how I was when I first trained. I was going to work abroad and live in different cities and build sites and teach . . . I'd just kind of assumed Adam was going to follow me, because that was what he'd always done. I'd gone to university, and he'd followed me, getting a flat and doing bar work as he tried to launch his band.

I had been the leader, forging ahead, and then suddenly, when the time came for our plans for the future to be solidified, I was on the back foot again.

I shook the thought away. But as if I'd summoned him, my phone beeped with a text.

Today is so boring! How's your day going, Tech Goddess?

I could hear Meera's and Bec's voices like alarm bells, as if each of them were sitting on my shoulder with a halo above their heads. The word flashing in front of my eyes was "boundaries." In five-foot, bright red capital letters.

I let my hand hover over my phone for a minute, watching Lucas in his scrum, how he wowed them. I remembered opening Dealbreakers on my morning commute to assess my next date and trying not to freak out that more and more of those faces and names were looking familiar. Oh God, had I already run through every available man in East London? Did I have to wait for the second wave to arrive, for currently married men to divorce and become eligible again?

I took a breath and responded to Adam. Talking to him had been simple, once.

It's a good day, I'm competing for that promotion.

I wanted to tell him my mother wanted to freeze my eggs for my birthday. It was the kind of thing we would have laughed at, back then. And he'd have stroked my hair and gone, "Oh Penny, always trying her best and doing her worst." And he was allowed, because he'd known my parents since we were children.

Except if we were still together, she wouldn't be looking into egg freezing; she'd be bugging him about grandchildren at Sunday lunch. Even that imagined scenario didn't make sense. Everything had changed.

What no one told you when you left a long relationship was how often you had random stuff that you just couldn't tell anyone else. No one got it. No one spoke that language. And then the language died.

Ours still existed by the thinnest thread, but I knew I should cut that tie. I just couldn't quite do it. Not yet. I tapped my necklace, angry at myself.

I was torn from my phone by a knock at the glass door, even though it was open. It was two of the guys from the sales team. I'd never learned their names because, quite honestly, we'd talked about the weather once when I joined the company, and we'd never found common ground since.

I jumped up. "Oh hi, do you need tech support?"

They looked at each other, quizzical. "No, we just wanted to say good job on the escape room. Sounds like you're a natural! If you ever fancy joining our pub quiz team, we go next door every Thursday. Pints and trivia, it's a laugh. Lucas said you guys might be up for joining us next week?"

Oh did he, now?

"I, uh, thanks! I'll keep it in mind!"

They nodded and waved as they left. Harriet chuckled, shaking her head. "Look who's suddenly Miss Popularity. Are you gonna start being mean to the geeks and stealing our lunch money?"

I smiled but shook my head. "Why would he tell them I might be interested?"

"Maybe he thought you'd like a pub quiz." Harriet shrugged. "Not me. I like my men huge and dumb. Give me a gym bro with a heart of gold any day. I promise I won't spend time trying to work out his *motivations*."

"Ah, to be young," I said reverently, hand on chest, looking into the distance.

"Even if you were . . . younger," Harriet ventured carefully, "you'd still be searching for that perfect person to snuggle up to in your pajamas on a Friday night, watching box sets and ordering takeaways. That's just you; you like the boring part. I am all about the fun at the beginning, before any of those messy soft bits like feelings get involved."

"Remind me to introduce you to my friend Meera. She is also not a fan of feelings."

"Smart woman."

I looked across at Lucas, now chatting to a different group of people—did this man *ever* work? Just as I was about to look away, he caught me and winked. It made my stomach flip.

"Smart woman indeed," I replied, and pulled on my headphones.

That evening was my first pottery class with Meera and Bec joining me. I wasn't really sure what Bec had been thinking with this idea. She saw enough of me in her home, so I assumed she and Matt relished the time I was gone.

Pottery was my thing. And . . . well, the truth was, I was terrible at it. Every week I tried my absolute hardest, and still I couldn't make a vase. I got books out of the library, I watched YouTube videos, I dreamed of the pottery wheel, spinning, spinning, spinning. No matter how hard I tried, it didn't seem to matter. But I refused to quit. I was going to make that vase someday, damn it.

My phone rang on my walk down to the secondary school where the pottery classes were held. Dad.

"Hello, sweetheart," he started, but I cut him off.

"I swear to God, if you ask me how much cinnamon to put in your apple pie, I'll scream." I laughed and waited to hear him chuckle. "You're allowed to just call me, you know."

"I'm making you feel needed. I'll expect the same in return some day," he said simply, and I heard him take a big gulp of tea. "You off to your art class?"

"Meera and Bec have joined," I said, the worry bleeding in.

"Oh boy, you three giggling in the back row making sculptures of God knows what. Just like you're teenagers again. That poor teacher."

"Dad," I sighed, sounding distinctly childish, "I'm a grown-up."

"Ugh, don't say that, what a horrible thought." I could hear some tinkering in the background and wondered if he was in his new shed at the back of the garden, fiddling with whatever bits and bobs he collected in there.

"What are you up to tonight?"

"Anniversary dinner," he said, and I suddenly realized the call was a warning.

"Oh no!"

"I told your mum there was a lot of delay in the post recently," he said, almost apologetically. "I mean, I think it's nonsensical to expect an anniversary card from your daughter, but you know your mother."

"*Etiquette matters*," we intoned together.

I took a breath against the rising sense of panic at disappointing my mother. "Thanks for calling, Dad." I tried to sound nonchalant. "Where are you going?"

"Gino's at seven p.m. Starter, steak main, share a tiramisu for dessert. Carafe of house red and a conversation about whether we should have sprung for a nicer bottle.

The same as every year for the past few decades, petal. You know that."

"Dad . . . would you like to go somewhere else?"

His pause told me more than I wanted to hear. "You know your mother, she loves tradition. I've got a bunch of pink peonies ordered and ready to go. The florist doesn't even ask anymore; we just set up a yearly standing order."

"Is that good?" I asked, wondering if that was an efficient way of pleasing my mother, or if it had taken all sense of joy from my dad. "I just want to make sure everyone's happy."

Dad chuckled gently. "You can be happy and wanting, Marina. You don't just find love and complete the video game and you're done, you know? I can be in love and happy and still want something else for myself."

I winced. "Like a mistress?"

The laughter that barreled down the phone was so loud it hurt my ears.

"What? No! Like . . . new memories. New favorite flowers. New stories to tell. New restaurants that don't charge twenty-five quid for an overdone steak just because it's tradition . . . but you know your mother, she loves our story."

"She loves you," I reminded him. "She'll go along with what you want."

"And here's me thinking you were the smart one in the family. I'll tell her I don't want to go to Gino's for our anniversary when you tell her you don't want to freeze your eggs."

"Um . . ."

"Yeah, um . . ." He laughed. "We're good, darling. You go live your life, I'll just be here, fiddling with my clocks."

"God, way too easy to mishear you."

He laughed again, that loud boom that made me feel like everything was all right. Like I would find my feet, and my flat, and a love that I deserved. Because Dad thought everything was okay.

And maybe he was right. I quickly used my phone to order an anniversary card and the chocolates I knew Mum loved. Okay, they'd arrive tomorrow, but it would stop the onslaught of hurt feelings. By the time I got to class I was positively giddy with the idea that *this week* would be the week.

I always got to class early to secure the best wheel. There were a few of them, but only one with a good amount of space around it and a good view of the teacher. We'd all started at the wheels at the beginning. Some of the others had moved on to different workstations, making sculptures or tiles. I was not leaving the wheel until I'd done something decent. So I went back to that same seat, week after week, refusing to move on. Probably why none of the other students spoke to me. I knew they went out for a drink after class most weeks, but no one had ever invited me. On the other hand, I was always too busy, slipping out while grasping my disappointing creation and trying not to cry. So . . . probably best for all of us.

"Darling!" Agatha, the teacher, clasped her bosom in faux surprise. "You're always so early, skulking in the shadows!"

"Just eager to get my spot," I said lightly, and watched as her eyes softened with something like pity. "My friends have signed up to join me."

"Ah!" Agatha waved her arms wildly, her voice full of relief. "Friends! Excellent!"

Meera and Bec bustled in, sitting on either side of me at the pottery wheel stations, giggling like we were back in school.

"This is going to be so fun!" Bec declared, and Meera gave me a look that said, *Clearly there is an "or else" attached to this statement.*

Agatha sat on a table at the front of the room, waiting impatiently, her multiple bangles jangling on her wrists as she tapped her watch. People filed in, said good evening, and she nodded, but she hated to wait. It was like she was just desperate to start. Like she'd waited all day for this. Her moment.

"Darlings, I want you to pick up that clay and chuck it down like you want it dead," she rasped, fingers holding an imaginary cigarette. "This clay ruined your life, broke your heart, took years from you." She jumped down from the table and gestured for us to begin. "Clay needs feeling, fire . . . you are the human kiln. You're giving it life, form, permanence. So do it with *gravitas*, darlings."

Bec exhaled under her breath. "Oh, I like her."

I chucked the lump of clay down on the wheel, hearing it thud heavily. I let out a sigh and did it again.

"Yes!" Agatha intoned, walking down through the room, looking at everyone's progress. "I want that clay not to know what's hit it! It needs to be as shell-shocked as my husband when I told him I was leaving him for a thirty-five-year-old I met in Santorini!"

I blinked and looked at Bec and Meera, then up at her in surprise (though really by now I shouldn't have been surprised by the snippets of information Agatha let slip), and she winked at me.

"Okay, my darlings on the wheels, remember: strength and softness, yes?"

She was constantly saying contradictory things like that, and somehow I found it all rather charming. Like this mess of a woman with her silver hair and bright eyes and proud chin, her gorgeous purple caftans drawing the eye . . . she could do anything with clay. It seemed to come to life in her hands and settle into the shape it always wanted to be. Like she was revealing it, rather than creating it.

I looked over at where Meera was skimming her fingertips on the clay as she moved it, looking at how her fingernail made a line that wobbled as she wiggled. She snorted to herself in quiet amusement. Bec was still with concentration but, as expected, made it look easy, her hands gently guiding until a funnel shape emerged. She smiled at me, toothy and delighted. I focused on my own wheel and huffed as the clay slipped between my fingers and the perfect vase I'd been attempting to make once again squished in the middle.

Lucas would be good at this. He'd sit there making jokes, knowing the exact pressure to use, when to be soft and when to be strong . . . going with the flow, responding instead of resisting.

He had nice hands.

The thought appeared from nowhere, and in surprise I put my thumb through the clay again. I clenched my fists, letting out a sound of irritation.

"Don't despair, try again. There are no failures, only lessons," Agatha breathed, emanating life-coach vibes.

"Tell that to my ex-boyfriends," a woman behind me called out, and a soft chortle echoed around the room.

"Well, quite." Agatha seemed amused, the corners of her mouth tilting up, leaving cavernous lines. I knew my mother would say, *Oh goodness, this poor woman has let herself go, hasn't she? Surely she's the same age as me, but she looks ancient!*

And yet, Agatha looked ancient in the way a tree looked ancient—wise and mysterious and full of life.

Oh God, Mum. I hoped the card, however late, could fend off the disappointment that I'd forgotten their anniversary. Mum's disappointment tended to be spiky and long-standing. Damn. Normally I was so on top of this stuff. I hoped Dad was at least pretending to enjoy his overpriced steak.

I struggled to get hold of the clay in front of me, clenching my teeth. Every time I tried to be soft, it whirled away, and every time I tried to be strong, it collapsed under my hands. Agatha stood watching me.

"Stop trying for perfection. It can feel how much you want to change it into something else. It's resisting because you're forcing it."

"Trying to stop Marina achieving perfection, you may as well get her to stop breathing," Meera said lightly, and Agatha considered her, then looked back to me, allowing me to give my side of the story.

"True," I admitted, and she shook her head sadly.

"Oh, what a curse perfectionism is." She turned to

Meera, assessing her relaxed posture. "You're the opposite—you don't care enough."

Meera frowned, then seemed to consider what Agatha said and shrugged. "Also true."

"Well, maybe care just a *smidge*, darling. It's not going to hurt you, I promise."

Meera looked a little cowed and nodded, head down.

Agatha looked at Bec's confident hands on the pottery wheel and nodded. "See this, this is synergy."

I huffed a little. "So I need to become one with the clay?"

Agatha quirked an eyebrow. "No, darling, you need to become one with yourself."

I almost vibrated with rage, waiting until she walked away to dare look at Bec and Meera, who were barely holding in their giggles.

"Oh, *boom*. I'll say it again." Bec snorted. "I like her."

"I *think* I'm glad you guys are here." I laughed. "Did you want to get dinner after?"

Meera shook her head, too quickly. "Busy."

"Oh really?" I tilted my head. "Doing what?"

"No one you'd approve of." She stuck out her tongue, and though I knew I was meant to laugh, I felt my shoulders drop.

"Oh God, Meer, not Tanya again?"

"Let me live my life, Marina," Meera said lightly, in a

voice that only I knew meant not to push. So, of course, I pushed.

"Last time she stole from you. *Stole* from you. And you always end up going on a weeklong bender and you turn up feeling wretched."

Meera raised her eyes to mine so slowly I almost cowered. "Sometimes I just need something that's familiar. Even if it's crap. Someone who knows my limitations, my situation. And she borrowed a tenner, for fuck's sake."

Her limitations. She meant her aunt. Arti had been diagnosed with MS when she was only a teenager. Meera's mum had looked after her sister with so much love and care, absolute devotion. But when her mum passed away and her dad moved back to Goa to find himself a new wife to take care of him, looking after Arti fell to Meera. She'd promised her mum, and nothing would stop her. She'd dropped out of uni, forgot about studying law. Forgot about anything but living in the moment and getting by. Plus, she loved her aunt, loved their life together, and would do anything to protect it. I might be too much with my five-year plan, but Meera didn't look more than five minutes ahead; she couldn't bear to.

"Fine." I shrugged, my hands still covered in clay. "Whatever you say."

"Thank you," she said, and the lightness returned to

her voice. "So, how is your battle with charm boy going? Find a way to smuggle an ax into that escape room?"

I let my fingers splay as I started to move the wheel again, focusing on my breathing. Maybe this was what I needed, a distraction in order to make it happen. To finally get it right.

"You know, he's really not that bad once you get to know him."

Meera slumped dramatically, clearly considering putting her head in her hands, but remembered they were preoccupied. "No."

"No?"

"No more waste-of-space men-children with no drive or direction wasting your time, remember? Like, I know I mock your need to immediately find and procreate with someone who is your specific desired level of boring but . . . you wasted fifteen years on a man with no backbone. Why would you do that again?"

"I'm not . . ." I yelped, shocked by the attack. "Sorry, did I not just get told off for having opinions about your love life?"

"I'm not gonna marry Tanya. I'm not gonna do anything but sleep with her a few times, go out to a few clubs, and absolutely regret it when I sober up in a few days' time and she's pawned my watch. I know what I'm getting into. You . . . you want people to fit your criteria so much you'll repaint them in your mind. This man is your nemesis, remember? Standing in the way of your picture-perfect flat and your stuff out of storage and a fancy title, running a team. Remember?"

I paused for a moment, unsure what to say. "I thought you hated my lists, my dealbreakers. You said I was too picky."

"You are, and I do. But being picky, having standards, being okay with being alone . . . that stuff builds character. Another Peter Pan with a nice smile and the easy ability to say yes to you . . . there's no growth there."

I turned to Bec to play referee, and she shook her head. "I'm here for the art, not the drama."

"I just meant it's tiring having a nemesis," I said lightly, eager to avoid an argument. "I have to be my cleverest, wittiest self at all times, on hand with a comeback, it's exhausting. Maybe I'll downgrade him to just *some guy*."

Meera didn't look up from her pottery wheel but nodded. I got the sense she was embarrassed. We usually didn't argue. Once, in the early 2000s, we got into a shouting match about the best episode of *Buffy the Vampire Slayer*, but . . . that was it.

I'd lost enough this year; I couldn't lose Meer, too.

Eventually, I forced the clay into something resembling a vase and exhaled as I put it on the side. It didn't look too shabby next to everyone else's. Meera's and Bec's vases were better than mine, but there was also the blue-haired girl who always carved little birds and the aging pub landlord who was obsessed with making the perfect tankard. A lot of them tried different things each week, but not me. I wouldn't let myself move on, not until I'd mastered the vase.

We then all walked over to the other table, where creations from the weeks before had been cast. I crossed my fingers that finally, this time, it would have worked.

My heart sank as I spotted my name on a piece of paper next to a clay vase that had a squat round base with thumb marks in it and a thin neck that loped off to one side, like a sad elephant's trunk. Somehow, I'd forgotten how awful it had looked. Maybe I'd thought the kiln would magically transform it.

I closed my eyes and sighed.

Bec tilted her head to the side. "It's cute."

"It's unique," Meera added.

"No failures, remember?" Agatha chortled next to me, and I gave her a look.

"It's entirely useless. How can anyone put flowers in that? It doesn't even qualify as a vase."

"Art should not be judged on its *usefulness*," she said, like the word left a bad taste in her mouth.

I rolled my eyes behind her back, took up my crappy little piece of "art," and turned to Bec. "Pub or home?"

"Home," she said, slipping her hand through the crook

of my arm. We hugged Meera good-bye at the bus stop, though I couldn't bring myself to wish her a nice time. Tanya. *Tanya.* The obnoxious, loud user who turned up only occasionally and took our friend away. Meera went from being this dry, funny, wonderful person to someone on edge, running from responsibilities. Resenting the promises she'd made. We'd spent years trying to convince her to get more help, a full-time nurse, or moving her aunt to somewhere with support, but I knew she thought that meant letting down her mum. She had a nurse come in at night when she worked at the pub, and during the day she was home, and she was surviving. She and Arti had their routines, their processes. Their video-game battles and Arti's novel that she was writing, a quiet, sarcastic companionship that Meera couldn't bear to change. Couldn't feel like she'd failed at. She might be spiky and sharp, but she was loyal till the end.

"Was I wrong to go off about Tanya?" I asked Bec as we waited for the bus.

She considered it, in that way she always did, weighing everything up. "Okay, so . . . Tanya is awful. But we don't live Meera's life. She does what feels right to her."

"But she deserves more."

Bec smiled. "She doesn't *want* more. And that's her choice. Are we veering a bit into Penny Spicer fix-everything territory? Not everything's fireworks and happy endings."

I saw the bus trundling up in the distance and put out my hand.

"But it was for you," I offered quietly. "And we never thought you wanted that."

Bec grinned and put an arm around me. "It wasn't fireworks, it was . . . it was this quiet, solid feeling that somehow I was home. I don't like all that jittery, nervous love stuff. To me, love is quiet and sure and steady." She paused. "And looks a bit like Clark Kent."

I snorted, stepping onto the bus and tapping my card. "Sure."

"He does!" Bec insisted as she followed me to a seat, swinging in next to me like we were still teenagers getting the bus home from school. "And just like you weren't right about Tanya, Meera may not be right about a certain annoying copywriter . . ."

I looked at her and made a face.

Bec took my hand and squeezed. "You're a smart cookie. You make safe, sensible choices. So don't worry so much. You always make the sensible choice."

Somehow, that made me feel worse. I didn't know why I wanted my friends to tell me to loosen up and make bad choices. Instead, it was like I was ancient, beyond risk, beyond fun. I just really wanted them to tell me to make a mistake that felt good. And I wasn't sure why.

When we got home, Matt greeted Bec with a kiss at the door, before realizing I was standing behind her.

"Oh." He blushed. "Sorry."

"Hey, your home, your wife. Do what you will." I held up my hands and sidled past, pretending not to feel awkward. I kept wanting to apologize for being in their space. But I couldn't bear to move into one of those crappy bedsits with the damp walls and mysterious stains on the carpet. No, my life didn't look how it was meant to right now. But I was not going to jump in the wrong direction just because I needed to make a move. A little longer, and I'd have my promotion, my beautiful flat, and the right guy whom I'd held out for.

When I got to my room I lay on my stomach on the bed, leaning over to slide a box out from underneath. It contained all my failed sculptures so far. I didn't want to, but I kept these ugly, pointless trophies that made me angry every time I looked at them.

I'd put all this time and effort into them. Raw materials had been used and wasted. And so they sat under my bed, taunting me every time I added a new one to the collection. But it was a promise, motivation that I'd be better, that it would work out if I just kept trying.

Dad still said that my stubbornness was exhausting. I was the kid who would be out in the garden till dark, insisting I could ride my bike without my stabilizers, but never going fast enough to get momentum. But I never gave up. Not until I did what needed to be done and proved (if only to myself) that I could do it.

I heard the telltale squeak of Bec's bedsprings and reached for my headphones, all too poised after a couple of months living with newlyweds. Some days, if Bec was being super cute, I'd find my headphones fully charged on my bed with a bottle of wine and a bow on it. She was a good friend like that. She knew this wasn't what we had planned. Or rather, it wasn't what I had planned. Move in briefly, go gallivanting, settle down, and move out. Marriage, kids, and no time lost. Bec had never really had a plan. She loved her job and her flat and Aperol spritzes on Saturday nights and karaoke Tuesdays and popping down to see her parents in Torquay for the summer, and that was it. The rest was open.

And now it was like I had the freedom she'd always loved, and she had the structure and safety I craved.

I looked at the vases, head tilted as I considered them, wondering what Lucas would make of them. That I was stubborn and ruthless in my need for perfection? That I was doing the same thing a hundred times over, expecting different results? That I was wasting valuable London floor space?

I was doing it, though, right? I was fighting for the promotion, I was looking for the right guy, I was trying to improve myself. Why not . . . have fun? Just for a few weeks? Why not take something for myself, something that wouldn't mean anything? To let myself be warm, cuddled and caressed and cared for, in between the sparks and jibes and one-liners.

I opened Dealbreakers to scan for more. Of course, as expected, there was a new one already. *He made me feel so special, I thought it was something real.*

Oh charm boy, when would you learn?

I scrolled back farther, refusing to admit what I was looking for.

He knew what he was doing.

He's a smooth operator.

Who could resist that smile?

I'm going to miss the sex.

Was there something creepy about the fact these women could be so open in their reviews? That I could log on and find comments about men I knew in real life? Was that what the funny feeling in my stomach was—something like loss, or regret?

Maybe it was the way Bec had told me I was safe and sensible, and Meera warned me off wasting my time again, that had me wondering. Or maybe it was that one dimple that had appeared in his cheek when he'd watched me find that sunflower on my desk?

I closed my eyes and clenched my fists. I was an idiot to

even consider this. How could I look at all these reviews from women who proved I was right about him and still think maybe I saw something they didn't?

You're sensible. You're safe.

Even if you were looking for love, you'd want the boring bit with matching pajamas.

Apparently my friends thought I wasn't capable of taking risks. Of doing something unexpected. Of choosing anything but a quiet, suitable relationship that met my end goals.

And it didn't make sense that I was standing in front of my wardrobe, carefully picking an outfit for tomorrow, choosing things with more intention than I had in months. That I was digging through my suitcases and boxes for my expensive perfume, wondering whether to curl my hair.

I'd spent the past year with no time to waste and nothing to show for it. So why not waste time, just for a little while?

I considered my reflection in the mirror, holding up my favorite dress in front of me. I would still go on my dates, and write up my Dealbreaker notes, and win my promotion.

So what harm could a little flirtation possibly do?

CHAPTER EIGHT

He swore all the time, it made me cringe. I need someone who can communicate on my level. But he was nice! No hard feelings.

I'd picked my favorite dark blue summer dress with the little stars printed on it and wore it with the denim jacket I'd found in a thrift store in a fancy part of West London a few years ago. My favorite summer outfit. One I'd never worn on a date in case it was forever tainted, like my black velvet dress, which now I couldn't look at without remembering Benji, who spilled soup on me, and Daniel, who asked what my favorite sexual position was before I'd sat down. No, no one was ruining my star dress.

I'd curled the ends of my hair, just a little, and tucked them behind my ears, frowning at my computer. As I stood behind my desk, closing down my station, a knock sounded at the door.

I looked up and caught the slight widening of Lucas's green eyes as they trailed me up and down. Well, that look was worth the twenty minutes I'd spent poking through my suitcases to find the dress. I tapped my star-and-moon necklace, then, irritated, tapped my collarbone.

"Well . . . you look fucking incredible," Lucas said lightly, as if he was commenting on the weather. "Hot date?"

I raised an eyebrow. "Very funny. Did you get the envelope?"

He waved it in front of me.

"I convinced Marie we didn't both need one. Save the planet and all that. You want to do the honors?"

I shook my head. "Go ahead." I watched as he ripped it, and then a huge smile erupted on his face.

"Oh God, what is it? Clearly something that works for your argument," I said, storming over. "Couples massage? Candlelit dinner?" I peered over his shoulder, then frowned.

"Cocktail making?" I laughed. "That is *so* a group activity! Some say the first hen do in ancient times was a cocktail competition."

Lucas snorted in amusement. "That's not true."

"Of course it's not true." I rolled my eyes and started out of the room. "But I'm still going to beat you."

"Is that why you're dressed like that?" He gestured. "To distract me?"

I snorted, hand on the doorframe as I waited for him to follow. "I have absolutely no idea what you're talking about."

"Marina Spicer, destroyer of men, stealer of hearts . . ."

"Maker of cocktails," I continued, feeling him fall into step with me, "winner of competitions . . ."

He laughed, that lovely lyrical sound I was starting to become a little addicted to.

"We'll see, Spicer. We'll see."

The worn sign above the door read "Mixology Wars," and I raised an eyebrow at Lucas, who shrugged and opened the door, waving an arm to let me go through first.

"Well, it's gotta be better than the magic wine." He laughed warmly.

Inside, the cavernous tunnels felt like we were heading underground into a hidden fairground. Artistic graffiti covered the walls, neon paint spattered across the floor, and carousel horses hung from the ceiling, repainted in crazy colors. It was so dark that I had my hands out in front of me in case I fell, and as my foot slipped on the uneven floor, I wobbled, tripping backward. I suddenly felt strong hands on my waist, propping me up against a solid chest. I could feel his breath tickle my ear. I should have moved, but I paused, just for a second, heart racing. Either from the slip or that damn intoxicating smell of soap and spice and how I could almost feel his stubble against my jaw.

"Whoa, you okay?" he whispered, still holding me close, hands resting on my waist like I might fall at any second.

I cleared my throat and stepped forward, out of his warmth. "Yeah, thanks."

"I think it's just ahead." Lucas's voice was unaffected, and I took quiet deep breaths as he got out his phone and used it to light up the floor. We slowly walked toward the circus-style booth at the back of the room, his hand hovering at my back in case anything happened. "Hello?"

"Ah, Joe said you'd be arriving soon! We've just about got things ready. Welcome to Mixology Wars!" a voice said from the dark, and a woman stepped out, her black bob swinging. She was dressed in dungarees and a rainbow T-shirt, and I wondered how she'd managed to make that look chic.

She ushered us forward. "Welcome!"

"Well, thanks!" Lucas launched into charm mode, that perfect smile fixed in place. "How are you doing today? I'm Lucas, this is Marina. We are super excited to be here."

She looked almost amused. "So I see. I'm Katrina, I'll be hosting your cocktail competition today. Joe mentioned you guys were already pretty competitive, so I hope this works for you?"

We looked at each other and grinned.

"Three rounds, three cocktails, best one wins."

I watched as Lucas smiled at Katrina, who smiled at both of us.

"Who decides the winner?" I asked.

Katrina pointed at herself. "Trained mixologist, right here."

"Afraid I was going to try to poison you, Spicer?" Lucas drawled, catching Katrina's eyes again as if to get her on his side.

More worried about you charming the judge.

"I worked in a pub throughout uni, I know my way around a bar," I said, and watched as he smirked. "What?"

"Nothing."

We followed Katrina to a room with two small bars set up next to each other, stocked with everything we might need. There were little wooden trolleys with an assortment of lemons and limes, fresh herbs, and all the different types of alcohol I could imagine. We stood next to each other, facing a larger bar in front of us, which Katrina walked behind and got out her supplies. Behind her was a scoreboard with flip numbers. Something about that fired up my need to win.

"Let's start it out easy—your first cocktail is an espresso martini."

She ran us through the ingredients, and at the beginning I made copious notes, afraid I was going to forget something. Yes, I'd worked in a pub during my uni years, but it had been mainly pulling pints of bitter and replacing the salt and vinegar crisps. The Gammon's Rest didn't even sell full-sized bottles of prosecco, just those little mini bottles that the occasional wives visiting at the weekends would buy and put a straw in. But he didn't know that. And it didn't matter—because Lucas didn't take notes. He was barely listening, just watching and smiling, in his usual relaxed pose as he leaned against his bar, unbothered. That bothered me. I felt his elbow nudge against mine as he stretched and held my breath. He didn't notice.

"Okay." Katrina smiled, and I suddenly paid attention again. "Your time starts now!"

Ugh, he'd joked that I'd distract him, and he already had me on the back foot. I hurried around, collecting my ingredients, following and double-checking the instructions every thirty seconds.

"Looking a little rattled there, Spicer. You know, for a former barmaid." I watched as Lucas shook the shaker and then chucked it up and over behind his back like a professional. I felt my jaw drop. Bastard.

"Oh, did I not mention I used to be a hired-out bartender for parties after I graduated?" He laughed at the expression on my face, and I clenched my teeth.

"Let me guess, it was a Butler in the Buff scenario?" I threw out as I looked at my instructions in panic. I heard the crash of the shaker.

"Who told you that?" He scowled, picking it up. "Did Harriet do a search on me? She always looks at me like she knows all my secrets."

Oh, darling, if only you knew.

"It's true?!" I crowed, clapping my hands in delight as he kneeled down to clean up the spillage. "I just assumed something where you could be the center of attention would appeal to you."

"Oh, here was me thinking you were just distracted by what was under my T-shirt," he threw back, and I knocked over a glass, catching it just before it fell. "Nice save."

This was a new type of warfare, a game of distraction that still somehow made my pulse flutter and my cheeks flush. I didn't reply and just shut down, focused on my drink. When the buzzer went off, I took my drink up to place it next to Lucas's on the main bar and watched Katrina with an eagle eye. As she sipped Lucas's drink she smiled, a quick flit of eye contact that told me she was impressed by him. She hemmed and hawed and wrote notes on a pad. When she tasted mine, there was none of that softness, just a forthright nod and a raised eyebrow, as if she was pleasantly surprised. Sure, she hadn't flirted with Lucas, but he seemed to have this effect on women; they softened around him, as if they automatically gave him the benefit of the doubt. The exact opposite of me.

"Very good first round, guys," she said with approval, flicking over the scores. I got an eight, and Lucas got a nine.

"I want to compare," I said suddenly, grabbing his drink and taking a gulp. Damn, it was better. She was actually being kind. It was so much better. Like being made with confidence imbued it with more flavor.

"Fair's fair," he said, and reached for my drink, his eyebrows raising as he sipped. "That's good, Spicer."

"You don't have to lie, it's patronizing."

He rolled his eyes. "It's called being polite. I know you've heard of it—I've seen you do it with every human except me. Besides, I wasn't lying. It's decent. You just needed less ice."

Katrina nodded sagely. "Exactly. Okay, round two."

This time, the process was in reverse—she gave us a drink she made, and we had to taste it, guess the ingredients, and try to recreate it. I sipped little and often, making notes.

"Need a clue?" Lucas offered, already reaching for the whisky, shaking the bottle in front of me.

"I don't cheat."

"Oh you, with your ever-solid moral compass. You know life's more fun when you bend the rules?"

"Rules exist to keep the world working." I sighed, sipping again. "Now shut up, I'm concentrating."

He laughed, loud and surprised, but did as I asked.

I knew the drink was an old-fashioned. I could see the cherry, taste the whisky, but everything else was a blur. It just tasted . . . strong. I sipped and sipped, until suddenly there was nothing left and I still wasn't sure what else to add. I grabbed a few bits in a panic and chucked them into a shaker.

Lucas placed his taster at the end of my table. "Here, have mine."

I looked at him. "You're so good you don't need to taste it?"

He deflated a little. "Not everything is a play. Everyone has that alcohol that tastes like a night you nearly died. For me, that's whisky."

"Wow." I laughed. "Dramatic much?"

He just tilted his head and looked at me. "Go on, you have one, too."

I closed my eyes and sighed. "Tequila. A house party at sixteen. Twelve shots with salt and lemon and then six hours throwing up."

He nodded effusively. "Yes! Exactly."

"And do I get to know about your night that tastes like death and whisky?" I placed my palms on the bar and waited for that dimple to appear as he laughed.

"Eighteen, a silly heartbreak, and an uncle who thought he was helping."

"Your family sounds supportive in interesting ways," I offered, and felt a little shine as he laughed again.

"Yep." He turned back to focusing on his process and presented the drink with a flourish. "Won't stop me, though."

I knew I'd failed at that round, even as I sipped on my final old-fashioned, having started from scratch multiple times. I got a four, and Lucas got a ten. Infuriating.

"What was that you were saying about going on a date with a sore loser?" Lucas laughed and wiped down his workstation with a towel, then threw it over his shoulder. I pressed my lips together and glared. He just laughed some more, hand over his heart like it was all too adorable for words.

"Okay, guys, last one—now you're going to create your own cocktail! Consider what you've learned about flavors, balance, and presentation!"

I felt the alcohol buzzing in my veins as I started slicing limes, aggressively crushing ice and picking up a variety of different spirits. It was like I was possessed, desperate to win, desperate to either wipe the smile off his face or put one there. I couldn't tell anymore.

I kept tasting, alternating, adding more. By the time I realized how drunk I was, it was too late.

"Time's up! Present your creations, my lovelies!" Katrina beckoned us forward.

"This is the Nemesis." Lucas smiled, that honey drip that always guaranteed one in return. Katrina's lips twitched, but she stayed neutral. "Rum, honey, and a smack of ginger. Guaranteed to blow your head off, but somehow you always come back for more."

Katrina used a straw with her finger over the top to pipette a sip into her mouth. "Well balanced, powerful, a bit edgy. It's good. I don't think I could drink more than one, though."

"I could." Lucas grinned at her, and I clenched my teeth again. He pushed it across the bar to me, as if daring me. "Go on. I need to be taken down a few pegs, clearly."

I ignored the straw method Katrina had used and just sipped from the glass. It was warm and sharp and there was a subtle sweetness right at the end. Damn. It was good.

I shrugged. "It's drinkable."

"Oh stop, I'll get a big head. All the fawning and compliments, I can't stand it." He grinned at me, and I felt myself smiling back before I could help it. Damn it, the dimple got me again. I was just like all those poor women leaving reviews on Dealbreakers, wondering how the hell Lucas Kennedy had spun them a beautiful lie.

"Go on, Spicer, you're up. Destroy me."

I put mine down in front of Katrina with a flourish. "This is ice-cold vodka, super-sharp lime juice, prosecco, and a blow-torched sugared lime on top. It's strong like a kick in the face, unrelenting, unnecessarily bubbly, and will probably get you in trouble if you're not careful. I call it . . . the Lucas."

I'd expected him to frown or huff or say something annoying, but he just guffawed, like I'd surprised him. Like instead of being offended, he was . . . complimented?

Katrina raised her eyebrows as she tasted it. "That's actually surprisingly tasty."

I pushed the drink over to Lucas, suddenly feeling like a dog nudging over a meatball, embarrassed and vulnerable. He sipped thoughtfully, nodding. "That'll definitely get you into trouble."

I narrowed my eyes at him, but he winked back, like this was a real date.

"Okay, so I'm gonna say Marina wins this round! But with the totals tallied up, Lucas wins overall." Katrina smiled. "Do you want a photo with your drinks?"

"No," I said, just as Lucas said, "Yes. That dress deserves the attention." I looked at him. "Or . . . good content for the website?" he corrected, unperturbed, and picked up his drink, ready to pose.

Katrina encouraged us closer, our heads together as we held our drinks, and I wondered what alternate universe this was. I felt the pressure of his hand on my lower back, warm and steady. I took a shaky breath and clenched my teeth into a smile. When the photo was taken and he stepped back, I still felt his warmth, like an imprint on my skin.

"So, included in the package, you get our little book of recipes with space in the back for you to add your own creations." She slid the books across the bar to us. "And you each get two drinks in our bar upstairs."

I followed him wordlessly as Katrina pointed out a spiral staircase hidden at the back of the room. My blood felt fizzy with nerves, like I was about to jump off a cliff.

The upstairs bar was completely different, like emerging from a cave into the light. It was snug and warm, with comfy velvet sofas and a long wooden bar. A couple of people worked on laptops or were sitting with huge sandwiches alongside their glasses of wine and cocktails. I blinked and then realized the huge glass wall at the other end opened out onto a terrace. A different world completely. It was still light outside, even though it felt like a whole day had passed down there, competing with Lucas and trying to hide my smiles.

We sat, and I gripped my menu, panicking about making conversation. Why was I panicking? This wasn't a date. And Lucas Kennedy could make conversation with a mannequin.

"Is it rude if I get a nonalcoholic cocktail?" I mused stupidly, and watched that smile light up his face.

"Rude to . . . the bartender?" He tilted his head. "You're adorable."

"I'm not." I frowned, only half joking. "I'm spiky and terrifying."

He shrugged. "Both things can be true. And to answer your question, no, it's not rude. To be perfectly honest I could go for a pint of orange juice and some toast."

I failed to hide my smile, tapping my lips with my fingers.

"I always see it, you know," Lucas said, and I kept my eyes on the menu. "It's a shame to hide a smile like yours."

I opened my mouth to say something stupid, but the bartender came over and I breathed a sigh of relief. I picked a fancy gin and tonic, thinking at least a drink that was mostly mixer would help me keep my head.

"You're feeling guilty about drinking when you should be working?" Lucas asked as soon as the bartender left.

"Does that make me a nerd?" I poured us each a glass of water and downed mine.

"No," he said, checking his phone, "it makes you a professional." He said nothing for a moment, frowning at his phone as I glowed at the most basic of compliments. God, I really was starved for male attention if a comment about my work ethic made me feel good.

I waited silently, remembering the multiple comments about him with his phone, taking calls, texting other women.

"Somewhere you need to be?" I gestured to the phone, and he looked up, frowning.

"Sorry." He put away the phone and paused, like he was deciding whether to give me ammunition. "It's my niece. She messages a lot . . . I'm thinking about moving here to be near my sister and her kid. My sister's going through a divorce."

"Oh," I said gently.

"It's hard on my niece. Like the bottom's fallen out of her world. I try not to leave her waiting too long when she messages. Everything's so desperate when you're twelve, isn't it? Like you don't get a response in thirty seconds and the world is over."

I blinked. "Being a kid is hard enough, let alone a divorce. What's her name?"

"Millie." He shone. "She's brilliant. So smart and witty and sharp. But she's hurting. My sister does what she can but . . . it's tough."

"It's nice of you to look out for her," I said blandly, unsure what to do with this new information.

He quirked his lips. "You about to pass out in shock that I can do something nice?"

"Maybe," I said lightly, putting together the comments about the phone calls to other women. Was it possible . . . ?

"My sister bought her a phone. Think she'd buy her damn near anything to keep her happy at the moment. But I tend to be the one she calls. I'm her safe adult. Which is hilarious." He paused to thank the bartender as our drinks arrived. I laughed at his choice, a bright pink pornstar martini served with a shot glass of prosecco.

"Hey, don't drink-shame me. It's mostly juice, and it tastes excellent. I'm secure enough to order a girly drink." He sipped as if to prove it, with a loud lip smack. "Perfect. So yeah, that's why I need the promotion. To be near Millie."

I have a good reason to beat you. I wouldn't do this otherwise.

I nodded, hearing it, and he twitched his lips in relief.

"Besides, it's time to leave the old scene behind. There's such a thing as being too close to your parents."

"Is there?" I asked honestly, and he looked at me.

"You're close?"

"I guess because I'm the only child . . ." I paused, but he'd given me some insight into his personal life, so I felt like I should share. Fair was fair. "We're an odd triangle. They're this perfect couple, met when they were teenagers, pure firebolt-out-of-the-blue-type love. They didn't really want kids, but I'm their 'happy accident.'"

"Accident's kind of harsh, even if it's happy." He nodded, and I saw his fingers twitch on his phone in his pocket, but he resisted. "Do you live with them?"

"My parents? No!"

He laughed at my horror. "What? It's a fair question! London's expensive. I'm sure lots of people in their thirties live with their parents. It's not something to be ashamed of."

"Well, it may be my only option soon enough." I tried to laugh. "I'm living in my newly married friend's spare room while I try to find a place that . . . meets my criteria. I can be picky."

"You? No!" He feigned shock. "Just taking the piss; you have high standards. That's something to be proud of."

I watched as a drop of juice dripped down his bottom lip and licked my own automatically. "Is it?"

"Of course. So many people settle because anything is better than nothing. You do not seem like someone who accepts less than exactly what she wants." He held eye contact, and it felt like a challenge.

"You make me sound like a nightmare." *Who would want to be with someone who expects the other person to be perfect?*

"Never." He smiled. "Can't be a nightmare when you

love dogs in socks and sunflowers and picking strawberries in the summer. Just not possible."

I closed my eyes and tilted my head back, exhaling. "You can take a day off, you know? From the charm thing? It must be exhausting for you."

"Funnily enough, telling a beautiful woman she's beautiful never tires me out."

I shook my head, blushing as my phone buzzed. *Adam.* I put it away, but clearly something must have shown on my face.

"So I was right, at the ax throwing. Some fucker broke your heart?" he said gently, no sense of triumph. "Hence the spare room?"

I considered lying. But his voice was soft, and the room was warm, and the copious alcohol made my tongue loose. I had exhausted this topic with my friends. And somehow I knew, even if I was handing him some power over me, Lucas would know the exact right thing to say.

"Well, my ex-boyfriend waited over a decade to tell me he didn't want children and then dumped me on my birthday. How's that?"

"What a wanker."

I snorted, looking at him in surprise. "I thought you were gonna try to wheedle me out of feeling bad about it."

He locked eyes with me, suddenly serious as he put down his glass and leaned forward in his chair. "Sweetheart, I would happily spend many hours making you forget that man ever existed."

I felt my lips make an *oh* shape, but no sound came out.

He waited, and I tried to think of a response. "That wasn't charming."

"Nope." He nodded and shrugged, sitting back in his chair again, as if the intensity had left his body. "Sometimes I can do blunt and honest. If that's what you want. No bullshit, no charm. No throwing snarky one-liners back and forth until my head feels like it's going to explode, when all I would really like to do is press you up against a wall and kiss that smart mouth."

I yelped, hands out in exasperation. "You can't say stuff like that!"

"You wanted honest!" He laughed. "So the kids thing, that's a dealbreaker?"

I blinked at the word, my heart racing as if I'd been found out. "What?"

"You want kids?"

"Yeah." I nodded, tapping my glass with a fingertip. "I know that probably sends most men running screaming in the other direction, but I'm in my thirties, I've got a plan for how I want my life to look, and kids are a part of that. Which means no more wasting time with people who don't want the same things as me."

Lucas considered this. "Even if it's really, really fun?"

"Especially if it's really, really fun." I laughed.

"Yes, you do seem like someone who's denied herself fun for quite a while now."

I gestured around us at the bar. "I'm drunk on a Friday afternoon."

"Yeah, because you were forced to be for work." He snorted, and I liked the curve of his lips as he leaned in closer. "You realize you could still be making the most of this time while working toward your picture-perfect life, right? It's not forward and backward; the joy is in the meantime. You're wasting the meantime."

"I thought you said it was good to have standards." I raised an eyebrow, and he nodded, leaning forward as if he was really eager for me to understand.

"Yes, have standards, have goals, have a dream. But enjoy stuff, too. Say yes, be surprised. Have fun." He smiled at me with affection. "You deserve it."

"You're charming me again."

"Yep, and buckle up because I'm about to say something mad." He downed the last of his pink drink and turned in his seat, intensely focused, his long legs caging me in on my stool. I covered how flustered he made me by raising my glass to my mouth.

"I think we should have sex."

I choked on my drink.

"Because . . . ?" I coughed, reaching for a napkin.

"Because if we don't, we're going to kill each other." He shrugged, as if he was suggesting an oil change or a systems update. A spring clean. Problem-solving.

I shook my head.

"Because it would be fun?"

I sighed, gave a small smile, and shook my head again.

Lucas paused, as if he was thinking. "Because I don't like how your eyes go sad and you tap your necklace when the arsehole who left you is clearly texting." He leaned forward, hopeful. "Because I think you're wonderful and should be worshipped. Because I cannot continue coming up with witty comebacks at this rate anymore. It's hurting my head. Take pity on a poor man, Marina."

I considered it. Just for a moment, I actually considered it, the alcohol running through my bloodstream and the pounding in my ears loud from my heartbeat. The way his green eyes seemed almost olive in the dull light, and how those dealbreakers now taunted me instead of warning me off. Yes, he never stayed, but they wanted him to. Because he was good at the things women liked.

"I . . ." I didn't even know what words were about to come out of my mouth when my phone rang. I rustled through my bag and looked at the screen. *Adam.*

Lucas looked at me sadly, shaking his head.

I paused, then stood. "Sorry, I've got to take this."

I escaped, grabbing my bag and not looking back as I

almost ran out the door in the direction of the garden terrace, answering as I went. A few smokers were sitting at tables dotted around, and I perched on a bench underneath a pagoda, vines trailing over it, flowers blooming in little pink and orange bursts.

"Is everything okay?" I asked, breathless.

"Did you see my text?" Adam asked, and I bit back an apology.

"No, what did it say?"

"Just thinking about the old days," he said, soft and morose. He did this sometimes, mourning our relationship's end as much as I did. We'd lost the person we knew best in the world. But he didn't want what I wanted . . . Besides, fifteen years, and he'd run away.

"Do you ever miss it?" he said, and I wondered if I should be angry about this. Meera would say yes. Bec would say yes. Lucas would definitely say yes. "Just, when it was you, me, and Meera, living down the road from each other, and everything was simple, you know? Like we knew exactly where our lives would go."

You're the one who changed all that, I wanted to scream. *It's you who messed up the plan.*

"Is something wrong, Ads?"

"Just wondering about life and choices and stuff, you know? Whether we end up where we're meant to be eventually. Even if we've made mistakes."

"Have you been drinking too much coffee again? You know it makes you all overthinky," I said lightly.

"You know me better than anyone, Rina. No one else knows the names of my pets, or my favorite aunt, or how hard it was when my granddad died. No one else seems to care about that stuff now, you know? Like it doesn't matter anymore."

"It matters," I said softly. "It all still matters." It suddenly clicked. "It's his anniversary, isn't it? Sorry, I normally remember."

A small part of me huffed at myself. *You remembered when you were his girlfriend. Which you're not anymore. Because he dumped you. This is not your job anymore.* If anything, I could imagine Meera standing in front of a big red button, threatening to press it if I didn't put down the phone. *Boundaries*, she would say. *Boundaries are key here. This man will keep taking until you have nothing left to give.*

"That's okay," he snuffled, then paused. "So how are you doing?"

"I'm . . ." *Considering sleeping with a man who makes my legs weak but I have no future with, thanks for asking.* ". . . Okay."

"Are you seeing anyone?"

I inhaled sharply and started coughing. "Um . . . I . . ."

"I shouldn't have asked." He laughed, suddenly much more cheery. "Bad ex-boyfriend behavior. But you're a catch, you know? I want to make sure you're with someone who treats you well."

The imaginary Meera sitting on my shoulder was screaming, *I'm gonna kill the bastard! How fucking dare he?*

Somehow, I found my voice.

"Adam, I'm really sorry, but I'm at a work thing, and I've got to go." I worked hard to let the silence settle around me but couldn't help myself. "But call me later if you're still upset and need someone to talk to."

No. I winced. *Don't do that.*

"Always looking out for me," he said fondly, "even now. We were always best friends first, weren't we, Rina? Nothing changes that. It can't."

I clenched my jaw and hung up.

The cheeky bastard. I thought about that last time I'd seen him, when he'd sadly wiped my tears away, tucked a strand of hair behind my ear, and asked if I was going to use the Lean Mean Grilling Machine or whether he could take it. How he apologized for the fact that I had assumed our plans were the same. That he felt so sorry that he was unable to give me something I wanted. As if I'd just made all this up. Like we hadn't talked about it over the years.

I thought about all the dates I'd been on, desperate to stop my life from staying stuck where he'd exited stage left, frozen in time. How many times I'd been insulted, negged, told I had "potential," stood up, talked down to, or made to feel ugly. All because I refused to compromise on one thing.

Soulmates.

He really *was* a wanker.

I closed my eyes and practiced breathing deeply, counting in and out until the rage and hurt left my body and my hands stopped trembling.

When I opened my eyes, I found Lucas sitting across from me, rolling a cigarette. I wrinkled my nose.

"Didn't think people smoked anything but vapes anymore," I said, feeling the need to put my rage and vulnerability somewhere and settling on his stupid bad habit. Smoking was a dealbreaker for lots of people, not just me. I watched as he ran the tip of his tongue down the edge of the paper, then rolled it up like he'd done it a thousand times before.

"S'only when I drink too much," Lucas said, lighting up, breathing deeply, and then holding it away from both of us. "Habit, more than anything. A bad one, I know."

"So why don't you stop?"

"You don't have any bad habits, Marina?" he asked gently, and then softened his voice even further. "Was it the wanker on the phone?"

I looked at my hands.

"My bad habit is probably doing the same thing over

and over again, expecting different results. Or expecting it to hurt less," I said, very quietly, focusing on the view.

"That's a good one. Shows consistency. Mine is probably not sticking around long enough to make the same mistakes." He took a breath and changed the subject. "It's beautiful," Lucas said. The golden light seemed to soak everything, making all those concrete buildings somehow sun-kissed and chosen. Special.

I nodded but said nothing, just listened to the sound of his breathing. The smell of the cigarette didn't bother me as much as I thought; it was the sadness on his face that I couldn't bear.

"Maybe I'm an idiot for wanting to move here. To stay here. I'd probably be better off jumping from place to place, starting over whenever I need. Sometimes I feel like this town is going to swallow me whole," he said quietly.

"Sometimes I feel like it already has," I replied. "Every day, every work meeting, every date is like waiting for something that never comes. Just replaying the same frame in a movie until I get it right. But I never do." I felt him smile in the silence, and when I turned, he grinned. "What?"

"Ever considered being a writer?" He smiled openly. "No, honestly, I think you'd be good at it."

"Thanks, but I like my code. Endless paths to finding a

solution, solving a problem in the cleanest, simplest way possible." I thought of my father with his clocks; all those moving parts were impacted the minute you changed one thing.

He nodded. "I take it back. Writers need to be okay living in the gray scale; you are all about the black and white."

"From the sound of things, maybe you could use a little more black and white."

Lucas shook his head and smiled. "Nah, the gray is where the magic happens."

I watched as he put out the cigarette and stood up to go.

I nodded, and we thanked our bartender before escaping through the front of the bar, down the spiral staircase, and finding ourselves at the side of the bridge, the road much busier than it had been earlier. Lucas stuck out a hand. "Well, I've enjoyed our cease-fire. But I guess we've got to go back to being enemies again. For the sake of a London studio with a garden."

"For the sake of my own set of brass cutlery and a mustard-colored sofa from Loaf," I agreed, shaking his hand. "Nice knowing you, but you're going down, et cetera, et cetera."

"Oh yes, you'll rue the day, so much ruing, and so forth." He kept hold of my hand, his thumb stroking it insistently as he grinned. As my bus arrived, and I took back my hand, Lucas called after me.

"Marina, think about my idea, would you, darling? I really think it would solve almost all our problems." He grinned, rocking on his heels, hands in his pockets. "Or create some rather splendid new ones."

CHAPTER NINE

I couldn't stop thinking about it. Frankly, having sex with Lucas was now the only thing I thought about.

Damn him.

This was not the plan. The plan was to find a nice, marrying type who liked watching *The Walking Dead* and wanted to make babies pronto. No tattoos, no swearing, no shagging about, no . . . no Lucas bloody Kennedy.

"You seem . . ." Meera started, and I jumped.

"What?"

We were eating lunch at La Cantina, a tiny Spanish restaurant we used to frequent as teenagers because it was cheap and delicious and they never really checked that we were eighteen when we tried our luck ordering sangria.

No matter what, we did this once a month. La Cantina

was down the road from Meera's house, so she'd only have to leave Arti for an hour or so, and I usually dropped in on my parents. Though, for some reason at the moment, I just really didn't want to. Maybe it was sensing Dad's frustrations, or Mum's desire to harvest my eggs, but I couldn't face it.

I sounded guilty, and Meera knew me better than anyone.

"Happy." She frowned, stuffing some tortilla in her mouth and chewing. "I was gonna say happy. Glowy, even."

"Oh." I gulped down some water. "New skincare regimen is working, then."

"I don't think it's that." Meera looked at me, raised a perfect eyebrow, and tapped her nose ring. "Whatcha hiding, Marina?"

"I don't think we should talk about it," I said lightly, and reached across for the meatballs.

She winced. "You fell in love with the copywriter."

I blinked. "Jesus, Meera. No. Nothing beyond verbal sparring. Which is totally innocent. I just . . . it's fun. I don't have to think."

"You do think too much," Meera agreed, and then reached across the table to take my hand. "I'm sorry I was mean at the pottery class. If you want to fall in love, you go ahead. I just . . . I don't want to see you hurt again."

"Bec said I'm too clever to get hurt again."

"Your brain never has much to do with it." Meera laughed, leaning back in her chair. "If it did, would you have chosen someone at fifteen who was a second-rate bass guitarist, had no vision, no goals, no nothing? Someone who never argued with you. Look at you, you love to clash. To fight your corner. To debate! Adam was . . ."

I held up a hand. "Adam was a fifteen-year-old who fell in love with another fifteen-year-old, and now we're here."

"No," Meera corrected, "Adam was a selfish narcissist who only ever cared about you making him the center of your world. And his jokes were crap."

"Then why were you friends with him?"

"Because he was fine if you weren't dating him! I've got loads of knobhead friends, present company excluded. I take people as they are. But not when they break my best friend's heart. You deserve to be a mum, Rina, you do. You'll be amazing at it. I want you to have someone who wants that, too. And someone who's honest about what they want. Who won't make you feel bad for wanting something for yourself." She paused thoughtfully. "And who isn't a massively selfish, self-involved, hypocritical, lying—"

God, I hadn't even told her about our phone call yesterday. I tapped the table, trying to change the conversation. "Is my glow diminishing?"

"A little," Meera agreed, patting my hand again. "Sorry.

Go throw an ax at that guy's head; that seems to pep you up."

I snorted a little. "You're right. I'm on my path, I've got my goals. I need someone who knows what they want and where they're going to be. A grown-up. No more Peter Pans . . ."

"But?"

I smiled a little. "I just quite enjoyed the idea of having fun and not thinking about the future. Just for a while."

Meera was quiet for a full thirty seconds. She just looked at me like she wasn't sure who I was anymore. I laughed and threw my napkin at her.

"Shut up! It was a momentary lapse in judgment."

"Maybe I'm all wrong about this. Have fun! Fun!" Meera almost yelled, then shook her head. "Wow. You think you know a person."

I laughed again. "Do you *actually* like me?"

"I love you more than anyone. And I like you as much as it's possible for me to like people."

We were quiet again for a moment, chewing away.

"So what did Tanya steal this time?"

"Spare change and, weirdly, a bunch of beach towels." Meera shrugged one shoulder, still focused on her food. "Go figure."

"Yeah, if that's what having fun looks like, I think I'll pass."

She rolled her eyes. "If you're not careful, you're gonna turn into your mother."

I gasped, loud and dramatic, pointing at her like we were in a soap opera. "You take that back!"

We collapsed into giggles, snorting into our water glasses.

"Seriously, though, the swearing and the tattoos? The no-smoking rule? Straight out of the Penelope Spicer handbook. Maybe you should shag the copywriter and turn up to Sunday lunch at Penny's on a motorbike. I think she was always a bit sad you never gave her the full teenage-rebellion treatment. Maybe there's still time?"

I laughed. "I'll put it on my list."

Later that afternoon I got an alert that the next installment on the blog was live. Working on a weekend. Surprising, from Lucas.

My glorious nemesis might disagree that a cocktail-making competition is a great date, but she still named her cocktail after me. Pretty romantic, right? Going head-to-head in some alcoholic action is a brilliant way to try to woo a woman. Besides, who doesn't fall a little in love with a capable bartender?

After three rounds of excellent hijinks, and more than enough insults thrown back and forth, our mixologist declared that I was the winner. We got a cocktail recipe book and two very ill-advised further free drinks in the beautiful upstairs bar.

Mixology Wars is a delightful way to spend an afternoon in excellent company, learning, laughing, and drinking way too much. While I will acknowledge that it would be brilliant for hens, stags, and work group events, there's something about going head-to-head with someone else that's strangely invigorating. So if you're dating someone you love to hate (hey, we've all been there), this is the one for you.

I couldn't stop thinking about how his eyes had twinkled as he'd asked me to bed. How he'd bitten his lip and inhaled a little as he complimented my dress. Had a man ever called me "fucking incredible" before? Maybe I was softening on the swearing. My mother might hate it, but the man knew how to make words mean something. Even the bad ones.

I shook my head. Even Meera thought this was a bad idea. Meera, who had encouraged me to shoplift as a kid and always took a handful of jelly beans from the cinema pick 'n' mix. Who happily slept with someone who stole from her and declared she'd never be in a relationship. Meera was all about the chaos and making yourself happy in the moment. And she thought it was a bad idea. I couldn't be trusted with just fun.

And she was right. The last thing I needed was Lucas Kennedy.

I opened Dealbreakers and purposefully didn't go to his page. Though I'd admittedly been checking to see if there were new reviews pretty regularly, to see if he was dating while he was in town. Just out of curiosity, of course.

But no, this wasn't about Lucas. This was about finding someone appropriate. Sticking to the plan. Finding the next step in my future. And sure, it was starting to feel like I'd had a fifteen-minute interview with every commitment-averse man in London, but . . .

Okay, there was someone new! Henry, thirty-seven, solicitor. Liked takeaways and cozy nights in, black-and-white movies, spending time with family. Looking for the picket-fence life. I almost passed out from shock.

I had found my unicorn.

No dealbreakers popped up on the app, though. So he clearly hadn't been dating for a while. Newly divorced and back on the scene? I didn't even hesitate. I immediately pinged him a message, saying that I thought we had a lot in common, and I'd like to meet. I didn't bother with back-and-forth; endless small talk and texting was a waste of time. Get them there in person, find out if they were who they said they were.

Thirty seconds later, I heard my phone ping and realized Henry had already responded. He spelled things correctly and in full, no LOLs or FYIs or any contractions at all. He agreed about not wasting time and meeting people in person and suggested dinner tonight. Maybe this was all I'd needed. Refocusing on what was right for me. Resisting temptation and sticking to my convictions.

I messaged straight back, and we agreed on a restaurant I already loved. This was it, this had to be *it*.

Fate, or just consistency in action.

As I jumped out of bed and started rooting through my suitcases, I heard my phone buzz again. This time it wasn't Perfect Henry. It was Mr. Most Certainly Not Perfect.

Did you see the article?

I huffed. Yes, it was very good. Pat on the head for you.

Did you want to get some food tonight?

I frowned. Had the Joes arranged another event, on a weekend?

Did we get an envelope? I didn't get an email or anything.

A long pause.

Do we need to be competing to hang out? I don't have any friends here and I don't know the good restaurants. Take pity on me!

I laughed and shook my head. Can't, date tonight. Go make eyes at a girl in a central London bar, you'll make a friend pretty quickly. Promise.

I paused, feeling a bit mean.

Also, for burgers go to Pat Pats, and for Italian go to Pacino's. They're not far from the office.

There was another moment, and then the reply came. I held my breath.

Thanks. Enjoy your date. Hope he's everything on your list.

I rolled my eyes and threw down the phone to return to my current conundrum. What do you wear on a first date that you desperately want to be your last?

. . .

"You do look beautiful," Henry said, smiling at me. I wouldn't have minded, but he'd already said it twice before, and I was running out of ways to say thank you. Especially as whenever he said it, he interrupted whatever we'd been trying to talk about.

"You're very kind."

He was. He'd greeted me with a kiss on each cheek, he'd pulled out my chair for me, and he'd picked a nice restaurant. I'd got no sense he was trying to rush me, like he was out dating every night. He was looking for the real thing, he said. And sure, he was wearing a jumper over his shirt, even though it was summer, and his teeth were a little too big for his mouth, and he kept accidentally interrupting me and then apologizing too much. But people deserved the benefit of the doubt. He seemed nervous.

I liked the way his dark hair flopped over his forehead and that he kept tugging on his sleeve. He was like a young Hugh Grant, a little foppish and posh, but sweet.

"So you're a solicitor," I said brightly, placing a napkin in my lap neatly. "Do you love it?"

He thought about it for a moment, tapping the edge of the table, drumming a rhythm with his index fingers. It seemed to be a nervous habit. "I guess so. I did, when I started. There's a good opportunity for progression, and I like . . . researching and solving problems . . ." He trailed off, and I wondered how he kept his clients engaged. Maybe when he spoke about something he really loved, he came alive. I looked over his shoulder at the group of young women clinking their glasses together, loudly bemoaning their lives and making appreciative noises as their food arrived. Next to them was a little old couple who looked like they'd been here a hundred times before, asking after their waitress's family. London on a Saturday night—vibrant, full of possibility. I wondered if Lucas had taken my advice and was charming some poor girl right this moment.

"So no plans to change jobs any time soon?" I refocused my attention back to Henry, who was failing to wipe a smudge off a glass and pretending not to care about it.

"Oh no, not really a fan of change." He made a face. "But I'd definitely take a step back when I had a family. I want to be involved in every second, there for all of it. Don't want to miss those special moments, you know?"

I smiled, warming to him.

Wow. He'd brought up kids first. I wasn't sure I'd met someone who planned like that, who wasn't afraid. Apart from me. And everyone always seemed to think I was super weird.

"You sound organized."

"Well, I'm coming to the end of my thirties. I know what I like and what I want. That's the advantage of dating like this, right? No matching with incompatible types or people who say they want one thing but want another."

"Here's to that." I lifted my glass and clinked it against his.

Henry spoke slowly, I thought. That would be my first dealbreaker, if I was going to write a list. But I wasn't going to. Because he checked off every single thing I wanted. Henry was my unicorn. If he was a unicorn that moved slower than a tortoise in a race with a sloth, so be it.

"You said you want the white picket fence?" I prompted. "What did you mean?"

"Well"—two creases appeared in his forehead—"you know, wife, kids, nice house. All those grown-up things people do." He smiled, hopeful, and I smiled back.

"Why do you want that?"

"It's what I've always wanted. It's what you do, isn't it? Settle down, make new life, make your parents happy as grandparents, and talk about the kids. You'd never be bored, would you? You'd always have something to talk about."

Okay. Not quite what I was expecting. I nodded. *Shut up, Marina. He wants what you want; you need the man to spell it out in skywriting?*

"So, tell me about you," Henry said, seeming to take forever to finish the sentence. "You work in apps?"

"I'm a developer for an events booking platform," I said, and then winced. "I've managed to make it sound boring, but it's not!"

"No you haven't—"

"I mean, it's . . . oh, sorry . . ."

"No, you . . . I mean . . . sorry. It's not boring."

I spoke more slowly, giving him time to jump in, and tried to make myself sound appealing. Upbeat and peppy. *Hi there, I'd be great as the mother of your children.*

But I kept thinking of the furious back-and-forth with Lucas, how I felt my cleverest, most "on" self when I was trading quips with him. Comparatively, this felt like very slowly sinking in quicksand. It was easier when I kept him talking about his own plans and interests. We both talked about the future a lot, which I liked. Henry was focused on where he was headed. He said he wasn't a man of huge ambition, but he was excited for the future.

When the date ended, he offered to pay, and though I offered to split it once, I didn't push it. He seemed relieved, like letting him pay meant I wasn't rejecting him. He kissed me on the cheek and walked me to the tube stop, giving my shoulder a sweet little squeeze. He was nice. So nice.

Sure, my dad would call him a wet blanket, and my

mum would panic about him not seeming happy enough at events, but he wanted the same things as me and on the same timeline. And he seemed just as thrilled as I was to find someone who was excited by having kids and life settling a little, having structure and an outline for adulthood.

And yet, at home that night, it was Lucas I was thinking about. Lucas, who I avoided calling or texting, but who I did imagine in my bed, leaving myself frustrated and overly warm.

When my phone buzzed as I was finally drifting off, the text wasn't from Lucas, but from Henry, thanking me for a wonderful time and asking to meet again. I didn't even hesitate. Not everyone got fireworks or butterflies. Some people got practical decisions.

My mother would hate it, but I didn't see how a perfect meet-cute thirty years ago was doing her much good in her marriage now. Too much razzle-dazzle wasn't good for you. Compromise and a little boredom, that was where the magic happened. I happily accepted Henry's offer of a second date.

But I didn't put my phone down after I hit send. I couldn't help it, like scratching an itch.

What did you end up eating?

Lucas responded instantly.

That burger place may be the best place in the history of the world ever. Thank you for introducing me to the true love of my life.

I snorted, and then another text came through.

Good date?

There's potential, I typed back.

Ugh. Potential. You need fireworks, woman.

I shook my head and decided to walk the line, just a little. My fingers hovered over the send button, but, hey, I wasn't having fun. Not really.

Stop trying to seduce me, Lucas.

You may as well ask me to stop breathing, darling. See you Monday for our next adventure.

And then he was gone, making me miss him, just a little. I rolled over, pushing my face into the pillow to hide the smile that hurt my jaw. Damn that impossible, charming, dangerous man. I was trying to pretend I wasn't made for fireworks, but it took half an hour to get to sleep, that fluttering, excited feeling creeping from my stomach up to my chest.

I wouldn't tell anyone, but I couldn't wait for Monday.

CHAPTER TEN

We went on three dates and I was starting to think I'd finally found the one. But he told me he didn't want anything serious. Shame he didn't tell me that before we slept together.

Walking down Carnaby Street in my vintage dress, I felt cute. More than cute; I felt in control and put together. I'd started dressing up for myself, and I felt good. I was rediscovering those pieces of my wardrobe I hadn't bothered pulling from the boxes, because there never seemed like a good reason to make an effort. I had my standard "date" outfit, and since I'd never been on a second date, I'd never needed another. My beautiful dresses and sparkly tops and embroidered bags . . . I'd missed dressing like myself, instead of a tech professional on a hunt for a husband.

Plus, there was nothing like a swishy dress and a bold lipstick to make an impression on a guy who threw around compliments like they were confetti. I wanted that reaction from him again, and maybe it was pathetic to chase compliments, but it had been a long while since I'd had a sincere one. I'd worked from home that morning, being the good housemate to wait for a plumber for Bec. And part of me was excited to make an entrance when I arrived at the venue.

What I was more worried about was dancing together, today's activity. My pulse had raced when Lucas placed his hand on my back. How was I going to hold it together while we were in close quarters? The only thing keeping me calm was the fact that swing dance wasn't particularly intimate.

I found the little door on a side street, buzzed, and was let up. When I got to the small practice room, Lucas was already there, looking the part, pacing back and forth. It was weird to see him not in his usual childish video-game T-shirts and jeans. Instead, he had beige trousers and suspenders worn over a white shirt that he had open at the collar, the sleeves rolled up. I could see the black-and-white tattoos that peppered his forearms, scattered randomly as if he were filling up a shopping list. Though, seeing them, it was hard to remember why tattoos were one of my deal-breakers. Because Adam had that stupid portrait of CatDog on his arse, and Where's Wally peeking out from behind his nipple? Because I'd sat through far too many dates in the early days where men talked me through their tattoos and the meanings behind them? On Lucas, I kind of liked them—they were like clues to a story I hadn't figured out.

He stopped pacing when he heard me and looked up in relief. "Thank fuck you're here, I— Whoa, you look spectacular."

I bobbed my head. "Spectacular's a big word, Kennedy."

He held up both hands as I chanced a look at him. "I only speak the truth."

"Sure, charm boy," I teased, taking a breath and feeling more like myself. I gestured at his outfit. "Looks like you got in the swing of it."

"Argh." He held his hands to his chest. "She's got a flower in her hair and she's making dad jokes. Help, my poor heart can't take it."

He'd slicked his dark hair back, making him look like he'd just walked out of a fifties movie, a young Marlon Brando, all sharp jawline and strong lines. My eyes went again to those patterned, muscular forearms, then flittered back to his face. All the moisture had disappeared from my mouth, and something fluttery and unpleasant was happening in my stomach. I took a breath. *Style it out, Marina. Come on, you're an adult, use your words.*

I rolled my eyes, desperate to appear unaffected. "You're usually charming the crap out of whoever is running our class by now. What gives?"

"Well, I know you're going to be terribly disappointed to hear this, as I know you were desperate for me to step on your toes for an hour, but our teacher is off sick." Lucas looked at his watch. "The owner was just running around to see if he could find a replacement dance tutor for us."

"Oh." I blinked, not sure how I felt about it. "Where would that leave us with our competition?"

He shrugged, hands in his pockets. "Guess we go get dinner and come back another day?"

I laughed. "Jesus, you're smooth."

"Too fucking right." He wiggled his eyebrows. "You'd have said yes, too."

I raised one eyebrow, very slowly, and said absolutely nothing.

"Friends! Friends!" A man in incredibly tight black trousers and a black tank top ran in, his tanned muscles bulging. "I'm so, so sorry for the mix-up! We wanted you to have the best experience here today, so you could write up something wonderful for the site! We're a new company, and Carnaby Street is expensive, and we just . . ."

"Hey"—Lucas held up both hands, his face open and smiling—"don't even worry about it, we're happy to be here, there's no problem. People get sick."

"Besides, this activity is for our internal . . . admin." I looked at Lucas, who fought a smile. "We're not judging your company. And everyone has sick days! So please don't worry," I said brightly, and the man looked slightly relieved.

"I'm Fernando," he said, with a strong Essex accent, "and Ginger Dance Studios is my baby. I just really need it to do well on your bookings app, you know?"

"We know," I said, placing a hand on his wrist, patting gently. "And it will. So we can come back another time if we need to."

He shook his head resolutely, and I noticed Fernando was wearing black eyeliner and making it look excellent. "Nope, you aren't leaving without a dance class today, not on my watch."

Lucas and I looked at each other, then back at him. "Okay, sure."

"The only thing is, I haven't got any of my swing teachers available. But I'd be happy to teach you?"

I actually saw Lucas gulp in fear. "And what do you teach, Fernando?"

"Only the best dance of all." He grinned at us. "Hope you two are okay with getting up close and personal."

Forró was a type of Brazilian partner-dancing, similar to salsa. At least that was what I thought Fernando said as he set us up, practicing steps on our own, back and forth in front of the mirror before he made us face each other. After all my earlier brave thoughts, I could barely look at Lucas, and it seemed like he felt the same. He offered me a shaky smile and an "I'll try not to maim you," and I laughed out a shrill hiccup that sounded like someone else.

"Closer," Fernando said, rearranging our arms. "This isn't ballroom, this is back alley, hot and sweaty dancing. You don't need to be stiff and upright; you curve around each other."

Lucas was like a furnace and his smell of soap and spicy aftershave was overwhelming, and as we practiced moving across the room in time, I felt his lips graze the back of my neck. I jumped, and he jumped with me.

"Sorry!" I yelped, feeling like a skittish horse as he took my hand again, almost looking guilty.

Even the brush of his fingertips was becoming a little too much as we swayed.

"I knew you'd want to lead," he mumbled against my neck, and the warmth of his laugh reverberated down my spine.

"Closer," Fernando urged, pressing on our backs. "You need to be able to tell when he's going to turn you, to read the signals of his body, right?"

He seemed to want an answer, so I squeaked, "Right."

"So, if your hips are connected, you can feel which way he's going to turn you and act accordingly."

"Hips?" Lucas half laughed, looking over my shoulder at our teacher, and I felt the exhale of breath on my shoulder.

"Mate, we're colleagues. We're also not professional dancers."

"You don't have to be professional dancers; you just have to trust each other."

Lucas swayed, and I followed, feeling confident enough to look over at Fernando and grin. "Ah, see, the thing is, we don't trust each other. We're mortal enemies."

"Aw, upgraded from nemeses," Lucas said, pulling back to look at me. "I'm touched."

"Mortal enemies, that's . . . new." Fernando tried to hide his amusement and failed.

"We're competing. I think these activities are better for groups of friends; he thinks they're better for dates."

"Oh, this is one hundred percent date territory," Fernando said immediately. "The closeness, the responsiveness, the trust. The sweat. Now push out and twirl . . ."

I felt Lucas grip my hand and push. Suddenly I was twirling prettily beneath his arm, and just as suddenly I was back in his arms, picking up the rhythm without a missed step.

"Hey!" I exclaimed in delight, a huge smile on my face as I pulled back to look at him. "We did it!"

Of course, that meant we were nose to nose, and I was stuck remembering that those green eyes were really green, like a field in the summer that seemed to go on forever, just the tiniest hint of jade and a little hazel around the center.

"Back to the hold," Fernando said gently. "Now just try to respond to the music, no expectations, just listen to each other and *follow*, Marina."

I huffed a little, irritated.

"There's no shame in following, you know. It's not weakness, it's strength. It's listening to signals and responding."

"And when do I get to give the signals?" I argued pointlessly. "When does *he* get to follow?"

"Ha, she says, as if I haven't been doing that from day one." Lucas laughed and twirled me again, letting me fall away before tugging me back to him and holding me against his chest, his head bent and curved into the arch of my neck.

"You're . . . good at this."

"You sound surprised," he mumbled, and I felt his lips vibrate against my skin again. It was getting a little hard to breathe.

"You're clumsy. You said it yourself."

"I know, I honestly have no idea what's happening. Maybe you're a good partner."

Before I could reply, Fernando jumped in. "It's about counterbalance. Being perfectly matched. And for mortal enemies, I see a lot of trust here."

When the music stopped, we paused, not quite stepping

away from each other. Leaving his arms meant I had to acknowledge that I quite liked being there. And I didn't want to do that just yet. Lucas's hand was sitting loosely on the small of my back again, and I met his eyes, almost daring him not to let go.

Instead, Lucas quirked his lips, took my hand, and twirled me into a final spin. When I stopped, my skirt still swinging around my knees, he lifted my hand and kissed it as if it was nothing but a performance. I blinked and he let go, taking two steps back as if I couldn't be trusted. Maybe he was right.

"I know it wasn't swing, but I hope you had fun?"

I was drenched in sweat, out of breath and shivery from the closeness, from the way Lucas's fingers had briefly caressed the column of my spine beneath my hair, how our thighs had touched, mine responding as he guided me which way to move.

"It was a great lesson, thanks," I said, smiling politely.

"Yeah, honestly, illuminating. And the first time I didn't feel like I had two left feet in years!"

How did Lucas sound so normal, so unaffected? Sure, a little breathless from all the movement, but there was no waver to his voice. He didn't even look at me, focusing on our teacher entirely.

"Let me guess," I said as I grabbed my bag, and Lucas held the door for me, "drinks in the bar?"

He laughed, following me down the hallway. "I hate to disappoint you, but there's no bar here."

I paused walking through the next door and he bumped into me, that warmth making me shiver again, my body still remembering the shape of his as we danced.

I dared to look back over my shoulder and found his brow creased, confused.

"Did you forget something?"

"Um, I just think we should talk."

"Here?"

I looked at the brightly lit corridor, busy with a passing class of baby ballerinas, who we were now in the way of. "No, um . . . here." I took his hand and dragged him into the nearest room, which appeared to be an empty studio with the lights off, the tiniest crack of light coming from the small window in the corner, and a bar along one wall, covered in mirrors.

I kept hold of his hand, perhaps gripping too tightly, based on the look of concern on Lucas's face.

"Hey, Marina. You okay?"

"Yes, I think so. I mean . . . you . . . you suggested something the other night. And I've been thinking that maybe it's not such a bad idea."

His eyes widened until he looked positively owllike, and I wanted to laugh.

"I thought you weren't about gray scale?" he whispered. "You're trying to find your perfect match and all that?"

"I am, and I haven't given up on that, but . . . maybe you were right about having a little fun."

"I was right?" Lucas shook his head. "Did you take an ax to the head when I wasn't looking?"

I tried to take my hand back, feeling rejected, but he kept hold of it, his thumb slowly stroking the side of my index finger.

"So I've convinced you it's okay to have fun?" he said, his voice suddenly low in a way that made my stomach itch and tremble.

I lifted one hand, holding my thumb and forefinger an inch apart. "Maybe just a teeny, ti—"

He kissed me before I finished speaking, swooping in to close the gap between us. His lips were gentle, hesitant at first, as if giving me the chance to step back, to change my mind or freak out. Instead, I heard myself let out this small sound of relief, like the magnets that had been pulling us together were finally satisfied. I sank deeper into the kiss, putting my arms around his neck and pulling him closer, taking tiny sips of air to remind myself to breathe. I was drowning in the smell and taste and feel of him, those strong arms around my back and waist, somehow pressing me up against the wall until I felt like I might fall down without it.

"Ahem."

I heard the sound just before the lights got turned on, frowning with the brightness as I looked over to the door. There was Fernando, accompanied by a gaggle of tiny tap dancers, their "click-clacks" across the room slowing down as they noticed us, their serious little faces concerned as they looked at each other.

Fernando raised an eyebrow, his arms crossed and his toe tapping. "Mortal enemies, huh?"

"It's . . . complicated?" Lucas offered, breathing hard.

"I blame the dancing!" I yelped, not looking at either of them, and rushed past Fernando to escape. I didn't stop until I got to the entrance on Carnaby Street and leaned against the wall, feeling the cool summer air on my skin.

Oh God, oh God, oh God.

"I know what you're thinking," Lucas said from behind me, his voice quiet and confident. I could hear that smile, but I didn't want to see it. It felt too much like him winning, like I'd given in somehow.

"I doubt that."

"You think there need to be rules."

I blinked and looked up at him. Okay, I hadn't thought of that, but rules might stop this from being awkward. "I'm listening."

"This is only for the duration of our little competition. After which it doesn't really matter anyway, because if I lose,

I'm probably back off to Belfast and you won't have to see me ever again." He held up his hands. "No awkwardness."

"And if you win, I'll be looking for a new job anyway, so we still won't be working together."

He looked shocked at that, but the minute I said it, I knew it was true. I needed more. If I couldn't get it at LetsGO, then I'd find it somewhere else, damn it.

"You can carry on dating your checklists, trying to find your perfect ready-made husband type," he said lightly.

"And you can keep dating women who think you're going to propose and then you dump them after one night."

Lucas raised an eyebrow. "Was that really necessary?"

"I'm just saying, this isn't personal."

"Of course it's personal," he argued. "What it doesn't have to be is messy."

"Does all the fun in your life have this many caveats?" I asked, long-suffering, and Lucas laughed so loudly it seemed to echo off the cobblestones. He offered a hand.

"Come with me and I'll show you," he replied, and I took his hand, tentative.

"One more rule: no needless charming me. I don't want either of us making this confusing."

"Spicer, I wouldn't dare to try to charm you. I know you're immune to my wiles." Lucas grinned, his thumb running along the inside of my wrist. "But that doesn't mean I can't have fun trying."

. . .

Trying to have sober sex with a man I had suddenly discovered I really fancied, on a weekday late afternoon, was somehow too cringeworthy to even consider. My mind was racing so loudly, Lucas suggested cracking open the minibar and putting on the TV. Which was how we ended up eating painfully expensive Kit Kats, drinking gin and tonics, and watching reruns of *A Place in the Sun* while we howled about the price of property in the Costa del Sol ten years ago.

"It's an absolute shithole!" he shouted, throwing a balled-up wrapper at the screen. "How dare they offer sixty-five grand!"

We were sitting on the floor, leaning against the end of the bed, our feast stretched out in front of us.

"I can't believe they paid for your hotel room." I laughed, looking around. "Even if *you're* considering moving to work for them. It's madness."

"Oh believe me, I agree, love." He slouched so his neck fitted the end of the bed perfectly and stared at the ceiling. "I have no idea why, but they offered and I thought, hey, at the very worst I'll get to see my sister and niece and piss off that gorgeous woman on the development team."

I huffed.

"It's not charm if it's true." He elbowed me gently and smiled at the ceiling.

"You just . . . you're too free with everything. Compliments and smiles and . . . everything." I sat up, swiveling to face him. "It's like I could be anyone."

He tilted his head, stroked a finger down my cheek, tucking my hair back. "You are most certainly not anyone, Marina Spicer. You are one in a million."

"Quite literally what you tell all the girls . . ." I paused. "I'm sure."

Lucas looked quizzical. "Where do you get this idea that I'm some sort of Lothario? Because I smile at people and chat bollocks all the time? I'm a friendly moron, I know. But apart from that and a way with words, it's pretty much all I've got."

"You're telling me you're not a casual dater, a one-night-stand guy? You asked me to bed, remember?"

"If you recall, I also asked you to dinner, but you had plans with Mr. Potential." He raised an eyebrow. "Look, I'm not saying I'm a blushing virgin here. I've dated a lot. I was trying to find something that . . . did not exist." I wanted to ask what he meant, but I didn't. "But you're not here for that either. You're here, even though you've got Mr. Potential . . ."

I closed my eyes briefly. "I'm conflicted about that. I don't do . . . this."

"Oh, I know, you're looking for the guy who asks for your parents' permission and proposes on one knee at your favorite restaurant, and you're not surprised because you already chose the ring and had a sensible conversation about it." He wrinkled his nose. "You want the marriage and the babies ASAP. You have a checklist and there is to be no deviating from it. I have been informed."

I opened my eyes and looked at him in horror. "Informed by *who*?"

"A bossy and terrifying redhead who has let me know I'm under no circumstances allowed to waste your time, because you're looking for Prince Charming and have no time for frogs." He reached out for my hand and inspected it, stroking the fingertips like he was thinking. "And yet, here you are. Even if I only get you for a little while."

I shook my head. "I wasted enough time looking for that love story. I'm a practical person. I can do without some things if I get the big stuff: I want a family; I want stability and someone who wants to move on to the next phase with me."

"Why?"

"Why what?"

"Why have kids now?"

I glared at him, and he laughed, shaking my hand. "It's an honest question! No judgment, I just want to know why it matters."

"There's a thing called a biological clock, have you heard of it?" I said snarkily. "We have different deadlines. Women have things that need to be done, and every time you make one choice, it impacts another."

He tilted his head and looked at me. "That's not the real answer."

"I . . . I just want to make a family where everyone belongs. Where no one feels lonely or alone, and everyone feels loved and accepted. And yes, there are fights and yelling and madness, but you've always got someone. Someone to play with, or talk to, or to tell you you're wrong, or celebrate your wins. I want . . . I want my own huddle of penguins, everyone warm and loved."

He looked at me, as if to tell me to continue.

I shrugged. "I was the third wheel to this huge, beautiful love story. And I love my parents, but it was just me. No aunts or uncles, no siblings, no cousins. I was like a little grown-up, right from the beginning. So I guess I want to have kids so they can *be* kids. So I can let them be exactly who they are." I looked at him, suddenly worried. "Does that make any sense at all?"

Lucas had this strange expression on his face, something I couldn't put my finger on. Half incredulous, half delighted. His eyes even glazed a little as he reached out a thumb and stroked my cheek.

"That's a very good thing to be picky for, Marina

Spicer. I won't stand in your way," he whispered, moving a little closer, until I could feel the warmth from his skin and smell that cologne. "But while you're looking for that, I could be something else? Just for a while?"

I felt him kiss my neck and tilted my head back, just a little.

I nodded.

"Is that a yes?"

"Mm." I sighed, nodding again.

He stopped, pulling back just a little until we were nose to nose, those green eyes demanding more. "I am going to need a more enthusiastic confirmation."

I reached for the collar of his shirt, gripping it tightly. "I want this. Take me to bed."

"Magic words," he said, and kissed me.

There was something about a London hotel room at night, the lights of the city visible from the huge windows as Lucas stood at the tiny kettle and made us tea. I liked looking at him in the darkness, lit only by the dull blinks of skyscrapers and buildings in the distance.

I was changing my mind about tattoos. Each one told a story, a moment in his life, something he wanted to remember. He had been places, seen things. The way I'd planned to years ago, before time passed and everything became a race to the finish line. Trying to outrun the fear of not getting what I wanted.

He passed me a cup, then slipped back under the sheets, resting his head on his hand as he looked at me.

"Freaking out?"

I put down the tea on the side table so I could shove him, knowing full well he'd pull me closer. I traced the rope and anchor on his biceps, just a black outline like a child had drawn it on a school desk. "Surprisingly, no. What's this one for?"

"I spent a summer as a deckhand on a yacht in Australia. Beautiful way to see things, but I chatted too much to the visitors."

I snorted. "Sounds about right." I pointed to a star. "This one?"

"I went to see the northern lights. Should have come up with something better for that." He winced a little, tapping it. "Not all decisions are good decisions."

"You've traveled a lot," I said, suddenly realizing how much I'd missed out on.

Lucas nodded, stroking a hand down my arm. "I had a very embarrassing and messy breakup in my early twenties, and after that I just decided to be incredibly selfish. See the things I wanted to see, do things on my own timescale. I could write remotely. I basically bounced around for ten years, just seeing stuff."

"And now?"

He considered my question. "Now I'm trying to be more constant, for Millie and my sister, and my parents, but honestly . . . I'm always on to the next thing. It's just how I am. I'm like a big dumb golden retriever, that's what my sister says." Lucas laughed. "She says I'm here for a good time, not a long time, and then I'm gone."

I nodded. "I get it, you don't have to start a whole thing with me."

Lucas raised an eyebrow. "You didn't want charm; you wanted honesty. So here's me, opening my heart and sharing my origin story. There's no game here, Marina. You are gorgeous and intriguing, and you fight with me better than anyone I've ever met. Even arguing with you seems to make me wittier and funnier."

"Good God, what were you like before?" I elbowed him gently, and he buried his head in my neck.

"You are . . . unlike anything else. But . . . I am not what you're looking for. You want that steady guy with the nine-to-five and the same day over and over. That's not me. And I'm not gonna take anything away from you. Someone did that to me once, and it's not fair."

I tilted my head. "You don't want kids?"

"I . . . don't think I'd be good at it. I'm good uncle territory, you know? Turning up unannounced with expensive presents, problem-solving. Being the one they want to run away to when they think about running away from home. I don't think it would be fair for someone like me to have a kid."

Before I could ask what that meant, he carried on. "Plus, I have that huge family you were talking about. That huddle of penguins. Three sisters, two brothers, endless cousins and uncles and everyone in your tiny house yelling at Christmas and giving you their hand-me-downs. It's possible to feel lonely, even when you're a penguin."

I tilted my head and ran my hands through his hair, enjoying the freedom that came with being able to touch another human being, feel close and soft and bold all at once. "Maybe you're not a penguin. Maybe you're a flamingo."

His laughter exploded like sunlight, and I joined in.

"Could have put money on you saying peacock there." He grinned and snuggled down closer. "So tell me about this guy, Mr. Potential."

I inhaled. "We just had sex and you want me to talk about some other guy?"

He stretched. "We're friends now, right? We can't be nemeses-with-benefits; it doesn't fit. So tell me. I'm not the jealous type, I promise."

A small fluttering in my stomach felt a little like disappointment.

"Well, we have similar visions of the future," I said

lightly, pulling the duvet around me and sitting up, my back against the headboard, "and similar timelines."

"He's desperate to get married and have babies immediately?" Lucas frowned, rubbing a hand across that light stubble that had so deliciously left marks on my neck. "And he mentioned this on a first date?"

I half shrugged.

"And did you like him? Was he nice to you?"

I considered it. "He was super complimentary and sweet. Speaks a little slow. He's a solicitor; he likes watching movies and relaxing at home."

Lucas closed his eyes, then sat up. My eyes followed as his bare torso was on display again. "Marina. I thought you said high standards? Likes watching movies? Relaxing? Those aren't hobbies! Those aren't real things. Does he cry watching *Casablanca*? Does he walk an extra fifteen minutes to get to the good Thai place? What would he do with a lottery win?" He snorted. "Likes movies. Probably also '*enjoys dinner*' and '*likes a good sit-down.*'"

"Okay, so not jealous but judgmental?" I rolled my eyes. "He's a unicorn. He's a man in his thirties who is ready for a family, open to talking about it, and not running in the opposite direction when you mention commitment."

"And do you want to fuck him?" he said lightly, and I coughed.

"Lucas!"

"What?! You're thinking about marrying the guy and you don't know if you fancy him?" He threw up his hands like I was impossible.

I raised a shoulder. Henry was attractive, in a foppish sort of way, and he had a kind smile and, well, no, when I thought of his hands I couldn't imagine them touching me. When I thought of kissing him, I screwed up my face a little. "Attraction can be built on getting to know someone."

"Bullshit, attraction is instant. It's fireworks and butterflies and mutually assured destruction." He gestured between the two of us.

"So if there were fireworks, it would be okay to talk about marriage and kids and all that?" I asked.

He looked out the window. "You know, somewhere out there are a couple of twentysomething kids meeting while drunkenly eating kebabs after a night out, looking in an estate agent's window and talking about which house they'd buy. And maybe they'll never see each other again, or maybe in ten years they'll be married with kids, in exactly the sort of house they pictured. But it's not about the house or the wedding or the kids. It's about them. It's about the fireworks. It's about that *moment*."

"Ha, you'd love my mum. She's all about the Big Story. If it's a boring meet-cute she thinks a relationship is doomed." I thought about how she told that story of seeing my dad across the room at a party when she was eighteen. I knew it almost word for word. But she never told stories now about him sitting tinkering in his shed and her watching from the kitchen window. The past was a prettier place. "She is all about the fireworks. I just don't think I'm that sort of person."

Lucas smiled to himself and splayed his hands. "Darling, I don't mean to be indelicate, but I promise you, based on our recent activities, you are *definitely* a fireworks sort of person."

"Yes, but *you* are a good time, and I'm looking for a long time. I'm willing to compromise on the fireworks to get the . . ." I trailed off, looking for an appropriate metaphor. I gave up. "Well, anyway, I'm giving him a chance. I'm seeing him on Friday, actually."

Lucas shuffled closer and took my hand, curling it so he could lean forward and kiss it. "Marina, I respect your choices. But could you do me a favor, sweetheart? On Friday, on what is sure to be a *super exciting* date with this wet tea towel of a man, ask him when his last relationship ended."

"What, why?"

"Because a man who talks about marriage with a woman he's just met is either infatuated or has recently left a long-term relationship. He's subbing you into his existing plans." Something about that clanged in my stomach in a way I didn't like.

"Believe me, I've been there." Lucas refused to let go of my hand, stroking my palm. "Almost ran off to Gretna Green with a manicurist who believed in astrology."

I want to know about this big breakup that changed your life. I didn't ask.

Instead I laughed, leaning into him. "Gretna Green! How romantic. More information, please."

"Her name was Mary, she was five-foot-nothing; hated sports, drinking, and parties; read her horoscope religiously; and organized furniture for a living. It was never going to work."

"You feel that strongly about horoscopes?"

"You think the pattern of the planets means that the hundreds of thousands of people born during a certain month are going to all meet a handsome stranger that week? Because if so, I've got a bridge to sell you." He grinned at me. "No, no mystical whackjobs, no extreme adrenaline junkies, no grown women with collections of dolls, teddy bears, or Beanie Babies . . ."

"Unless that last one is a genius moneymaking scheme?" I offered.

"Oh, it never is, Spicer. It never is." He shuffled, then nudged my shoulder with his nose, tracing a thumb down my spine. "Go on. Your turn. What's your *absolutely not* list?"

"My dealbreakers?" I asked, and winced. "Um . . . no tattoos . . ."

He laughed. "Go on."

"No smokers . . ."

"Even just ones who smoke socially when they get too drunk?" He nuzzled my shoulder.

"Lives nearby . . ." I winced. "Likes dogs . . ."

"Ooh, okay, I got one!" Lucas laughed, and I frowned at him.

"I thought you hated dogs?"

"Why would you think that?"

"I . . . don't know?" *Because a bunch of other women complained about it online?*

He wrinkled up his face in confusion. "I mean . . . I'm allergic to a lot of them. But you know some dogs are hypoallergenic? Weird, right?"

"That is weird."

"So my dreams are not completely dashed!" He laughed, and I tried to laugh along. "Go on, continue your list of reasons I'd never be right for you."

"That's not what—"

He kissed my cheek. "I'm not taking it personally. You want some straitlaced, upstanding guy who will be painfully honest when you ask how you look in some ugly dress."

I blinked, pretending to be horrified. "You wouldn't tell me if I looked awful in an ugly dress?"

"No." He shook his head, kissing my shoulder, lingering. "I would seduce you out of it, let you know you were the most beautiful woman in the world"—he kissed me again—"and then convince you to wear something else if you really insisted on putting your clothes back on."

I considered that, lips pursed. Didn't sound too bad, really . . .

"Ah, suddenly she's not so against charm."

"I could be coming around to it . . ." I smiled. "Feel free to keep convincing me."

I put my arms around Lucas's neck, stretching out fully against him, letting him know this conversation portion of our evening was over. After all, we knew what we were. Completely incompatible. Here for a good time, not a long time.

Even if he did like dogs, and only smoked when he was drunk, and the tattoos inked into his skin told a story. Even if he made me laugh as he kissed me, until that desperate need started to thrum. Lucas Kennedy was never the man who would get down on one knee, or get nervous waiting for an answer, or even talk about wanting kids. He was the shooting star that moved into your orbit ever so briefly before your real future arrived. And he knew it, too.

But at that moment, as his fingers stroked my skin and his teeth traced my jaw in a dimly lit hotel room, looking out over a bright city that was just coming to life, I really didn't care.

CHAPTER ELEVEN

He was fun. So fun. But that's all he was.

"I'm so glad you agreed to get together again!" Henry said, pulling out my chair for me.

We were in another lovely restaurant, Italian this time, but something in the back of my mind kept yelling for attention, tapping me on the shoulder. Lucas's words kept repeating over and over: Could I imagine sleeping with this guy? *Get out of my head, Lucas.*

I kept looking at this perfectly handsome, kind man who was sitting opposite me in a beautiful restaurant on a Friday night and wondering what this future I'd imagined would actually *look* like with him. *Feel* like with him.

No, I most certainly didn't need fireworks. But could I imagine Henry stroking my cheek and asking questions about my life in the dark of a hotel room or calling me in my favorite dress "fucking spectacular"? No. Probably not.

But . . . that wasn't the stuff that was meant to matter. That wasn't the stuff on my list.

Henry would bring flowers and remember anniversaries and give me a kiss on the cheek in front of the kids at Christmas. I was trying to focus on that.

My phone beeped, and I partly expected it to be Adam. But it wasn't. It was Lucas.

> Good luck with Mr. Unicorn. Hope your date goes well. But if it doesn't, you can always come over . . . X

"Sorry to check my phone. You know how work can be." I shuffled in my chair and tried to shift my smile from my screen to Henry. Forget fireworks. I was going to make an effort. I put my phone away. "I'm putting it on silent."

He just shook his head, amenable as ever. "It's fine, I'm sure if your colleagues are as rubbish at tech as I am, they're calling you every five minutes to fix things. Turn it off and turn it on again, right?" He guffawed, and I tried to dispel the strange feeling crawling up my body that told me I did *not* want this man to touch me. I tried to imagine sex, but all I could say with complete certainty was that he'd definitely keep his socks on.

I didn't bother explaining I didn't work in tech support, just smiled with a clenched jaw, gripping the edge of the chair with both hands. I desperately tamped down on the horrible realization: I had discovered the Ick. Oh no.

The waitress arrived, and Henry sat up straighter.

"Shall I order the wine?" he offered, and picked a bottle immediately, without pausing, and the waitress nodded and disappeared.

"Have you been here quite a lot, then?" I asked, and watched as a peculiar look crossed his face. "I don't really know much about wine—I'm always intrigued by how people know what to order." *Especially before we've thought about what we're going to eat.*

"Oh, it's what we always get when we're here," he said mindlessly, flipping through the menu, then paused. "I mean, used to come here. I used to come here regularly and always ordered the pinot grigio. It's really good."

Oh God, Lucas was right.

"Oh, does your family like this place?" I prodded, and he paused again.

"An ex." Henry's eyes met mine, and he seemed to crumble. "I'm sorry, I probably shouldn't have brought you here, but it was the one place I knew was really nice, and I should have thought that it would have memories associated with it. I mean, God, we had our fifth anniversary here, and . . ." He suddenly looked up in panic. "I didn't bring you here to make her jealous or anything. It's just that you mentioned Italian food, and when I think of dates, I think of this place."

I closed my eyes briefly, everything clicking into place.

"How long ago did you break up, Henry?"

He sighed. "About two weeks ago."

"Two weeks?!" I tried to control my voice and resumed in a whisper, "And you'd been together five years?! You have to know that's too soon?"

He shook his head, but his bottom lip wobbled like a child. "She didn't want to get married, wasn't sure she wanted the three kids and the house in the country. She said she liked our life the way it was. Without a shared vision for the future, what's the point?"

I winced and caught the eye of the waitress as she brought the wine over. I shook my head and she nodded, holding back. Goddamn, Lucas had been right. He was always right.

"But you love her?" I asked, and that was the final straw. He hid his tears behind a coughing fit, honking as he furiously searched for a hankie in his pocket. The one he pulled out with a flourish had little smiling cupcakes on it. Oh God, my unicorn unironically owned a handkerchief.

"And she loves you?" I said, trying to get some words from the man.

He just coughed louder, the people at the tables near us looking intrigued, some scowling at me as if I'd brought patient zero to their dining experience.

"Henry, some words, please?" *I should feel disappointed, but instead I feel relief.*

"We didn't want the same things," he said quietly, staring at the table like a scolded schoolboy.

"But . . . surely there's some compromise?" I asked gently. Henry took deep breaths, watching me wide-eyed. *If I'm your romance guru, pal, I'd reconsider your life choices.*

"But . . . I knew what I wanted my life to look like . . ." he said softly.

"But wouldn't you rather she was in it?"

He nodded, as if he was just coming to that realization himself. Then he stood. "I think I'd better go . . ."

I nodded back, relieved. "I think you should. Good luck, Henry."

"Thank you. I'm sorry . . ." He shrugged helplessly. "Thanks."

As I was sitting in the chair, watching him run to the door, already holding his phone to his ear, I felt . . . at peace. Like I'd been helpful, a bridge toward what was always meant to happen. Shouldn't I have felt loss, irritation . . . like I was once again back to square one? I supposed so. I'd been annoyed enough at the child-accountant, and the man who wanted a barefoot baby mama, and the tens of other men I'd met who weren't who they said they were or who weren't really what I wanted.

But a failed date meant I could go back to that hotel room with the beautiful view across the city and curl up alongside someone who would laugh and swear at rubbish television shows and ask me what I thought and how I felt about things. Tell me I was spectacular and amazing and one in a million.

That definitely took the sting out.

The waitress came over tentatively, holding a tray with a small glass on it.

"Bad date?"

I smiled, shaking my head. "For me, but not for him. I just helped him get back with his ex-girlfriend."

She placed the glass on the table. "That's what I thought. This is on the house."

"Oh, that's so kind, but I'm really okay." I held up my hands and smiled at her. She scanned my face seriously, and some of the professionalism dropped from her voice.

"Wow, you really are, aren't you? I've been on three shit dates in the last month—that would have broken me." The waitress looked hopeful. "What's the secret?"

Mind-blowing sex with a man who's not right for you?

I shrugged hopelessly and then reached in my bag for a pen and grabbed a napkin off the table, scribbling down a URL. "I haven't really figured it out either, but if you're looking to save yourself some time on the duds—most of the time—try downloading this add-on to your dating app. It's not foolproof, though."

I slid the napkin across the table. The waitress looked at it, then back at me, a surprised smile on her face. "Intriguing. Well, if dating's gonna be crap, it may as well make for a good story, right?"

"I tend to agree." At least, now I did.

As I left the restaurant, I went into my messages to reply to Lucas.

You were right.

The response was instantaneous.

Come over so I can say I told you so in person.
Slowly. A few times.

I laughed to myself as I walked to the tube station, pulling my jacket around me. Early-summer nights in London were often sweaty and sticky, but on the odd occasion a breeze fluttered through and I remembered there was always the chance of rain. I quickened my steps, looking at the sky. *Don't even think about it.* Just as I was about to make it inside the station, my phone started ringing—Adam. I paused. It felt like there was a choice here. Listening to the man I had loved for half my life and commiserating about the past like we were both hurt, even though he was the one who had left. Letting him still have that little part of me.

Or I could . . . well, it wasn't moving forward. But it was having fun. Just for a little while. A break from searching for my future. A break from planning and scheming and reading reviews and working. Just to adore and be adored, for a little while. Until this ended. And I'd go on to my promotion and my search for a dependable adult, and he'd go home to Belfast and then probably on to his next amazing adventure somewhere magical.

And I'd pretend not to miss him.

I pressed the cancel button, and Adam's call was cut off.

For the smallest, silliest step . . . it felt like something huge.

"Do you think the concierge thinks I'm a call girl?" I said, lying on Lucas's bed, naked under the duvet, eating Hula Hoops. "He gave me a dirty look when you came to meet me."

"Yes, because your date night ensemble was very lady

of the night." He raised an eyebrow at me. "Seriously, you gave me shit about my Care Bears T-shirt—why are you dressing like an old lady tonight?"

"Rude."

"A beautiful, sexy old lady . . . but still, what gives? I've seen you in some really great dresses. This is . . . not you."

Okay, well, my brown spotted wrap dress was one of my mum's castoffs, but still . . .

"I'm trying to convey that I'm serious about things."

"Believe me, darling, no one needs help believing that. You pretty much shout it down a foghorn." He leaned across and kissed me, then pressed his lips together. "Whoa, salty."

"You about to tell me you hate crisps?" I widened my eyes in faux horror.

"Is that on your list, too? No savory snack haters?" He shook his head sadly. "I never had a chance. Are you ready to talk about the date?"

I winced. "Do I have to?" I curled into him, pressing my nose into his neck and smelling that cologne I had started to really love. All spice and promise. "Instead, why don't you tell me about the woman who sent you almost running off to Scotland with an astrology buff?"

I felt him shake his head.

"Come on, you know all my secrets—it's not fair. Plus,

we've got to go back into the office on Monday and pretend to be all normal."

"So?"

"So, it's our last activity, and our time together is almost up."

"Well, that's your fault for wasting so much time hating me." He trailed his fingertips down my arms, leaving goosebumps in their wake. "We could have been doing this from the start."

I rolled my eyes. "You hated me, too. No one sends that many annoying emails if you don't hate someone. All those times you'd write these *huge* demanding emails, and I'd reply with lots of detail and you'd just send back 'k.'" I threw up my hands. "Just 'k.' Like you'd never cared about any of this and I was insane."

Lucas screwed up his face and had the good grace to look embarrassed. "Call me immature, but sometimes boys do stupid things to get a girl's attention. Playground hair-pulling. I always read what you said, even when I pretended I didn't. I just liked how passive-aggressively polite you became." He wiggled his eyebrows and pinned me to the bed. "And see, it worked out very well for me. Don't underestimate a 'k'—it sends a message."

I laughed, looking into those green eyes, and felt something in my chest expand and contract. Oh God. Dangerous.

I rolled away gently. "Come on, tell me your story. I want to know who Lucas Kennedy was before he became the charming Lothario I love to hate."

"I'm not a Lothario!" he yelped, but sat back against the headboard and lifted an arm for me to snuggle under. "Fine, in an effort to humanize myself, I will give you my tale of woe."

He stroked my shoulder, whirling circles as he talked. "Once upon a time, there was a silly young boy who believed in Romance with a capital R. And he fell for his sister's best friend."

"Ooh," I interjected, and he tapped me with a fingertip.

"Hey, quiet in the cheap seats," he said lightly, but took a breath. "She was super impressive. A trainee doctor. I adored her. She was more practical. With me she got the big proposal, the expensive ring, the chance to start wedding planning in her early twenties, beating all our friends . . . and, in my family, she got the family she'd always wanted. It never occurred to her she was meant to adore me back."

I felt my lips shift to a pitying pout, and Lucas shook his head. "None of that. I knew what I was getting into. I was a sap. Loved big romantic gestures, being that perfect guy."

I snorted and he winked at me quickly. "Yes, I know, not exactly in line with who I am now. But every lowly womanizer has a villain origin story, right?"

I nudged him with my elbow. "A big public proposal?"

"Oh yeah, big party in her favorite restaurant, all our family and friends there."

"Brave, if you thought she might not say yes?" I said, tracing lines on his stomach.

"Oh, I knew she'd say yes. She wanted the wedding planning and the 'secretly' recorded video. I was giving her exactly what she wanted. And my family adored her. They couldn't have been more thrilled. Sure, I dropped out of uni and wasted my loan on clubbing, takeaways, and poker games, writing my silly little stories, but marrying Sarah? It was like I'd finally come good."

He was silent for a moment.

"And then?"

"I guess I thought I could love her enough for the both of us. I was completely prepared to spend my life with the scraps she offered me." He twisted away from me, pulling himself up and fluffing the pillows, plucking at threads. "She cheated on me with someone from work. And pathetically, I forgave her. I was willing to put it down to cold feet, but she realized it wasn't meant to be that way. If you're excited to get married, you don't go sleep with some random guy. She realized she wanted the wedding and not the marriage. And she was right."

He looked down at me, took one look at my expression, and laughed. "What, what is that look? Is that pity? You never believed the man who charms the knickers off every woman in a five-mile radius actually had a beating heart? What?"

I snorted. "I mean, it's definitely a ten-mile radius, but no . . . your face looks weird when you're being sincere."

"Oh good, kick a man when he's being all vulnerable."

I pulled back to look at him. "It's hard to imagine that version of you."

"Is it?" He tilted his head, his big hand on my face. "It feels like he keeps appearing more and more these days. The poor, hopeless bastard."

He held my gaze as if he was trying to tell me something, that thumb tracing my cheekbone. I held my breath but wasn't sure why.

The moment was broken by my phone ringing. I reached over to the side of the bed and looked at the screen. Adam. Again.

"The wanker? Or have you already lined up a date with the next picket-fence-loving stable adult who'll talk your ear off about mortgage rates?" Lucas said lightly.

I frowned at the screen, canceled the call, and turned to him. "Hey, unfair."

Lucas just looked at me.

"I didn't answer. Don't I get points for that?"

He shrugged. "I don't know, do you?"

"Yes! I have been available to him whenever he wants for too long! And now I'm not. So . . . yes. Go, me. Woo and hoo. Et cetera," I said very seriously, with a straight face.

Lucas smiled and shook his head. "And about the search for Mr. Picket Fence?"

I sighed, pulling my clothes on and looking for my stuff. "It will resume after our competition ends. When I win and you head off on your next adventure."

"You're still certain you're winning?" he asked, his eyes following my every movement.

"You think just because you pretended we were on dates and now we're having sex, you're going to win?"

He considered me seriously. "I guess maybe I'm hoping . . . yeah. Maybe I'd like to stay awhile. Do you really have to quit if I win?"

"If I move up, then I'll stay. If I'm back to where I was, stuck in the same place . . . I can't do it. I can't stay stuck anymore. I've got—"

"A plan," he said softly, his smile almost painful. "I know."

As I looked at him, this gorgeous man with stories inked onto his skin and eyes that told me to stay, I felt something click into place. This different version of Lucas, one who followed a woman like a puppy, taking the little she offered and making it enough, I could see him in that moment, even as his older self smiled at me, sharply vulnerable.

I pulled my apparently ugly dress over my head and sat down on the edge of the bed, on top of the rumpled duvet. His eyes traced my movements, as if I was saying something.

"How did you recover?" I asked softly, watching him. "How did you say good-bye to a life you had planned and family who loved her and . . . history?"

Lucas considered the question, his head tilted back as he stared at the ceiling. I wondered what version of him would answer: the glib, sarcastic guy who didn't take anything seriously, or the quiet, hurt man who sat there in the dark hotel room with me.

In the end, it was a mixture of both.

"Well, I guess at first I tried to replace her as quickly as possible. I dated women who looked like her, who had the same interests. Who wanted the things we'd always said we wanted. And you know why that was so fucked up?"

"Why?"

"Because I'd changed," he huffed slightly, tapping his fingertips together. I wondered if he wanted a cigarette. "I was trying to choose the same things, even though I was completely different. I'd been betrayed, I'd been left, I'd clung on like a pathetic sad sack, I'd begged her to stay . . ." He bowed his head, ashamed, and I reached over to stroke the back of his neck, feeling those soft, short hairs like bristles against my fingers. "I was a completely different person, even if I didn't want to be. I couldn't want the same thing. I had to adapt."

"Into a charming Lothario who leaves a trail of broken hearts behind him?" I asked, only half joking.

Lucas grinned. "Into a happy-go-lucky guy who's around for a good time, not a long time. I'm always honest about that. No one has any feelings or expectations." He paused. "Problem is, I've been doing that so long I'm not sure what I'd do if feelings did come along."

"Send you running, I imagine." I smiled and patted his hand. He grasped it, bringing my palm to his cheek and holding it there.

"I'm more worried about the opposite," he whispered, placing a kiss on my palm and then releasing my hand. We stayed like that for a moment, two statues on a bed, frozen in a moment where no good could come of any possible response.

"I think I better leave," I said gently, and Lucas shook his head.

"Ah, I scared the lady off. All that adoration, it can be overwhelming." That wry tone was back in his voice, and I watched as a mask dropped over his face. I had briefly seen the boy who existed before Lucas Kennedy learned his own power, and now he was scared away again.

"Probably better not to stay overnight," I said, pulling on my shoes. "Keep this what it is, right?"

If I don't leave now, I could stay here forever.

I could feel his eyes on me. "You the expert in hookups now, Spicer?"

"Learned from the best." I gestured and grabbed my bag. "I'll see you on Monday."

He cleared his throat, and I looked at him, half naked in the middle of that huge bed, suddenly vulnerable.

"Did you . . . did you maybe want to do something on Sunday? A Sunday in London can feel a little lonely."

I looked at him, suddenly unsure of what he was offering. He was clearly busy on Saturday, but that was none of my business. "I'm seeing my parents. Aren't you going to see Millie?"

He nodded. "Yeah, I just thought . . . she really wants to work in tech when she grows up, thought it might be nice for her to meet a woman kicking arse."

I smiled softly, something warm and fluttery in my chest. I had to get out of there. "Next time." I nodded. "Always want to encourage the next lot of young women coders."

"Next time, sure," he said, a smile playing about his mouth like he didn't believe me.

"And I'll send you a list of my personal favorite Sunday lunch pubs," I threw in, somehow unable to fully refuse him.

I watched as he stood up, pulled one of those hotel

robes on, and followed me to the door, hand pausing on the handle as he reached past me to open it.

"There's just one thing before you go . . ." he said, and I only caught a glimpse of his smile before his lips were on mine, his hand tangled in my hair, the other still on the door so I was contained in his arms. It didn't even occur to me to resist, or that I was sending mixed signals. I trailed my hands down his arms, squeezing his biceps slightly. He let go of the door and wrapped his arms around my waist, actually lifting me off the floor.

I yelped against his mouth, and he laughed against mine, putting me back down and slowly backing away.

"What was that?" I sighed, touching my lips and staring at him.

He grinned lazily and leaned against the wall. "*That* was a thank-you for your list of lunch places. And . . . encouragement to come join me at one of them."

"Lucas . . ." I sighed, and he held up his hands, the look of a man who was dedicated to getting what he wanted.

"It's just lunch, Spicer. But I bet you miss me by tomorrow night." He winked, then opened the door and patted me on the behind. "Okay, get out of here before I drag you back to bed like the helpless Neanderthal I am."

"Self-knowledge is so important," I teased, and pretended I could feel his eyes on me as I walked down the hallway to the lift, refusing to look back. When it arrived and I stepped in, I dared to glance back and found the door closed, the hallway empty. I couldn't tell if I felt relieved or disappointed.

As I stood in the lift going down to the lobby, braced against the wall, I looked at myself in the mirror. Lips kissed plump and red, hair tousled by gentle but demanding hands. A blush on my cheeks, a sparkle in my eyes. I looked like a completely different version of myself. Someone who slept with a man she had no future with and asked awkward questions and defended her boundaries and her plans. Someone strong, fighting for what she wanted.

So why, more than anything else, did I want to run back to that bedroom and into his arms?

And why did these fizzy feelings in my stomach feel so much like fireworks?

CHAPTER TWELVE

I did miss him. But I'd never tell him that. I filled Saturday with brunch—me and Bec drinking too much prosecco and then aggressively tidying the flat while Matt looked on in confusion—and then every errand I could think of. But I didn't call Lucas, so it felt like a win.

Plus, Sunday lunch with my parents had been mostly delightful. We had the same thing we had every month I went home: roast lamb and Dad's special gravy and Mum's crispy (totally charred) roast potatoes. We drank the same wine, and we talked about the same things, and they cracked the same jokes, finishing each other's sentences in the same way they always had.

Halfway through the meal, I found myself day-dreaming about living abroad. What would I be doing if I lived in Spain now, or Italy? Even a different city—what would my life look like? Where everything was unexpected and upended. What was Edinburgh like this time of year? Could I imagine myself on a boat at sea for a whole summer?

"Marina, darling, are you okay?" Dad touched the back of my hand as he passed me the washed-up serving plate to dry.

"I'm fine." I smiled. "Just thinking."

"Always thinking, always scheming." Dad laughed. "You ever considered just *being*? It's very nice. Relaxing, even."

"Don't get on me with all that zen *live-in-the-moment* stuff."

"The moments you live in are the ones you remember, that's all I'm saying." He shrugged, moving on to the next plan. "Spent a year planning our wedding and can remember my vows and not much else. Couldn't tell you the color of the bridesmaids' dresses or the flowers or what we had for our meal. But that time I posed for a photo on the beach in Málaga and got hit by a wave, and me and your mother laughed until we cried? That was fifteen years ago, and I could tell you what she was wearing, what her laugh sounded like. I'll remember that joy for the rest of my life. And it was, what? Nothing. A moment, a breath."

I briefly thought of Lucas's hotel room, the view of the

city out the window, the sound of his slow exhale when he first saw me undressed. How his eyes darkened when I said something sarcastic. How he'd leaned against that desk in the near darkness just watching me, and sighed, "Fucking hell, Spicer. You're killing me." How my stomach flipped as he closed the space between us, his eyes still light even in the darkness. How I'd never known it was possible to taste a smile before.

And then I shook it away, like a wish on a breeze.

"I'll be sure to meditate on the taste of my chocolate-chip cookie at lunch tomorrow, I promise," I said dryly, and Dad bumped me with his hip.

"I just . . ." He paused. "Don't take this the wrong way, but I want more for you."

"I know, that's what I've always been working on. Good job, responsibility, nice house, good family. I'm going to have more."

"I want more for you *now*. More laughter, more light, more . . . silliness. Waste more time, kid, I beg of you. Waste it, because you can't bank it. You've got twenty-four hours a day to spend, and once they're gone, they're gone."

I narrowed my eyes. "I'm investing them."

"Boring!" Dad hooted. "Just . . . do something crazy, please, for your old man? Something unexpected and spontaneous, so when you wake up and you're sixty and most of your story is already told, you can look back and be proud."

I paused. "Are you having a midlife crisis? Because I think you're about twenty years too late."

"Cheeky cow!" he exclaimed, and splashed me, laughing.

Of course, Mum came down and got grouchy that we were making a mess (or more likely that we were having fun without her), but it was one of those moments he was talking about. I would always remember standing there, drying a frying pan as my dad told me to take more risks.

Just before leaving I checked my phone, and there were four more missed calls from Adam that morning and some accusatory texts about why I was ignoring him. They ranged from irritated to pleading. But I didn't want to respond. I felt proud, like I'd finally done something right. I wanted to call Bec and Meera and tell them. And then I tapped the star-and-moon necklace on my collarbone. The final hurdle.

I would take it off when I got home. I would. That promise he'd given me when we were sixteen, the big adventures that never happened, the proposal that never came, the children we'd never have. So much meaning attached to a twenty-quid necklace from Argos that a thousand lovesick girls across the country probably got on Valentine's Day. I would stop wearing it. And that would be the end, finally.

Instead, I texted the person I wanted to hear from: Lucas. How's Millie?

He texted back a selfie of the two of them. I didn't realize twelve-year-olds were already into makeup.

He had a solid amount of black eyeliner on, and I kind of liked it.

Tell Millie she's very talented. I can't do a smoky eye like that.

"Who are you smiling at?" My mum appeared at my side, squeezing my shoulders. "Is there someone we should know about?"

I shook my head. "No one permanent."

Her face dropped. She looked like I'd told her I murdered kittens for fun.

"Darling, why won't you just settle down? I know you career girls these days value your independence, but I just want to see you cared for, settled."

It was that word, "settled," that got me. The compromises I'd made, the men I'd read reviews on, the effort I'd made on nights that went nowhere. I'd built a whole damn app to be more efficient, for God's sake, and the one man I'd met who fit the criteria was probably on his knees begging his ex-girlfriend to take him back right now. And the one man who was completely wrong for me was the only one who made me smile.

"I don't think I want to *settle*, you know, Mum?" I said thoughtfully. "I think I want to be adored."

Mum exhaled heavily. "Having high expectations is very noble, Marina. But being realistic is safer."

I nodded, kissing her cheek. "Yeah, but it doesn't sound very fun, though. I'll see you next month, okay?"

"But . . ."

She looked so confused as I stood on the front step of the home where I'd grown up and slowly closed the door behind me. Standing up for what I wanted felt like . . . something. Growth? A new start? An end to my stuck era? I leaned against the front garden wall for a moment, doing what Dad had said and just soaking it all in. Did I still want the picket fence and the two-point-five kids? Sure, and was I worried about missing it? Absolutely. But just for the smallest moment it felt good to breathe and know there was someone out there who was thinking of me. Who thought I would inspire his niece and made me laugh and made me feel awkward and tingly and my smartest, sassiest self. That version of myself I saw in my future plan. And okay, he wasn't staying, but he *existed*. It was like I'd remembered I could have feelings, I could be attracted to someone, even if they were wrong for me.

It wasn't all algorithms and reviews; sometimes a pair of pretty eyes and a dimple could be enough.

I started my walk back to the train station and decided, in a fit of confidence, I wouldn't avoid the route past Adam's parents' house today. I'd walked the long way around ever since he left, in case I bumped into his parents and had to deal with their awkward apologies and how much they missed me. But no more nonsense. I did not take the long way around anymore.

I couldn't wait to tell Meera and Bec about my mum's expression as I told her I deserved more than to settle. "To us young ladies and our high expectations," Bec would say, and pop a bottle of champagne in celebration.

As I approached Adam's parents' house, I allowed myself a brief moment of nostalgia. That house with the cornflower blue door and the ivy up the side held so many memories. Watching Adam's band practice in the kitted-out shed at the end of the garden. The parties we'd throw when his parents were away. The Christmas Eve drinks his mum hosted where my parents came and drank too much, and Mum always moaned about her hangover when getting the turkey out on Christmas Day. Afternoons spent watching movies, playing video games, doing nothing at all. Hell, I'd lost my virginity in that house. And now it was just a door on a street I never walked down anymore.

As I walked on the opposite side of the road, the door

opened and I watched, almost in slow motion, as two people came out. All hugs and kisses and loud good-byes, the way Adam's parents always were. Somehow I wasn't afraid of them seeing me anymore.

But then I saw that flash of dark hair, that curve of his neck, and that navy shirt I'd bought him for his birthday a few years ago.

Behind him, a woman stepped out. Beautiful, her long dark hair flowing over her shoulders, her dress a light blue that caught in the breeze, turning as she revealed a huge baby bump at the front. They held hands, him helping her down that uneven step, and then she let go, both hands resting on her stomach.

I stopped breathing. I couldn't look away, taking in every detail of the scene. Dad had wanted me to live in the moment, and here I was, categorizing everything from her silver earrings to the twin looks of joy on Adam's parents' faces. She had to be six or seven months pregnant, at least.

But . . . but Adam didn't want kids. That was what he'd said.

I wanted to run, wanted to move, but I was rooted to the spot. A statue in a black dress, staring from across the street, a wordless extra as the life I'd wanted played out in front of me with another woman in the starring role.

It was almost as if he felt my stare, because he looked up. She was still talking to his parents, but we shared a moment between us, him looking at me in shock and guilt and fear. He took a step forward, mouth open, as if to come over, and I shook my head once, firmly. Adam paused and nodded, and when he turned back to his parents and the mother of his child, I walked away, head held high, and didn't look back.

In stoic silence, I boarded the train, sat quietly through the ride back, then walked all the way to my tiny bed in my friend's extra room, surrounded by suitcases and boxes and plastic bags . . . where I finally cried.

Because when Adam had blown up my life and all my plans and hopes, I had been broken and angry, but I'd accepted it. You had to let people make their choices. But he didn't leave me because he didn't want a family. He just didn't want a family *with me*.

And now someone else was living my life.

And he knew! All these months calling me, texting me, reminiscing like there was no one else, like maybe there was still a chance for us to work it out . . . like he missed me as much as I'd missed him. Missed us.

Oh God, that was it. I'd thought there was still a chance. I'd been on all these dates and I'd created a fucking app to weed out the liars and fakes, and here he was, still in my head all these months later. I was a fool for the ages.

I fiddled with the clasp on my stars-and-moon necklace, almost strangling myself in the process of pulling it off. I threw it across the room and stuck my face into my pillow.

Okay, I needed a plan. Clearly I'd been wrong about everything, and I'd been distracted. I'd let a pretty face and a smooth-talking mouth distract me. In the battle of the exes I was losing, and I needed to refocus. Henry wasn't the one, but there had to be someone out there for me. The panic that I'd wasted time, that I'd lost my chance, that the vision I had of me with kids and a house and a dog and some faceless man who loved me . . . maybe my life wouldn't be like that. Maybe I'd tried my best and I couldn't control it anymore.

I looked at my phone and saw four missed calls from Adam. Endless texts I didn't open. Instead, almost out of habit, I opened Dealbreakers and went to Lucas's profile.

There was a new review.

Quite the charmer. Said he wasn't interested in anything serious, though. Typical.

Well, he'd told me Sundays in London were lonely. I'd turned him down. He didn't owe me anything. And yet, I was upset. Dad always said people showed you who they were, it was your job to believe them. I'd fallen for the charm.

God, I was just like all those other women. I'd thought I'd seen something underneath, but there was no underneath. Peter Pan had an origin story and loved his niece. Didn't change anything. Except that I'd changed. I'd felt passion and desire and . . . *need.* There was no other word for it. Lucas had awoken this thing in me I'd been insistent I didn't have or need in a relationship. Passion. Attraction. Spark.

I had loved Adam for over a decade, but I'd never demanded he take my clothes off. I'd never lost my breath at the sight of him naked or felt my knees buckle when he kissed my neck.

It was meant to be fun, but I'd been playing a game I was no good at. And now Lucas had ruined me. The idea of finding someone else who could make my pulse race and my mouth go dry, while fitting my other criteria? It didn't work; it didn't make sense. Dealbreakers only worked if I was okay without spark. And worse than realizing I couldn't have a relationship without it was the idea of having it with anyone but him.

He'd ruined me. And I'd let him. I'd been weak and lonely, and here I was, almost a year after the worst breakup of my life, and I was no closer to marriage or children or anything real. I was playing make-believe in a hotel room with a man who never stayed. Never.

Tomorrow was our last activity, and all I had to do was keep him at arm's length. Protect myself. I couldn't do anything about Adam, but I could finish what I'd started. And that meant beating Lucas Kennedy once and for all.

CHAPTER THIRTEEN

The next morning, I was focused on working quietly at the office. When she arrived, Harriet took one look at me, my headphones already on, barely raising my eyes when I nodded hello, and knew not to push me. She simply sat down and got to work, surreptitiously pulling a chocolate bar from her desk drawer and sliding it over to my desk without saying a word.

The envelope for our final activity sat on my desk, and next to it was a takeaway hot chocolate with too many marshmallows. It had already been sitting there when I got in. I could feel his eyes on me from across the room and pushed the drink away to focus on the bright blue envelope. One more task.

One more day of holding it together. And then I

could do my presentation, win my promotion, and Lucas Kennedy would be gone from my life, on to his next adventure.

He bounded over, those bracelets rattling on his wrist giving him away before he even entered. Today's T-shirt demanded its audience "Wake up and smell the coffee," and I mentally thanked him. I had done what the T-shirt had said; well done, T-shirt. Wake-up call achieved. No more nonsense.

"Good morning, lovely people," Lucas seemed to boom obnoxiously loudly, then zeroed in on me, his forehead creasing into a frown. "Hey, you okay?"

I nodded. "Ready for our last task?" I chucked the envelope at him with a little too much force. I watched as Lucas's eyes moved between me and the untouched hot chocolate, trying to decide whether to say something. For probably the first time in his life, he chose to say nothing.

"We are"—he paused, letting the full force of his disappointment hit—"hiking. Just what everyone comes to London to do. Why would anyone pay for that when you can walk around for free?"

Normally I would have made a joke about the apparent love for hiking on people's profiles and how it wasn't a real hobby, it was just walking with good branding. But I didn't engage.

I held out my hand wordlessly for the envelope, then

found the company listed on our site. "It's an hour's train ride out of London. A walking tour around a national park with history, snack stops, and a meal at the end. Not quite a hike."

"Walking for no reason is walking for no reason." Lucas shrugged. "Are you sure you're feeling all right?"

"Yup," I said tightly. "I'm just going to get some work done, and I'll meet you at the train station in about an hour."

"You don't want to walk over together?" He seemed almost hurt.

"I've got stuff to finish off," I said, and looked back to my screen, dismissing him.

Oh God, I was being unfair, I knew I was. The rational part of my brain looked up as he walked away, exchanging a look with Harriet, who responded with the smallest shift of her shoulders. He'd been clear, he'd never promised me anything. Was I just projecting my anger at Adam on to him? I kept going back and looking at those dealbreakers.

He was charming.

He made me feel special.

I felt like I was beautiful when I was with him.

He told me I was one in a million.

He said he didn't see it going anywhere.

He said he wasn't available for anything serious right now.

It may not have been his fault, but I'd been played. I'd

fallen for his charm and nonsense, and now here I was, further from my goals than ever. Wasting time with someone who didn't want the same things as me at all. Just like I'd been doing for fifteen years.

Adam was going to have a family, and I was still here, stuck in amber. Frozen. Right where he'd left me.

But I could hold it together. I'd always been good at that.

All I had to do—I told myself—was go on a long walk with the guy who had made me feel so special and try to pretend that it hadn't all been for nothing. Okay, it wasn't real, but maybe it wasn't all fake.

I got my work done, occasionally glaring at that takeaway cup of hot chocolate, and took deep, calming breaths as I headed to the train station. I marched, breathing in time, and with every out breath I convinced myself I could do this. That I was being sensible. That I wasn't hurt, or upset, or transferring my feelings.

I dodged people on the street, getting more irritated the more I had to move out of their way. Why, for once, didn't they move out of *my* way? Didn't they see the scowl on my face? Didn't they know enough to be afraid of a woman who'd discovered she was a fool?

When I slipped through the open entrance to the train station, I scanned the concourse, sure it would take a while. But there he was, easy to spot even in a crowd, those jeans and beaten-up red Converse, the bright blue T-shirt. He wore his trusty beanie, which I now hated more than ever, because I loved how wild those curls were when they were let loose. How they sprang softly back beneath my fingers.

I was going to miss him, I realized. And that made me angrier than ever. In a little under a year, Adam had started a whole new life path. I had . . . wasted even more time. All that talk of fireworks and butterflies, stuff that had never applied to me, and now I felt them with the wrong person.

"Hey, you!" Lucas looked so happy to see me, his face lit up as he waved. I dismissed it; he was happy to see everyone. Hope and wariness flitted across his face as I approached, as if he didn't know how to deal with me.

We fell into step toward the platform, Lucas handing me a paper ticket.

"Thanks," I said quietly, not looking at him.

"I got you a cronut." He handed me a small paper bag.

"A what?"

"It's a mixture of a doughnut and a croissant." He shrugged. "I'm a gentleman; ladies get gifts."

I stopped suddenly, my hands clenched into fists.

"Why would you say that?"

He stopped beside me and just stared, his face open, innocent, like he had no idea what I was talking about. People milled past us, irritated at our sudden stop.

"What?"

"We're not dating, we're not anything. We're just wasting time, right? That's what you do?" I felt the words spewing up like vomit, unable to keep them in. "For all I know, this was just you making it easier to win our little competition. Playing to your strengths."

Lucas looked like I'd hit him with a hammer, but he came back fighting.

"You know that's total horseshit." Those green eyes stared me down. "But I support this whole having-feelings thing, instead of just scheduling a breakdown for later when it's more convenient. Come on, then, if you need to get angry, get angry. I can take it."

"This is a waste of my time." I tried to push past him, but he reached for my wrist.

"Come on, Marina, don't be a coward. You want to say your piece, go for it."

I whirled on him. "Fine, you want me to be honest? You are wasting my time. You are getting inside my head and messing it up when we both know you don't commit, you don't stick around, and even if you did, you are not what I'm looking for."

"Because I swear too much and smoke when I drink and get a rash when I pet a dog?" He rolled his eyes, knowing it would wind me up further. "Yeah, believe me, I know I'm not your dream guy. Nothing to tick off your neat little checklist here."

"We have nothing in common! Like, what was even the point of all this? You'll move on to the next woman, and I'm still sitting here waiting for someone who actually wants kids."

"I never said I didn't want kids! I just said it was fucking insane to expect them with the first moron you meet!"

"You said it was selfish to have them!"

"You're twisting my words and you know it!" he yelped, pointing at me. "No one forced you to sleep with me, you made that choice, you took that step. I've been nothing but honest with you; you're the one who's been pushing me away."

"Honest?" I snorted. "You want honest?"

I riffled through my pockets for my phone, and before I could stop myself, I pulled up Dealbreakers, went to his profile, and showed it to him. "A hundred women, in the six months since I created this app. A hundred reviews from women who thought you were awful to them. Whether you meant to be or not."

"'*Too clumsy, trod on my foot . . . told me he really liked me . . . always on the phone to other women.*'" He frowned at the phone. "What the fuck is this?"

"Reviews," I said with triumph, crossing my arms. "Dating reviews."

He was quiet for a moment more, scrolling through.

"You made this?" he said quietly, looking at me like I was a stranger.

Oh no, you're not turning this around on me. I'm not in the wrong.

"People are so rarely who they say they are or who they think they are." I shrugged, glaring at the people around us, who seemed to enjoy the drama in the train station concourse. "It seemed sensible to let people who'd actually met the men behind the dating profiles speak for themselves."

"I can't believe you'd create something that reduced people to *things* like that. Like you just bought a watch online." His eyebrows creased as he continued scrolling. "You're not like that; you love people's stories and what makes them human. You *see* people in that special way—"

"Don't try to charm your way out of this. I'm not special; I'm not anything except late for my life." I shrugged, staring at the ground, suddenly worried I was going to lose my steam. "You can see why I can't trust what you've told me."

"Because a bunch of random women on the internet said I sneezed too loudly or they didn't like my shirt?" Lucas shook his head, and when he looked up, I saw deep disappointment in his eyes. I tried not to feel it, but it stung.

"I should have known. No nuance, all black and white. Good or bad. No differing perspectives, no other points of view. You couldn't even let yourself be real with someone who was crazy about you, who wanted you so badly. You just clung to your checklist for your perfect future with a guy you're not even sure you want to fuck." Lucas snorted. "You're a coward."

"At least I'm honest."

"Is this honesty? Creating this app to judge and bitch about men? What about those guys who went home thinking they'd just been on a really good date? *Honestly* thinking they'd connected with someone. You don't see people, Marina; you just see problems and solutions. I can see how those comments would make me look horrible. But you've met me, you've known me. I've shared things about my life with you."

I opened my mouth to argue but found I had no defense.

"You know I smoke when I'm stressed or I'm drunk and trying not to make a fool of myself in front of a woman who hates me and who I can't stop thinking about. You know I'm allergic to dogs but I still want one. You know the only girl I spend all my time on the phone with is twelve years old and going through a hard time. You know I get clumsy when I'm nervous and am pretending not to be. And you, more than anyone, know that the charm is a crutch for someone who opened his heart up and had someone stomp all over it. You know *me.* And you would still rather believe strangers on the internet?"

"I . . . I mean . . . it wasn't . . ." There was nothing I could say. The damage was done. "You were with someone yesterday, she put a review on and . . ."

He looked at my phone and shook his head. "A woman I met in the park, one of Millie's mum's friends. We chatted while the kids played on the swings. She asked me out and I said no. The woman I told"—he looked down at the screen and quoted—"'*said he wasn't interested in anything serious, though*'? Why do you think I said that to her? I wasn't available because I'm seeing you!"

Lucas looked me in the eyes, shaking his head like I'd let him down. "Maybe this started as something casual, but I have tried time and again to make it clear that I like you."

I opened my mouth to say something but couldn't find the words. I knew if I didn't say something now I'd regret it, but nothing came to mind except pointless excuses and Adam's girlfriend's round belly and how hard I'd cried that first night in Bec's spare room, muffling the sound with a pillow and then drying my eyes and smiling when she asked if I wanted a cup of tea. No weakness. No hurt. No signs of brokenness.

"Marina, you never even considered that. Considered me. Because I wasn't exactly what you wanted."

He shrugged, as if this was all too boring for words. *You win some, you lose some. No big deal.* I'd lost him. I knew it as soon as I saw that smile creep back on his face. All charm and no reality. No vulnerability, not anymore. A pretty mask to hide behind.

"I can see that I was clearly a waste of your time. I'm sorry about that. I wish you the best with your checklist dates. I really hope they make you happy, truly."

Lucas walked away without looking back, and I didn't blame him. I watched him disappear into the train station crowds, swallowed up by the movement, my own feet stuck to the ground.

What had just happened?

And if we'd really just been wasting time, why did it hurt like this?

CHAPTER FOURTEEN

I didn't want to go to my pottery class. Why did Agatha have to move our session this week? I knew Bec and Meera would take one look at me and see that I was falling apart. And I'd already had one very embarrassing public "moment" today.

But also, something about the clay was therapeutic. I was crap at it, I could hate it. It was always there to give me the tiniest bit of hope that I might come out on top, and then, bam, make me look like an idiot. But every week I went back. Because of the hope.

"You're concentrating so hard I'm worried you might get a headache," Bec whispered, and I smoothed out my forehead as I focused on the pottery wheel. If I could do this, if I could finally conquer this stupid challenge, I'd be fine. I'd be able to feel happy for Adam. I'd be able to apologize to Lucas and tell my mother I didn't want to freeze my eggs. I'd be able to say good-bye to that future I'd been obsessing over. If I could just make this vase. I knew I was so close, it was starting to take shape, I was sure of it . . .

It collapsed in my fingertips.

"Fuck it!" I growled, clenching my teeth and starting again.

"Didn't even think you *knew* the f-word." Meera chuckled, then sighed as I didn't respond. Around us people were laughing and chatting as they sculpted, the teacher giving them advice and tips.

Agatha's soft voice floated over my shoulder. "Stop taking it so seriously. The more you try to control the clay, the more it resists. Just . . . relax with it. Let things happen."

I looked up, pressing my lips together, but failing to stop myself. "No, you know what, if I relax, things don't happen. Nothing happens unless I make it happen, and so the clay is still clay. It's not a vase. It's not a vase unless I make it a vase, is it?"

Agatha looked at me curiously. "I don't know, darling, is it?"

I clenched my fists together and said nothing. Agatha paused, as if she was trying to find the right words. "It's just meant to be a bit of fun, darling. You can't make a vase; I can't commit to one man or ever remember my PIN number. We've all got our foibles." She patted my shoulder and floated off.

"You"—Meera leaned in and pointed at me—"step away from the wheel."

I considered resisting but sat back. I just looked at her, letting everything free. The hurt, the heartache, the damn exhaustion that came with trying to start over, to convince everyone you were fine. To not be bitter, to be the bigger person. To keep hoping, keep working. Keep trusting that your dreams weren't done. I just looked at her and let her see it all.

"You know, don't you?" she said sadly, wincing a little. "Did you see it on Facebook?"

"You knew?" I shook my head. "I saw them. At his mum's house." I felt the tears rise and looked up quickly, taking a deep breath. No, I had already lost my temper in a train station today; I wasn't going to cry at a community center art class.

"Oh honey," Bec said with such pity in her voice that my bottom lip wobbled. She reached out her clay-covered hand to hold mine.

"Fuck it," Meera said, and joined hers to the pile.

For some reason, seeing our messy hands piled up on the pottery wheel made me laugh.

"I'm an idiot."

"You're not, he's an arsehole," Bec said vehemently.

"I hope that baby doesn't let him sleep through the night until it's twelve," Meera said. "I'm sorry I didn't say anything. It just seemed . . . cruel somehow. You were working so hard on starting a new life . . ."

I laughed. "I wasn't, though, was I? I was just . . . looking for a substitute so I could finish the game. Besides, he's happy, he's allowed to be happy. He's allowed to change his mind." I took a breath. "God, Mum's gonna lose her mind. She told me I'd have solved the argument by faking a pregnancy."

"Your mother needs to stop hanging out with the middle-aged theater nuts who live for drama," Meera said seriously. "You know what's harder than having a baby? Having one with someone who doesn't want one."

I nodded and thought of Lucas. "I know. I absolutely know."

"You still thought he was coming back," Bec said, and I nodded.

"I don't think I realized, but . . . yeah."

"And yet," Meera noted, head tilted, "you're not wearing your necklace."

Her and Bec looked at me, eyebrows raised, as if they expected me to break out into a dance solo and express myself.

"I think . . ." I took a breath. "I think I may have a bigger problem."

"Is it, by any chance, a six-foot Irishman who has terrible taste in T-shirts and is absolutely obsessed with you?" Bec offered, making a face. "Just a wild guess."

"I told you, you can't do casual," Meera said sadly, patting my hand. "So of course you pick the Lothario who is incapable of commitment."

"I'm just . . . I'm not sure he is that person." I winced and held up my messy hands. "I know that sounds pathetic and like I'm trying to fix him or fit him into the life I want, I just . . . he wasn't really those things. He was sweet and kind and had his own stuff he was working on. And he kept trying to know me, and I kept saying he wasn't what I wanted. He wasn't what I planned for."

"Plans change," Meera said lightly. "Maybe they should."

"Isn't that just . . . lowering your standards? Giving up your dreams for some guy?" I shook my head. "Isn't that the worst thing we can do?"

Bec laughed. "Babe, I met a man who literally thinks lines of letters and numbers are the coolest thing ever and collects those little wobbly headed *Star Wars* action figures. And I married him! So instead of getting shit-faced at three a.m. on a Thursday on margaritas, I'm at home eating homemade pizza and learning to crochet while I watch season fourteen of some insane show I would never have even turned on without him." She laughed, her beautiful face full of joy, blowing those strands of hair out of her eyes. "I never intended to get married. I never intended to slow down, or stay in one place, or fucking *crochet* a Christmas present for my husband's family corgi. I compromised a life I had planned for one that arrived, because I felt like I couldn't risk missing out. Not on him."

"But don't you get . . . don't you miss the life you wanted?"

"Honestly"—she shook her head—"not really. I pretend I do for the girls at work so I don't sound like a boring old cow. And when the mood strikes I have you two to drink under the table on a weeknight and pretend we're still in our twenties."

"Ugh, no thank you." Meera made a face. Then she turned to me. "Look, I know I talk a good game about not taking bullshit and standing for something and being who you are. But sometimes I talk absolute crap."

I honked a laugh, eyes still tearful.

"No, really." She looked at me, brown eyes wide and honest. "I was wrong to drop out of law school. I was wrong to refuse help and to insist I didn't do relationships just because I didn't want anyone to walk away because of my responsibilities. I didn't want to resent my aunt if I couldn't have something like everyone else. So . . . I kind of became this tough character. And now I'm thirty-one and I have no fucking clue how to be vulnerable or honest with someone. But . . . I'd like to."

I felt my jaw literally drop open, like I was a cartoon character.

"Wow, I didn't think people did that in real life." Meera snorted.

"You admitted you were wrong *and* that you'd like a relationship," Bec yelped. "I'd be less surprised if you said you were a pod person."

"An alien sent to Earth to report back," I added croakily.

"A cyborg sent from the future to destroy us all," Bec added. "We could go on."

"Well, thanks." Meera smiled sarcastically. "But I revealed this to push Marina on a moment of growth, so let's go back to that, shall we?"

I looked between them, and Meera gave a wide, toothy fake smile, and Bec put both thumbs up.

"Come on, baby, you can do this." Meera nodded, like I was a child learning to take her first steps. "You've been dating in a panic like it's musical chairs and you're gonna be left on your own. But you're the one playing the music. You decide when it stops."

"Ooh." Bec pointed, nodding. "I like that. You should write that down."

We stopped talking as Agatha clapped her hands loudly,

over at the far side of the room. "Darlings, your creations from a couple of weeks ago. Now, as always, some do not survive the kiln. It is the nature of creation! Death is, itself, a form of transformation . . ."

Meera rolled her eyes. "This one should join your mum's drama group. Instant hit."

We walked over, and I crossed my fingers and took a deep breath. I was the last one to arrive at the table. And there it sat, my sad little squat attempt at a vase, the neck unstable, the base already cracked. The three of us stood there long enough, looking at it, for the room to empty.

Agatha saw my look of despondency and squeezed my shoulder. "I think you'd be *marvelous* at ashtrays," she said, and walked out of the room, shutting the door behind her.

Then it was just the three of us, and I took a deep breath.

"I'm going do something super embarrassing, and I'm going to need you guys to pretend this isn't happening."

They nodded, and I picked up the stupid failed lump of a vase, raised it above my head, and slammed it down as hard as I could, shrieking as it smashed onto the floor with a satisfying clatter. I felt it, in that moment, how every bit of anger and frustration and utter, utter sadness coursed through me, from my noisy head and broken heart, down and out through my fingertips. There was no room for embarrassment, even if it was a mad banshee moment. As I heard it crack, I opened my eyes and breathed a sigh of relief.

It was done. The mess on the floor was just crumbs and dust, almost like a treasure map.

“I feel better,” I said, smiling at my friends, and then went to find the dustpan and brush. Yes, I’d had a literal breakthrough—didn’t mean other people had to clean up my mess.

“If this was just a class where you *destroyed* shit instead of having to make it first, I would have been a *lot* more enthusiastic,” Meera said, looping her arm through mine as we left the building. “Now, let’s go talk about this fantastic new future of yours.”

CHAPTER FIFTEEN

We all stayed at Bec's, curled up on the sofa with duvets and sleeping bags, pink wine and black tea and packets of biscuits from the corner shop, the way we used to before. Matt poked his head around the door, said goodnight, and chucked a bag of Maltesers at us before he left.

"How did he find my secret sweet stash?" Bec had cried, before shrugging and tearing open the bag.

We watched reruns of all the noughties rom-coms we used to love and talked about silly stuff, and when I woke up the next morning I was sandwiched between the two of them, Bec holding my hand, and Meera resting her palm on my forehead.

I disentangled myself, showered, and got ready for

work. I left them both sleeping, sticking a Post-it note with a huge lipstick kiss on the kettle for them to find. *Thank you.*

On the train in to work, I blocked Adam's number. A small, measurable moment of success.

The remaining issue was Lucas.

What to do about Lucas? I mean, apologize, obviously. But after that? Well, I guessed it wasn't just about what I wanted. Maybe that was the mistake I'd been making. Assuming that what I wanted was the only thing that mattered.

When I got to the office, I could feel eyes on me. Not the same way I had when his blog posts were released, like I was a low-level celebrity people recognized. This was . . . disapproving?

I sat down at my desk and peered over to his across the hallway. I couldn't see that tuft of hair from underneath his beanie or those tattoos snaking up his arm as he twirled a pen and leaned back in his chair.

I knew it was going to be hard, the apology I had to make, the explanation of what Dealbreakers was, how it was well-intentioned. That I was wrong. But it was better to get it out of the way sooner rather than later.

I took a breath, stood up, and walked across the room, leaning on the doorframe of his office and peering around, like he'd done so many times to me. But he wasn't there. Instead, Martha looked up tiredly. "He's gone. I thought you'd have known that."

"Gone?"

"Back to remote work. Said he didn't think he was the settling-down-in-one-place type after all." She shrugged, taking off her glasses and cleaning them on her jumper. "It's a shame, he was so . . . bright, you know? Liked a chat. Made my days a bit nicer. It's rare someone asks about how your cat's operation went and actually listens to the answer," she said, and looked back at her screen, dismissing me.

I turned back around, and everyone in the middle of the office seemed to have eyes on me. Even from beyond those glass walls, it was like they were all holding their breath.

Marie walked up, holding her laptop. "Marina? Have you got five minutes? The Joes want a word."

Oh God.

I tried not to panic, and nodded, smiling even as my lip trembled. I followed her along the corridor, watched as she knocked once, poked her head around the door, and then gestured for me to enter.

Going inside the Joes' office was always stressful. It had been designed by someone who wanted to show how *powerful* and *dominant* our leaders were, so there were two huge desks, facing each other from across the room, and then in the middle a basketball hoop over a bin, a massive aggressive black canvas, and, in the corner, a bright blue leopard that I really hoped wasn't taxidermied. Bad enough to stuff a poor creature, let alone make its corpse live out its days bright blue and in this office.

"Marina Bambina!" Joey yelled, standing up. Joe stood up from behind his desk, too, tilted his head slightly, and asked, "How are you?"

"Fine! Good! How are you?" I rambled, too enthusiastic.

Joey bounded over, waving away the question as if it was inconsequential.

"Now, Mr. Kennedy sadly had to return home and has decided to stay remote and freelance. We did offer him a contract regardless of whether he won the bet, because we felt he really brought a good energy to the business and we liked his content, but ultimately he said he didn't feel it was the right fit," Joe said, standing behind his business partner, watching for my response.

"Oh, that's . . . surprising."

"It is!" Joey agreed. "It really is! He also apologized that you weren't able to complete the last task together. He had a family emergency and had to get back ASAP."

"Did he discuss any of this with you?" Joe asked, a slight frown creeping up to his forehead. I shook my head. "Hmm."

"Anyway, I know this probably wasn't how you wanted to win, but seeing as it was your project in the beginning anyway, all's well that ends well, right?" Joey bounced on his heels, his round face eager for me to be just as enthused as he was. "So you can get your title, you can work on your group-outings project, and you can add one developer to the team this year. If we like what we see, we'll look into adding two more next year."

"That's . . ." *Everything I ever wanted. And I got it by hurting someone who cared about me.*

"Oh, and a raise, to go with the title, of course!" Joey blathered on. "Can't have a new title without the money to go with it!"

As my bosses made small talk, I managed to nod along and eventually blurt out a thank-you before returning to my desk.

"You look like your dog's died," Harriet said, eyes wide with concern. "You okay?"

"He's gone." I looked over at the single sunflower sitting in a pint glass by the window. "He just . . . left."

"That's his thing, though, right? He comes, he has a good time, he leaves when it suits him. That's what all the Dealbreakers reviews said." Harriet shrugged.

I blinked. "You looked him up on Dealbreakers? You *know* about Dealbreakers?"

Harriet rolled her eyes. "Marina, you put it on a female coding forum. We are both female coders. I use it! Or I would. I'm taking a break from online dating right now. Seeing how many meet-cutes I can engineer in real life."

"I . . . Why didn't you say anything?"

"Assumed you wanted to keep it private. You do that with a lot of stuff. I mean, I adore you, but you're a hard person to get to know."

I suddenly thought of that night in the park, Lucas's smile beaming in the dim early evening light as he told me it was good to finally meet me. I guess I knew what he meant.

I looked at Harriet, trying to process everything. "You know that little Italian place on New Grafton Street, where you're obsessed with the gnocchi?"

"My sole reason for existing. Yes?" Harriet replied, frowning. "Oh God, don't tell me it's closed!"

"It's got like a hundred one-star reviews."

She relaxed and rolled her eyes, leaning back in her swivel chair. "Yeah, because people go in there and they think it's gonna be all fancy, and they want five-star service and a crazy wine list. And instead you have Paolo telling you all about his wife's niece's hairdresser's kid and how many Pokémon cards he's collected, and telling you that no, you don't want the linguine, the linguine is for idiots, you want the fettucine." Harriet shook her head. "The food is amazing, but you can't go in thinking it's going to be like everywhere else. It's not."

I looked at her and raised an eyebrow, willing her to get it. "So you don't trust those hundred people?"

"I think they probably went in with the wrong expecta— Oh." It dawned on her. "You think Dealbreakers isn't working."

"I think I tried to make something that worked for me, to stop me having to be vulnerable. And maybe, yes, it cut out a lot of bad dates, but it probably cut out a lot of really good ones, too."

Harriet made a face. "I don't know, I think it was a sound idea. Maybe it just needs a little tweaking. A fresh perspective."

I nodded, frowning, as I turned back to my computer screen and tried to settle down to work, but my mind was racing. There was planning to be done, and hiring, and I could make an impact here. But all I could see was Lucas's look of disappointment as he frowned at those reviews on my phone, reducing him to an object rather than a person.

"And what about the other thing?" Harriet asked, and I looked up.

"What?"

"Your little Italian restaurant that's been misjudged." She raised an eyebrow. "Are you gonna go get him?"

"He's gone. He could be in deepest darkest Peru by now, for all I know."

"If you say so." Harriet shrugged and turned back to her screen.

. . .

That night, I logged onto the infrastructure behind Dealbreakers and decided to do some research. Looking at it from the side of a creator, rather than a user, I could see the problems instantly. I lay on my bed, on my stomach, laptop in front of me, and briefly rested my head on my arms.

"Shit."

The whole system was corrupted. Except it wasn't the code, or the app, or the interface. It was people. In trying to make women safer, and save them time, and stop anyone else from having to listen to Nick from Dalston as he talked about his truly innovative podcast on why we needed to invent "wife school," I had forgotten one important fact: people loved to talk shit on the internet.

I did some language analysis, and 98 percent of the reviews were negative. Not even just negative, unkind. Complaining and mocking and sarcastic. Threads of women who'd been on a date with some unknowing guy, laughing about the size of his nose or how he mispronounced "specific."

This was not what I'd meant to do. But my intentions really didn't matter. If you could trust anything, it was that people would ruin stuff. This was meant to be about girl power, the sisterhood sharing secret knowledge. Giving out good-egg badges, helping each other find the right person for them. Knowing that every date with Mr. Wrong put you one step closer to Mr. Right.

But maybe Lucas was right about that. There was no Mr. Right, not really, no matter what all the movies and storybooks told us. Maybe there was just being as happy as you could for as long as you could, and then letting it go with a little grace when it was over. I hadn't particularly mastered that bit yet.

As I shut down the app, I sent out a message to all users:

This program was a social experiment that has unfortunately been corrupted. We will be shutting down the app. We at Dealbreakers encourage you to maintain your high standards and be true to what you want. But also be aware that you may not know what you want until it walks up to you, says something you didn't expect, and completely upends your life.

Please, above all else, in a world where we're all looking for connection . . . be kind.

And then it was over.

I was left wondering what Lucas would have said about my decision. I knew how upset he was, but I also knew he would have asked me how I felt as I shut down the thing that gave me purpose through those months when my dreams had seemed lost.

That night, I went down and sat with Bec and Matt as they watched TV. I hadn't since I'd moved in, fearing I was interrupting their time together. But Bec looked up in delight as I curled into the armchair in the corner of the room, and Matt gave me a surprised smile.

They were curled up on the sofa, still working their way through all the seasons of *The Walking Dead*, most of which Bec missed because she was scrolling on her phone/crocheting a misshapen purple hat/munching on Skittles. They were so incredibly mismatched, him all quiet and composed with his scruffy facial hair and focus on problem-solving, her with her reality TV, love of being around people, and flawless style. And yet, there it was: love. A future. Simple. How had I known to put them together? Because I could see it. How fun their life would be. How conversations would become perfectly witty dialogue, looks would become chemistry, obligatory parental visits would become road-trip adventures. Some people just made sense that way.

Some people just made everything an adventure.

God, I missed Lucas.

I missed someone having the perfect reply to everything I said, so quick and witty that I had to fight laughing sometimes. I missed how that little dimple appeared in the side of his eyebrow when he raised it, and how he always smiled when I said something unexpected. I missed those stupid T-shirts and how those hands had stroked my arms, down my spine, until I felt completely relaxed, like a cat sleeping in the sun. I missed being seen. Having an equal and an opposite. Now it was like the seesaw was uneven, and I was stuck in the air, with no way of getting down.

I had wasted an entire year looking for something that didn't exist anymore. And I'd spent weeks pretending something wonderful wasn't for me.

I imagined Lucas, goading me, asking me what I was going to do now, all mocking grin and confrontation, daring me to do better.

And in my head, I answered him.

It was time to begin again.

CHAPTER SIXTEEN

"Ready to make some magic today, doll?"

Agatha smiled at me as I walked into my class that evening.

"You mean, ready to let the energy roll through me and land in the clay, whichever which way it pleases?" I grinned, and she snorted.

"But of course." She paused, putting a hand on my shoulder. "Fail, fail well, fail often. Reward yourself with wine."

"I've definitely got the wine part down." I winked, and called over to Pete, our resident living-life-to-the-fullest septuagenarian widower. "What do you say, double or nothing?"

The past two weeks, we had bet on whether my latest

creation was going to explode in the kiln. And the past two weeks, it hadn't. Each time, Pete said, rather less than kindly, that it might have been better if it had. But he always topped up my glass of wine and gently elbowed me in the arm, so I didn't mind.

Besides, I'd stopped making vases and started making . . . art. I suppose that was the only word for it. A series of little ducklings that I'd painted and glazed for Bec, all punky pink mohawks and huge eyes; a mouse for Matt that looked half like a computer mouse, half like an animal. He was way too polite when he received it, so I knew it was awful, but he seemed pleased to be included.

And last week's monstrosity, an attempt at salsa dancers for my parents. Pete had been right, total disaster. Today I'd decided to make something for Harriet, maybe a bowl, or a mug, something to say thank you for being a real friend, not just a work friend.

"You know what's funny, pet," Pete said, looking over my shoulder. "You stopped being shit the minute you stopped trying to make anything useful. Although I suppose that mouse might scare the town cats away."

"Good thing I'm not the sensitive sort, eh, Pete?" I offered, throwing down the clay with a thud. He just winked.

I'd created a little group of friends for myself. An odd assortment of people who all had their own stories. I'd channeled Lucas on that first pottery class back, asking questions, listening, nodding. They'd invited me for drinks, and the rest was history. As easy as that.

But as much as I'd made it through the workday and to my pottery class, and shortly after I'd be meeting Harriet at the pub to celebrate her promotion . . . today, my head wasn't in it. And neither was my heart.

It had been three weeks since he'd left. I'd sent emails, apologizing, explaining, sharing my recent understanding of the weird year I'd been through. No response. Well, that wasn't entirely true.

I'd sent another email last night and I'd promised myself it would be the last one.

> It was my birthday three days ago. Thirty-one. Weird that I'd been so panicked about time passing, about losing out on this invisible race with other people, like I had to hit these markers in my life when I hadn't even asked if I was ready for them. And guess what? It wasn't a big deal. I blew out a candle, ate some cake, magically got one year older at midnight, and . . . nothing changed. Well, nothing except this feeling of relief. It's not a race. It's not a sprint. I'm enjoying my time. I thought you'd like to know that; it was you who taught me how.
>
> The people at work miss you. They don't say it, but I can tell. I've tried to make up for it. I ask Martha

about her cat and Tony about his stepdaughter's issues with school and I nod and "hmm" the way you did with Keith about his (entirely nonsensical) kraken-mermaid love story comic book. I'm not as good at it as you, but I think it makes the office a little nicer to spend our days in.

I know I've said I'm sorry before. Those embarrassingly huge emails, solid walls of text because I just can't find enough words to explain everything. I wonder if you read them with a mental red pen, crossing out anything you don't believe, the words that don't sound right. I wonder if you read them at all. I wouldn't blame you if you took one look at the name on this email and deleted it. I judged you, and used other people's judgments of you, and the closer you got and the more I liked you, the more I hid. Because I wasn't ready to let go of what I'd lost yet. I'm not sure I was ready to let go of being the victim.

My parents have taken up Hobby Thursday, where they go try one new thing every week together, to find some new common ground, learn together. I got the idea from us, our competition. Being forced to work together, find a space where we made sense. They seem happy, forging new stories.

That's a comfort, right, that people don't have to be defined by their beginning? Don't you think?

I can't keep writing to you, this fake version of you in my head who I wonder about. I think about what your response would be to my emails, if you'd be honest and vulnerable in that brave way you are, or if you'd be sharp and infuriating just because I deserve it.

So this is my last letter, I guess. There are only two things to say:

I'm still sorry, and I still miss you.

M

x

I'd felt a twisted relief when I'd pressed send at one a.m. Like scratching an itch you'd been trying to resist all day. Like finally letting that square of chocolate you said you'd leave untouched melt on your tongue. At least I'd said what I needed to.

And though these one-sided emails had become like letters in a bottle, full of far-fetched hope, I'd still had to blink when I'd seen a reply that morning.

My heart had raced, my finger hovering, trying to give it enough time to load, afraid of what it would say, of what it must say. *Don't email again. I don't forgive you, I don't want your apologies.*

When it had loaded, I'd stared at it for a full minute and then started laughing.

Lucas Kennedy, celebrated copywriter, was at his most effusive.

K, he'd replied. Just *k*.

The most lazy, passive-aggressive, infuriating reply a girl could ask for.

And that one little letter had reignited hope.

I was just figuring out what to do about it.

I allowed myself a quiet ten-minute bus journey from class to the Treasure, just thinking about that single letter. *K. K. K. K.* And then I stepped off the bus, took a deep breath, and pasted a smile on my face. Because I was celebrating Harriet, and that was all that mattered.

She was already sitting at the bar, chin resting on her hand, laughing with Meera.

"Hey! Here she is!" Harriet yelped, jumping up to give me a hug. "Hello, big fancy head of development lady."

"Why hello, Miss Very Important Senior Developer, good to see you." I slid onto the barstool next to her, and Meera placed a glass of wine in front of me without even pausing.

"Hey," she said, smiling. "Have you showed Harriet your new digs yet?" She tilted her head, and Harriet held out her hand for my phone. "Show me, show me!"

I passed it over, and she swiped through the photos.

"Oh my God, it's so cute! It even has a breakfast bar!"

It did. No garden, but a balcony overlooking the water.

Who was I kidding anyway? I could barely keep a cactus alive.

"Just FYI, I'm not the help-you-move-home type friend. Do not call me on moving day, I will not be swayed by free pizza." Harriet grinned at me, handing the phone back. "It's beautiful, though. Please tell me you're going to fill your home with neon signs, a bar cart, and furniture incompatible with children?"

"What . . . like a sex swing and a pole?" Meera leaned over the bar, grinning. "Not really your style, hey, Rina?"

"I was thinking more like a white sofa or a glass coffee table?"

Meera shook her head. "Wouldn't work, I spill things a lot. And I plan to be there *all the time*."

My new flat happened to be near the college where Meera was going back to finish the course she'd missed studying. She'd asked her cousins to come spend some time with her aunt and had hired extra help. It was finally time. That sleepover at Bec's hadn't just been transformative for me apparently.

"And I'm clumsy. I'd go right through that coffee table," I lied, thinking of someone else. Imagining him sitting back on the sofa, throwing up his feet, and smashing them through the glass, his face a perfect picture of horror.

Meera went off to serve a patron at the other end of the bar, and I watched as Harriet leaned in, her voice low.

"So . . . your friend Meera . . ."

"I know she can seem a little fierce, but she's the warmest, loveliest person I know. Loyal and sharp and funny. She's great."

Harriet gave me a look. "I know. I was going to ask if she was seeing anyone."

"You want to set her up?" I frowned. "I don't know . . ."

"No, I was asking for me," Harriet said, raising an eyebrow and waiting for me to say the wrong thing.

"You . . . you date big-muscled men who can barely spell their own names and speak in three-word slogans."

"Correction." She grinned. "I sleep with big dumb men. I date sharp, funny, bartending future lawyers who care about their family and look after their friends and deny all of it because they're pretending to be tough. When I can find them, that is."

"Well . . . no harm in trying."

"You think she's going to say no," she said, unoffended.

I looked at her Harajuku-inspired getup, her pink fingerless gloves matching her nails, and half shrugged.

"You're a bit more colorful than her usual type."

"Some people are looking for a bit more color and beauty in their lives," she said haughtily.

"Did I say beauty?"

"You missed it out." Harriet grinned at me. "Anyway, I've got a present for you."

She tossed me her phone, already open to a rudimentary app.

"Meet My Friend?" I frowned, looking back up at her.

"I took what you started with Dealbreakers and tweaked it."

I held up my hands and shook my head. "Oh, no, Harriet, I . . ."

She widened her eyes. "Just hear me out?"

I nodded, feeling this strange sense of panic.

"Dealbreakers was a good start, but it was corrupted by the inevitable awfulness of people. So let's work with that. Just like how you put Bec and Matt together, now we help other people help their friends. They write a recommendation for the person they love, to help them find a date. Like a testimonial."

Harriet splayed her hands like a magician cutting a deck of cards and waited for me to be impressed.

"You designed this?" I flicked through the features, clicking and navigating. "It's good."

"It's rough, and I'm no designer. But together . . . we could do something good, right? Make dating more like that excited feeling when your friends know you like someone cute and everyone gets giggly. Make it . . . community based. Everyone I know, their love lives are a mess. We all make terrible choices when left to our own devices.

You're the perfect example. Takes a village to meet the right person and be open to meeting the right person."

I raised an eyebrow. "Ignoring the dig at me for the moment . . . it needs a better name. My Friend Thinks You're Cute dot com or something. Mates and Dates . . . Bec will have loads of ideas, she's much better at brand stuff."

Harriet grinned at me. "So you're in?"

"Sure—not like I can do much more damage. Why not celebrate your friends knowing you better than you know yourself? Seeing what you deserve and demanding it for you? I like that."

Meera returned, looking at us quizzically.

"What's just happened?"

"We're going to change the dating world," Harriet said confidently, and suddenly I saw the tilt of her head, the set of her jaw, as she smiled at Meera. Huh.

"Wow, big day." Meera pulled up her own glass of water from behind the bar to cheers, and we clinked the glasses together. "To Harriet, who was promoted and still wants more, like the best sort of woman."

"And to Marina, who knows what she needs to do next," Harriet replied, raising an eyebrow.

"Make you lots of money in this new business venture I apparently joined thirty seconds ago?"

"No . . ." She rolled her eyes. "Accept that you met the right person for this version of you. You met someone fun and warm and relaxed, who forced you to try new things and be okay with being bad at stuff and give people a chance. You're actually not shit at small talk anymore. I heard you talking about the weather in the lift with Clive yesterday. You didn't exclaim how boring it was once!"

"You can't say all my growth is down to one man," I argued. "Not fair."

"But we can blame your static year on a different one man?" Meera sided with Harriet, smiling at me. "Come on, go be brave. Make your move."

"Look." I paused to down half of my wine. "I'm learning from this year. I'm growing. And I'm not going to chase things that aren't for me. I'm not going to sit and be the victim. I'm moving on, I'm making my life something full on my own terms."

"And we're really proud of you . . ." Harriet started, looking to Meera to add something.

". . . but he made you happy, and the sex was good, and you laughed a lot."

"Plus he's pining for you on every page of our website." Harriet laughed, and I turned to look at her so quickly I hurt my neck.

"What?"

"His blogs, about your dates. There's a new one."

"But . . . we hadn't even finished our last task." The desire to check my phone was overwhelming, but I resisted. "Look, this was meant to be about your promotion, and it's turned into whining about my love life again. Let's focus on you."

"Twist my arm." Harriet laughed, then turned to ask Meera about herself. Harriet was straightforward, good with who she was, and didn't play games, and Meera was the same. They both had a softness but could be strong when it was needed. Meera scared drunk idiots into leaving the pub most nights, and Harriet shut down one of the sales guys with a thirty-second pitch-perfect explanation of why he shouldn't call her "darling." But how understanding would Harriet be about Meera's limits, her life with her aunt, how little time she had? And would Meera want to date someone younger, who still went to festivals and spent significant time sewing her own epic Halloween costumes each year? It didn't seem like an obvious fit.

But I watched Meera's face, that lazy smile around her lips as they laughed, throwing jokes back and forth. How her shoulders relaxed and the tension slid from her. Maybe Harriet's idea wasn't such a bad one. After all, people have been setting up their friends since forever. It was as good a start to a story as any.

I promised myself I'd wait until I got home. Until I

was safe at Bec's, curled under my duvet, surrounded by those boxes that were packed up for the *right* reason this time.

I didn't even make it to the bus stop. I slipped out of the door, letting Meera and Harriet continue their smiling but sharp dialogue, and snuck around the corner into the staff garden. That little patch of fake grass where I'd sat with Meera more times than I could remember, eating bacon sandwiches and moaning and watching her vape.

I leaned back against the cool brick wall, briefly closed my eyes, and took a fortifying breath, unsure what I wanted to see when I loaded the website. Actually, that was a lie. I knew exactly what I wanted to see. I just didn't know what I'd do about it if I did.

Lucas had his own page for his blogs about our exploits that he'd named "The Fake Dates." I'd read all of them, scanning his words for hidden meaning, for nuance and suggestion and, on some level, to see myself through his eyes. He'd made me kinder and funnier and sharper than I'd ever considered myself.

But he hadn't written about our last encounter, and I didn't know how he'd planned to explain it.

"Stop being a coward, Marina," I huffed at myself quietly. "Read the damn thing."

Once I started, I couldn't read fast enough.

To our readers: Alas, the time has come to say good-bye to "The Fake Dates." The competition has ended, and our time together is drawing to a close. These activities are only a few of the wonderful and wacky things you can try out on our site, whether you're going out with friends or, as I was, trying to impress a girl way out of your league. Maybe it's very important to show off for an anniversary, make a splash with a proposal, or simply show your ex on social media that you're having a better time than they are.

I will say this—choose a partner who will take part fully in everything, who won't back down and will meet you ax for ax, or twirl for twirl, or tequila shot for tequila shot. It makes the whole thing sweeter. We guarantee a magical night no matter where you're going, because boxing class or historical pub crawl, there's no better way to fall in love with someone than to see them be absolutely terrible at something and still laugh their arse off.

So, be careful out there, intrepid adventurers. You may win at date planning, but you may lose your heart in the process.

My hands started shaking before anything else. I looked

at the publication date on the post: that morning. A few hours after my e-mail and that solitary "k."

I could be cautious and sensible and wait . . . but I was tired of waiting. I was tired of doing anything but going for the things I really wanted. To know that there was some happiness out there and not be bold enough to make a move was excruciating.

He'd said he was always here for a good time, not necessarily a long time. But as terrifyingly vulnerable as it made me feel, if a short time was all we got, I'd take it. Just to know I'd been brave. He was worth being brave, no matter how long I got with him.

Seven minutes later I was booking a flight to Belfast International Airport.

CHAPTER SEVENTEEN

I'd forgotten how much I hated flying. I couldn't remember the last time I'd taken a flight, and certainly not alone. But I kept my eyes closed, my fists clenched, and kept practicing what I was going to say.

Joe and Joey had been surprisingly positive about my plan when I'd called them at six that morning, and when I made a case with numbers, they couldn't argue. Okay, there'd been a few surprised sounds and some gentle concern as they asked if I was sure, but this was who I was now.

Unembarrassed, painfully vulnerable, human. Still, there was wearing your heart on your sleeve and there was putting it on your head like an apple, demanding people take a shot.

But at least the journey was exhilarating. With no certainty that I wouldn't get there and find I'd completely created this scenario in my head.

But I didn't care.

After a cab from the airport, where the cabbie desperately wanted to talk to me and I couldn't bear to let him down, I was there, standing on his street, looking at the front door of a very ordinary house, clutching a letter in both hands like I was desperate. And, well, who was I kidding? I was.

I knocked on the door before I could chicken out and stood there, clutching a purple envelope in front of my lips, trying to hide my face. Oh God, if I'd got this wrong . . .

When the door opened, I peered over the envelope to see his green eyes widen in shock; then, as he recovered, his face carefully neutral, he raised an eyebrow.

"Well, this is quite the surprise, Spicer. On my doorstep, no less."

"I'm here on official business." I waved the envelope, hating how sharp I suddenly sounded.

His lips pressed together, but only slightly. He still leaned in the doorway like there was nowhere else to be. "I didn't assume otherwise."

Yes you did, you liar. And you should have.

"As per their usual shenanigans, Joe and Joey have a

proposal for you, but they need us to complete the last activity we were meant to do." *Please buy this stupid nonsense I've come up with. I'm trying.*

"They expect me to haul my arse back to London to drive out to the Chilterns and hike?"

"Nope, luckily enough there's apparently somewhere nearby. Cave Hill? Up for it?"

Don't turn down a challenge, Kennedy. Be bold, be stubborn. Be you *about the whole thing.*

He shrugged, reached back for his coat in the hallway, and stepped out, closing the door behind him.

"Don't overwhelm me with your enthusiasm," I said, pretending to be the version of me he'd claimed to like. His lips twitched, and I counted it as a win on the tally I was keeping in my head. But he still said nothing.

I started walking, expecting him to follow, but he stood in the street, refusing to move.

I frowned, and he raised an eyebrow, neither of us saying anything. This was new, arguing in silence.

He clicked his keys and his car unlocked; then he gestured to the car and got in, waiting for me.

"Unless you fancy taking a two-hour bus ride for the craic."

I pressed my lips together, huffed, and got in the car, pretending not to be elated as I noticed a small smile on his lips, for the briefest moment. We were being us. Different, a little more careful, but still a version of us.

He was a careful driver, which was unexpected, and clearly not making small talk was killing him. Lucas fiddled with the mirrors, tapped his fingers on the steering wheel, turned up the music and hummed. All as if he didn't have a care in the world. But I knew him. His silence was a tell.

This small fact made me smile, which I hid as I turned to look out the window, watching as the houses got farther apart and the slashes of greenery became visible.

When we arrived, he held out a hand in front of us, as if for me to lead the way.

"First of our excursions you're not here before me to thoroughly charm our guide and get them on your side," I said, trying to bait him.

He raised an eyebrow but said nothing.

Okay, then.

I picked a direction and started walking. I looked back and found he wasn't following, a half smile on his face.

"You clearly have no idea where you're going."

I riffled through my bag. "I printed out this map . . ."

"Do you want me to lead?"

I paused in my scrambling and said nothing, just met his eyes and nodded.

He nodded back, and just as I thought he was going to

say something meaningful, like he really understood what I was trying to tell him, he picked another direction and strode off.

"That dance teacher was right about you learning to follow," he threw over his shoulder, and I faux-glared at him, hoping he'd turn around. "And don't spend the next hour ogling my arse. I know what you're like, Spicer."

That little flicker in my chest came to life again. Hope. I trudged behind him, saying nothing, until he slowed. I followed him up the trail, taking a deep breath, trying to figure out how to start this.

After another five minutes, he seemed to slow until we were walking side by side. I finally had the chance to look at his T-shirt and noticed it had Scooby-Doo on it.

I hid a grin.

"What?"

"Nothing."

"What's wrong with my T-shirt? Too childish for someone of your esteemed grown-up . . . ness?"

I looked at him, letting the humor flash across my face. And then I grinned. "No, I missed your stupid T-shirts, that's all."

The look on his face was priceless. It was like I'd announced I was moving to Zimbabwe to study the ocarina.

"Oh," Lucas said faintly, and carried on walking.

Right, left, right, left. Trudge, trudge. I knew the silence was killing him more than me. I was just buying time. But for Lucas, who thrived on people and conversation and activity? It was too much.

"I called a few of the girls I dated and apologized," he said suddenly, his voice serious. "I didn't realize what I was doing. I mean, on some level maybe I did. I thought if I said something up front, then I'd done my job. I'd been honest. I didn't think about . . ."

"How painfully charming you can be?" I offered, and his lip quirked. My heart kicked wildly.

"How charm can be dishonest. I guess after the engagement . . . I'd been avoiding some stuff. I don't want to be someone who makes people feel bad. I don't want to be the guy those women described on that app. I thought I was better than that."

I had to tread carefully. "I think you are." He went to interrupt, but I didn't let him. "Apart from the clumsiness. You really are horrendous."

"Says the woman who nearly chopped my head off."

"The important word there is 'nearly.'"

We walked in silence for a bit longer, nodding at walkers around us, seemingly much more prepared than we were. I hadn't quite considered the real-life ramifications of a romantic gesture that involved being so out of breath and sweaty. And not in a good way.

"How's Millie doing?" I asked, searching for topics.

He offered me a brief but real smile. "Actually, really good."

"Even with you being . . . here?"

He winced. "Fulfilling everyone's expectations. Never staying. She forgives me, possibly because she's the best person in the universe. Did you find your fancy flat?"

"I move in next week. It's nothing like I'd planned." I smiled to myself.

"No ground-floor flat with a garden, and lots of light, and a breakfast bar, and near a good shop and . . ." He raised an eyebrow, and I snorted.

"Third floor, balcony, not much light, but I got my breakfast bar. My new neighbors gave me a bag of Italian cookies, and I can see ducks when I have my morning coffee. It's perfect."

"Perfect! When it has almost nothing on your list?"

We fell into a companionable walk, side by side, and I took a breath. "Sometimes the list needs amending. Sometimes your idea of perfect changes."

Lucas looked out at the distance, then back at me. "I feel like you're building up to something here, darling, and I can't feel my legs. Can we sit for a bit?"

I sighed in relief, hearing him say "darling." It settled around my shoulders like a blanket, and I nodded. He walked over near the edge of the hill and flopped down on a bench, looking out at the distance.

"You don't mind the heights here?" I asked, and Lucas shook his head.

"As long as I'm not being asked to throw myself off it. You okay?"

I peered over the edge, then scuttled back. "As long as I don't look down." I flopped down next to him, getting out my water bottle from my bag and taking a few sips before offering it.

Lucas took it without question but didn't drink. Instead, he simply held the bottle and looked out at the view of Belfast.

"So did the ex have the baby . . . ?"

Quite the test, Lucas. Excellent.

"Apparently they had a little girl. She's cute, according to my mother." I paused. "I mean, you're meant to say that, right? If you say she's got kind of a cone head and really distinct eyebrows it sounds bitchy. Mum bumped into his mum. He's happy. I'm happy. I blocked his number. We've got nothing to talk about anymore."

"Hard to cut out history like that."

"Not when you realize how much it's holding you back." I gestured to my neck, and he looked confused. Then he seemed to get it.

"He gave you that necklace."

"Promised me forever." I laughed. "A terrible thing to promise someone."

"You meet my parents, sometimes it's not a promise, it's a threat," he said, and I laughed, an awful nervous noise that skittered out of me.

"Sorry, I don't know what that was." I coughed, taking back the water bottle.

Lucas turned to me, meeting my eyes fully for the first time since I'd landed in Belfast and turned up at his door. "So how much longer are you going to torture me?"

"*Me* torture *you*?!"

"You came here to say something. Just say it. I don't know how much longer I can take this distant politeness. That's not us."

"Oh, the offer." I got out the envelope again. "Sorry, of course. The research shows your idea was solid. The bosses want you to come back and set up your own division, project managing the date side of the site. Fancy title, money that could let you live near your sister if you still want to . . . the chance to keep writing your articles. A lot of people really liked them."

"Oh, they did?"

"Very much," I said earnestly.

"And why would I move back to London?"

I threw up my hands. "Because it was what you wanted? To be near your sister, away from your ex? To do a great job? Because you've been proven right? Because I miss you?"

His eyebrows rose, and he took his time thinking, the bastard. "Hmm, some compelling reasons in there. Care to elaborate on that last one?"

I glared at him, but the delight that played around those lips made it worth it.

"Look, I have this very strong feeling that you might be my person."

"Butterflies and fireworks?" he ventured, hope in his voice as he scooched closer on the bench.

I grinned. "Fluttering and booming like absolute fuckers."

"And swearing, too." He smiled, moving closer still. "I'm a terrible influence."

"Oh yeah, you've absolutely destroyed me," I said. "So come home and do it forever."

I saw the look. Like he wanted to reach a hand to tangle in my hair and kiss me. Like he was barely holding himself back, vibrating with need to close that gap between us. I leaned a little closer, feeling the warmth from his skin, the smell of him.

"Forever, hey? I thought that was a terrible promise to make," Lucas said so gently, like he wasn't sure he believed me. "And what does that forever look like, darling? Immediately getting married, having a bunch of kids, that house in the suburbs you'd imagined with him? Fitting me into your existing plan?"

Here was my moment.

I shook my head and took his hand. "Nope. It looks like you and me going places and doing stupid things and laughing and drinking too much and having sex in normal beds where people don't leave chocolates on your pillows."

He laughed, a full belly laugh, squeezing my hand as he rocked back and forth. "You romantic."

I looked up at him, suddenly hopeful, but Lucas put a little bit of space between us even as he kept holding my hand, kept stroking his thumb over the inside of my wrist.

"Are you ever going to really trust me? Trust that you know me better than some random strangers on the internet?" he asked. "Because I have spent a damn good amount of time trying to show you who I am, and if I come back and that's not enough . . . I'd prefer an ax to the head, Spicer, you know?"

He looked so vulnerable it was all I could do to stop myself from reaching for him. He'd left signals, breadcrumbs. I could see it now. All those little things he did that I dismissed as charm, or persuasion, or just friendliness and boredom.

I untangled my hand and put it on his cheek. "I think we're asking the wrong questions. We've been asking what my plan is this whole time. But I'm not the only one who matters. What would you plan?"

He smiled, almost bashful. "It's stupid."

"Good." I stroked his cheek. "Tell me."

"I want to take you to Venice because I can see your face lighting up when you get into a water taxi." Lucas smiled softly at me, those green eyes like a spring field. "And I want to go sledding in Finland and watch the northern lights and hear you truly swear like a trooper because that night sky deserves it. And I want to sit at your breakfast bar and drink coffee with you on a Sunday morning, talking about what we're going to do with our day. And I want to make love to you. As often as humanly possible."

I pressed my lips together, torn between tears and laughter.

"You were really turning on the sincerity until that last one."

He pulled me closer. "Believe me, darling, I'm very sincere about that last one, too. But I've spent a decade only thinking day-to-day. Give me a chance. I can come up with some great plans for forever."

I leaned closer. "To me, it looks like the two of us, fighting, figuring it out, following the fireworks. Just seeing where they lead us. For as long as we're happy."

He mirrored my earlier movement and reached for my cheek, stroking it gently with his thumb as his voice dropped to a whisper.

"How casual of you, Spicer. Here I was expecting a

twelve-point plan ending with a prenup and a list of children's names."

"I'm trying this romance thing. Don't think I'm doing a good job, though . . ."

"Darling, you're doing just fine," he said, and kissed me. Finally. My heart pounded wildly in relief as his lips touched mine, his fingertips tracing my jaw so gently. Each kiss was a message.

I've missed you.

I'm sorry.

I'm glad you're here.

I forgive you.

But was he saying the one thing I wanted him to?

I pulled back, breathless.

"You know," Lucas said, putting an arm around me and pulling me into his side, nestling in close, "if this was one of those perfect movie moments you're obsessed with, there'd be a crescendo of fireworks in the distance as the camera panned out to views of the city."

I rolled my eyes and reached into my bag, pulling out a packet of sparklers.

"Hey, smart-arse, I think I love you. You in or you out?"

His laugh was electric, his kiss was a promise.

"I'm in, Spicer, I'm all in." He pulled back to look at me, eyes shining, laughter on his lips. "Fucking sparklers, you gorgeous, mad woman. I'm completely in love with you."

EPILOGUE

NINE MONTHS LATER

Oh God. This was not the plan.

It was not the plan to be pacing back and forth in our very nice but affordable holiday apartment after the most perfect few days in Santorini, freaking the hell out. Lucas had gone down to get some ice cream from the little shop on the seafront. A task I'd given him so I could test a theory and freak out in peace. That rumbling nausea and panic threatened to overwhelm me. I'd just needed a minute. So I could figure out how I'd feel and what I'd say to him. Wrap my head around this idea for a moment.

Things had been perfect. *Perfect.* Lucas had his place, I had my little flat. We spent most of our evenings together, and my friends had adopted him into the fold. Matt was relieved to have another guy around, and they found an odd, shared appreciation of local ales and *Star Wars* Lego kits, in that way boys have of zeroing in on the specific weird thing they both love.

Meera had gone back to school and was dating—yes, actually dating—Harriet. Harriet, who'd grown up with a mum who had MS, she'd confided lately, and understood Meera's obligations to her aunt like no one else in the world might have. They made sense, so unexpectedly, the way most couples I looked at suddenly seemed to.

We had created DateMyMate for fun, but I'd left LetsGO London last month to work as a trainer for women in tech. It was my dream job, building a new generation of female coders, all hungry to prove themselves and be the best in the business. Harriet took over my job, and Lucas was still there, leading his way, writing his blogs, charming the pants off everyone in the building. He was enjoying the consistency. I kept thinking he'd get itchy feet and want to do something new, but every time he got the urge, he just booked us a weekend away.

"Have you ever tried calamari fresh from the Aegean?" he asked one Tuesday evening, and this weekend I did. We had been lazing in the sunshine, sand on our toes and sea salt on our lips.

It had been magical. More than I ever could have imagined. We still had that edge, poking fun and being silly, but it was softened by the fact that I was allowed to kiss the man any damn time I wanted. I could reach out for his hand and know he'd trace his thumb down my palm before giving a little squeeze. I could have done this forever, living in the beautiful now, not worrying about the future.

And now the future was looking back at me from two blue lines.

"Fuck." I sighed, putting my head in my hands, collapsing onto the bed.

"Language, darling," Lucas mocked as he walked in, holding two cups of ice cream. "You know there are *far* more appropriate ways to express your frustration."

I looked up, not even sure how to start the conversation.

Would he think I'd trapped him? That I'd planned this? That I'd promised I was okay with seeing where everything went and had just . . . lied? He'd said he wasn't ready. He was the fun uncle, and I saw him with Millie, the way he loved her. We'd take her somewhere fun and feed her sugar and listen to her talk about things we really didn't understand.

And then we'd come home and put our feet up and

open a bottle of wine, not talking for an hour as we recovered from a day out with a very outgoing preteen.

But those two blue lines called to me. A baby with Lucas's eyes. The idea made my stomach flutter, my bottom lip tremble. Too much uncertainty for fireworks, but . . . hope settled, quiet and certain, like a sparkler or a birthday candle, shining in the dark.

When he caught sight of my face, Lucas's smile disappeared and panic took its place. He set the ice cream on the side table, walked over, and dropped to his knees in front of me, placing a hand on my leg. He looked at my face, reaching out to feel my forehead with the back of his hand. "Are you okay? Are you not feeling well?"

No, actually, now that you mention it, I do kind of want to throw up.

I shook my head.

"You know how we said we weren't going to make plans for the future . . ." I said quietly, barely able to find the words.

Lucas offered a small, concerned smile. "If this is about going to my family's for Easter, I promise you, that romantic view of a big family of siblings who love each other is going to fall apart. But we can still go, I don't mind. They're even better at taking the piss out of me than you are."

I shook my head and closed my eyes, pointing to the bathroom.

"You're freaking me out," he said, and I felt him get up and heard him walk into the bathroom.

When the silence went on for too long, I opened one eye warily.

I would remember Lucas's face in that moment for the rest of my life. Shock and fear and . . . joy? There were tears in his eyes as he walked back over to me, taking my hands and pulling me up.

"Is this for real?"

I grimaced. "Apparently so."

His features curved back to concerned and cradled my cheek in his palm. "Aren't you happy, darling?"

"I don't know." I shook my head. "Everything is so good right now. And I'm not prepared! I haven't been taking vitamins, and I've been drinking way too much coffee, and I just started this job, I won't get maternity benefits. Oh God, your parents! Your mother is going to freak out that we're not married, and you said you weren't ready, and . . . I just . . . this wasn't our plan."

Lucas smiled at me, so full of affection I thought my heart would burst. "Love, you know I think that sometimes the best things happen when the plan goes out the window. Besides, when you do a lot of the terribly fun stuff that makes a baby, you can't be surprised when one turns up."

He wiggled his eyebrows at me until I laughed, shaking my head. I took a breath, exhaling slowly.

"Are you happy?" I whispered, puzzled. "You look happy. You aren't even sure if you want kids."

He smiled and pulled me in close for a hug, enveloping me. "I said I didn't know if I'd be any good. But it's you and me, Spicer. We will fight about it, freak out about it, and figure it out. Besides, you know what you call good news when you don't plan for it?"

I frowned, unsure where he was going with this. He pulled back so he could smile at me.

"An absolute fucking miracle."

And that was it. The fear floated away as the man I loved laughed with tears streaming down his face, thanking me for this beautiful, unexpected moment.

So instead of panicking that we weren't married or we might not last, that this might be a terrible idea and neither of our flats was any place to raise a baby . . . we sat on the balcony, looking out at the ocean, eating ice cream and holding hands. And then the charming bastard pulled out a pen and paper and said, "Come on, Spicer, time to make a list. A nine-month plan? A list of baby names you absolutely hate? Parenting approaches you absolutely won't consider? All the things you're worried about? All the stuff we need to get?"

I laughed and squeezed his hand, shaking my head,

looking into the distance with complete calm as the sun started to disappear into the horizon. I knew I'd remember this moment forever, like all the others I'd stacked up as wondrous, unexpected, and absolutely perfect.

"Isn't it weird how life can look nothing like you planned," I said suddenly, grinning at him, "and isn't it fucking fantastic?"

Lucas tugged on my arm, so I was pulled into his lap, his hand still holding mine as he raised it to his lips. "Well, not to put too fine a point on it, darling, but I think you have yours truly to thank for that. And for your degenerate language."

"Well, thank goodness for charming men with pretty eyes." I leaned down to kiss him, safe and certain that whatever the future held, it was going to be wonderful. His arms went around my waist, one resting oh so gently on my stomach. "Ones who smoke and swear and have tattoos."

Lucas raised an eyebrow and tapped the nicotine patch on his shoulder, sitting oddly among those inked memories like it wanted to belong.

"Fine," I said, running my fingers through his hair, "ones who swear and have tattoos and have been *very good* at not smoking, however much they would like to after a bottle of wine with dinner."

"Damn straight, you're not the only one capable of making changes." Lucas laughed. "And *I* would like to say thank goodness for beautiful, ax-wielding women." He paused before reaching up a hand to guide my lips to his. "If they miss your head, they'll get your heart."

My life was nothing like I'd planned.

Thank goodness for that.

ACKNOWLEDGMENTS

Huge thanks to Kate Dresser, Tarini Sipahimalani, and the team at Putnam for making this book what it is. Thank you to my agent, Hayley Steed, who has always been my champion and puts up with my "distracting myself from edits by asking a hundred irrelevant questions" emails at all hours.

To the writer friends and writer groups who provide support, friendship, and a friendly ear, I couldn't do this job without you. Lynsey, you know I can't write a book without mentioning Team Cheerleader. Always.

And to my son, who was the main barrier in getting this book finished, in that he was a few months old when I started it, and having him completely destroyed my brain and my concept of romance. I was very tempted to write a book where the main character gets to shower and no one touches her or talks to her for forty-eight hours, the end.

So big thanks to my husband, my parents, and everyone who congratulated me on managing to write a book while having a newborn, and reminded me I could do it.

And to that now-one-year-old, my Theo: you helped me prove that no matter what else I did with my glorious life, whoever else I became, the stories would still come. And that is a huge relief.

Finally, as always, my lovely readers—thank you for taking the time to try out this book. There are so many fantastic stories to read out there, so I really appreciate you spending a couple of hours in my imagination. I hope it made you smile.

DISCUSSION GUIDE

1. From self-obsessed novelists to the ever-churning stream of loud-chewing men, Marina deals with her fair share of disaster dates. Which would you deem her worst date, and why? How do her dates compare to your own experiences? If you feel comfortable, share your worst date with the group.

2. Marina and Lucas play the role of each other's enemies before they meet in person. Do you believe Marina might have received Lucas's disruption differently if they hadn't had this history? In what ways can their "meet-hate" be considered a "meet-cute"?

3. Marina is a highly focused, ambitious, type A woman while Lucas is a natural connoisseur of life's simple pleasures. In what ways does their dynamic inform

your definition of compatibility? What did you discern to be their most immediate point of connection? How does their relationship evolve through the course of the story?

4. Marina and Lucas butt heads mixing cocktails, throwing axes, and tackling escape rooms together. In what ways is competition conducive to the building of intimacy? Discuss which activity would personally appeal to you.

5. In addition to her dating checklist, Marina also has a list of qualities she desires in a home. With everything so meticulously planned, why do you think Marina has so much trouble achieving her clearly imagined dream life?

6. Pottery class helps Marina blow off steam throughout the novel. How does the process of sculpting clay mimic the experience of dating? What does Marina's collection of trial-and-errored clay vases tell you about the way she navigates her love life?

7. From offering unsolicited updates about Adam to leading the charge on Marina's fertility plans, Marina's

mother no doubt keeps keen tabs on Marina's life. It's easy to see the ways in which Marina and her mother are different. In what ways are they similar? Discuss whether these similarities could be perceived by Marina as stark differences, and if so, why?

8. Marina's friends play a vital role in her navigation of grief and loss. To what extent do our friends' opinions and observations inform the way we see ourselves? Identify a scene that includes Marina, Bec, and Meera, and assess their self-perceptions based on the responses they give each other about themselves. How should a good friend ideally consult one on their love life?

9. *Dealbreakers* speaks to the trials and tribulations of modern dating and the often self-inflicted complications of love. What part of Marina's dating journey spoke to you most?

10. Amid the humor and lightness, *Dealbreakers* also touches on some heftier topics. How big of a role does Marina's biological clock play in her urgent search for a life partner? What did you make of the way Marina talked about family planning with regard to dating?

11. The novel opens with Marina struggling to heal from a fifteen-year-long relationship. Discuss Adam's appearance on the page. To what extent do you think Marina and Adam's breakup was overdue? What appeal does he hold for Marina, and how is he different from Lucas?

12. In *Dealbreakers*, author Lauren Forsythe deliberates the functions of turnoffs as well as the significance of correctly identifying them. In which scenarios can dealbreakers be helpful, and when can they do more harm than good? In what ways does the Dealbreakers app skew Marina's impression of Lucas? What does this say about people's proclivities when it comes to dating? If the Dealbreakers app were real, would you use it? Why or why not?

ABOUT THE AUTHOR

Photograph of the author © Kaye Ford 2021

Lauren Forsythe lives in Hertfordshire with her husband and son and a cat that gets more spoiled by the day. She works in marketing, studied English and creative writing at the University of East Anglia, and spends too much time trying to work out how she can retroactively add pockets to every piece of clothing she owns. She is the author of *The Fixer Upper* and *Dealbreakers*.

VISIT LAUREN FORSYTHE ONLINE

laurenforsythewrites.com
LaurenForsythe_Author
LaurenF_Writer